BEST
MARITIME
SHORT STORIES

BEST
MARITIME
SHORT STORIES

EDITED BY
GEORGE PEABODY

FORMAC PUBLISHING COMPANY LIMITED
1988

Canadian Cataloguing in Publication Data

Main entry under title:

Best Maritime Short Stories

ISBN 0-88780-068-8

1. Short stories, Canadian (English) — Maritime Provinces. * 2.
Canadian fiction — 20th century. I. Peabody, George.

PS8329.5M37B47 1988   C813'.01'089715   C88-098619-0
PR9198.2M37B47 1988

Published with the assistance of the Nova Scotia
Department of Tourism and Culture

Formac Publishing Company Limited
5502 Atlantic Street
Halifax, Nova Scotia
B3H 3G4

Printed and bound in Canada

CONTENTS

CREDITS

The stories in this collection are used with the permission of the author and the original publisher of each work.

"The Boat" from *Lost Salt Gift*, by Alistair MacLeod. Used by permission by of the Canadian Publishers McClelland and Stewart, Toronto.

"Passages" *Transfigurations*, Janice Kulyk Keefer, Ragweed, Charlottetown, 1987.

"Corn Flakes" *Leaping Up, Sliding Away*, Kent Thompson, Gooselane, Fredericton, 1986.

"Voyage Home" from *Township of Time* by Charles Bruce. Used by permission of the Canadian Publishers McClelland and Stewart, Toronto.

"Another Country", Ann Copeland, *The New Quaterly*.

"The Clumsy One" from *Rebellion of Young David* by Ernest Buckler. Used by permission of the Canadian Publishers, McClelland and Stewart, Toronto.

"Major Repairs" *Billy Botzweller's Last Dance*, Lesley Choyce, blewointmentpress, 1984.

"Did You Ever" *The Book of Fears*, Susan Kerslake, Ragweed, Charlottetown, 1984.

"Paradise Siding" *Paradise Siding*, Gooselane, Fredericton, 1984.

"Oh, Think of the Home Over There", Robert Gibbs, *Journal of Canadian Fiction*.

"Nels", Veronica Ross, *Canadian Fiction Magazine*.

"Skipper" from *Will Ye let The Mummers In?* by Alden Nowlan. Reprinted with the permission of Irwin Publishing, Toronto, Ontario.

"An Arch for the King" *An Arch for the King*, Michael Hennessy, Ragweed, Charlottetown, 1984.

"A Beautiful Woman" *The Apostales Tattoo*, J.J. Steinfeld, Ragweed, Charlottetown, 1983.

"The Tunning of Perfection" from *As Birds Bring Forth* by Alistair MacLeod. Used by permission of the Canadian Publishers McClellan and Stewart, Toronto.

INTRODUCTION

Writing an editor's introduction for a book entitled *Best Maritime Stories* is, in part, an exercise in explanation, even a defensive move. There are sixteen stories in this volume, written by fourteen Maritime authors. The stories are representative of the best work of some of the best writers of short fiction in the region, but the list is not definitive, not an attempt to say "these and no others are the best there are." The choice, like that in any anthology, is personal. Of the hundreds of short stories I read in making this collection, dozens might have found a place on someone's 'best'list. My 'best' are those stories which spoke to me: as a writer, as an editor, as a Maritimer.

Is it valid to speak of a distinctly Maritime literature at all? Over the past two decades, Canadian literature has become legitimate and accepted both in Canada and internationally. It is a branch of world literature, not just a variant of American or British writing, any more than Canadian culture is just a variant of American or British culture. In some ways Maritime writing and Maritime culture exist as Canadian culture and literature did twenty years ago. That is, we are in the early stages of the process of defining ourselves and our literature as distinct, sharing characteristics with other cultures and literatures, but formed and informed by distinct and different realities.

In her *Under Eastern Eyes* (University of Toronto Press, 1987), Janice Kulyk Keefer — whose "Passages" is included in this collection — argues persuasively for "the fundamental coherence of the

Maritime ethos and vision, and also its significant points of difference from other regional cultures and from what we have been taught to think of as 'the distinctively Canadian.'" *Under Eastern Eyes* itself, as "a critical reading of Maritime fiction" contributes to the developing public awareness of Maritime literature.

This awareness is one aspect of an overall move toward an understanding of the existence of a Maritime consciousness. This 'Maritime-ness' is shaped by the unique historical experiences of the region and the people who live here. It is also shaped by our more recent attempts to recover and re-interpret our history. The process has accelerated throughout the 1980s: each year has seen the publication of books and articles exploring the history, the economics and the culture of the region from Maritime points-of- view. We are not so much re-claiming our history as re-claiming our right to tell it.

This is not, of course, a phenomenon unique to the Maritimes. Some theorists have described the late 20th century as the last gasp of nationalism. They foresee the coming century as one in which nation states will gradually be replaced, both by supra-national entities such as the European Community and by a revived regionalism. Celebrating and reinforcing a Maritime identity is part of this revival of regionalism. Discovering and appreciating a distinctively Maritime literature deepens our awareness of ourselves.

Defining a Maritime identity is a touchy proposition. As part of the editorial work for the Maritime Studies textbook, *The Maritimes: Tradition, Challenge & Change*, I read some hundreds of short essays by grade 9 and 10 students on the theme "What Is the Maritime Identity?" The defining characteristics which emerged in essay after essay are that Maritimers are a friendly people, polite and helpful to tourists. Not, on the surface, much on which to build a distinctive regional identity. Yet, underneath, there is a recognition of a positive difference: we see ourselves as open and welcoming, willing to go out of our way to make sure that strangers feel at home, feel part of the community.

This emphasis on the importance of community runs as deep in Maritime literature as it does in the Maritime consciousness. From Cape Breton to Madawaska, Maritimers like to be able to place each other within known family and community contexts. Maritime poet, essayist and writer of fiction Alden Nowlan once commented that this need to know family and community connections is as important to

Maritimers as it is to the British aristocracy — and is found in few other cultures. The Charles Bruce story in this volume is taken from his *The Township of Time,* an interrelated collection of stories tracing family and community history through two centuries. Variations on the themes of family and community and place crop up again and again in Maritime writing.

In other ways than the thematic, the stories in this selection will be recognizable to Maritimers as 'Maritime'. Characters, situations, settings, language may all strike chords of familiarity. In style, of course, they are as individual as the authors who wrote them, shaped by and contributing to developing literary traditions as diverse as those represented by Kent Thompson's enigmatic 'postcard' stories and the rich emotionally charged narrations of Alistair McLeod.

As I began assembling stories for this collection, and discussing the project with friends and relatives, I found a common reaction to be "Sounds interesting, but are there really enough Maritime writers/stories to do that?" The previous two and a half years immersed in Maritime Studies had left me with the conviction to give an unqualified "yes" to that question. But as I tried to find the stories I knew were there, I understood a lot more about the basis for asking the question. Many of the volumes where these stories were originally published are out of print or no longer in bookstores, even those few which make a deliberate effort to carry the work of the region's writers. Most libraries do not identify Maritime work as such, either on the book or in the classification system. If one is not already familiar with writers as 'Maritime' and not willing to put some effort into locating their books, one could be readily forgiven for assuming that not much Maritime writing exists.

The reality, however, is the opposite of the assumption. The problem with Maritime short stories, as with Maritime novels and Maritime poetry, is not lack of either quality or quantity; the problem is getting the wealth of existing writing to Maritime readers. For the best of Maritime short stories, which can take equal rank with the best work of any other culture, speak first and deepest to Maritimers. The rise of regionalism will, perhaps, provide an opportunity for more Maritimers to discover just that.

— George Peabody
Debec, N.B.

ALISTAIR MACLEOD

Alistair MacLeod is a native of Inverness County, Cape Breton. His short stories have appeared in a number of literary magazines and anthologies in Canada and elsewhere. They have been collected in *The Lost Salt Gift of Blood* (1976) and *As Birds Bring Forth the Sun* (1986), and have been translated into Russian and Urdu, among other languages. MacLeod is currently a professor of English at the University of Windsor where he also serves as fiction editor of the *University of Windsor Review*. He is working on his first novel.

THE BOAT

Alistair MacLeod

There are times even now, when I wake up at four o'clock in the morning with the terrible fear that I have overslept; when I imagine that my father is waiting for me in the room below the darkened stairs or that the shorebound men are tossing pebbles against my window while blowing their hands and stomping their feet impatiently on the frozen steadfast earth. There are times when I am half out of bed and fumbling for socks and mumbling for words before I realize that I am foolishly alone, that no one waits at the base of the stairs and no boat rides restlessly in the waters by the pier.

At such times only the grey corpses on the overflowing ashtray beside my bed bear witness to the extinction of the latest spark and silently await the crushing out of the most recent of their fellows. And then because I am afraid to be alone with death, I dress rapidly, make a great to-do about clearing my throat, turn on both faucets in the sink and proceed to make loud splashing ineffectual noises. Later I go out and walk the mile to the all-night restaurant.

In the winter it is a very cold walk and there are often tears in my eyes when I arrive. The waitress usually gives a sympathetic little shiver and says, "Boy, it must be really cold out there; you got tears in your eyes."

"Yes," I say, "it sure is; it really is."

And then the three or four of us who are always in such places at such times make uninteresting little protective chit-chat until the dawn reluctantly arrives. Then I swallow the coffee which is always bitter and leave with a great busy rush because by that time I have to worry about being late and whether I have a clean shirt and whether my car will start and about all the other countless things one must worry about when he teaches at a great Midwestern university. And I know then that that day will go by as have all the days of the past ten years, for the call and the voices and the shapes and the boat were not really there in the early morning's darkness and I have all kinds of comforting reality to prove it. They are only shadows and echoes, the animals a child's hands make on the wall by lamplight, and the voices from the rain barrel; the cuttings from an old movie made in the black and white of long ago.

I first became conscious of the boat in the same way and at almost the same time that I became aware of the people it supported. My earliest recollection of my father is a view from the floor of gigantic rubber boots and then of being suddenly elevated and having my face pressed against the stubble of his cheek, and of how it tasted of salt and of how he smelled of salt from his red-soled rubber boots to the shaggy whiteness of his hair.

When I was very small, he took me for my first ride in the boat. I rode the half-mile from our house to the wharf on his shoulders and I remember the sound of his rubber boots galumphing along the gravel beach, the tune of the indecent little song he used to sing, and the odour of the salt.

The floor of the boat was permeated with the same odour and in its constancy I was not aware of change. In the harbour we made our little circle and returned. He tied the boat by its painter, fastened the stern to its permanent anchor and lifted me high over his head to the solidity of the wharf. Then he climbed up the little iron ladder that led to the wharf's cap, placed me once more upon his shoulders and galumphed off again.

When we returned to the house everyone made a great fuss over my precocious excursion and asked, "How did you like the boat?" "Were you afraid in the boat?" "Did you cry in the boat?" They repeated "the boat" at the end of all their questions and I knew it must be very important to everyone.

My earliest recollection of my mother is of being alone with her in the mornings while my father was away in the boat. She seemed to be always repairing the clothes that were "torn in the boat," preparing food "to be eaten in the boat" or looking for "the boat" through our kitchen window which faced upon the sea. When my father returned about noon, she would ask, "Well, how did things go in the boat today?" It was the first question I remember asking: "Well, how did things go in the boat today?" "Well, how did things go in the boat today?"

The boat in our lives was registered at Port Hawkesbury. She was what Nova Scotians called a Cape Island boat and was designed for the small inshore fisherman who sought the lobsters of the spring and the mackerel of summer and later the cod and haddock and hake. She was thirty-two feet long and nine wide, and was powered by an engine from a Chevrolet truck. She had a marine clutch and a high speed reverse gear and was painted light green with the name *Jenny Lynn* stencilled in black letters on her bow and painted on an oblong plate across her stern. Jenny Lynn had been my mother's maiden name and the boat was called after her as another link in the chain of tradition. Most of the boats that berthed at the wharf bore the names of some female member of their owner's household.

I say this now as if I knew it all then. All at once, all about boat dimensions and engines, and as if on the day of my first childish voyage I noticed the difference between a stencilled name and a painted name. But of course it was not that way at all, for I learned it all very slowly and there was not time enough.

I learned first about our house which was one of about fifty which marched around the horseshoe of our harbour and the wharf which was its heart. Some of them were so close to the water that during a storm the sea spray splashed against their windows while others were built farther along the beach as was the case with ours. The houses and their people, like those of the neighbouring towns and villages, were the result of Ireland's discontent and Scotland's Highland Clearances and America's War of Independence. Impulsive emotional Catholic Celts

who could not bear to live with England and shrewd determined Protestant Puritans who, in the years after 1776, could not bear to live without.

The most important room in our house was one of those oblong
old- fashioned kitchens heated by a wood-and coal-burning stove. Behind the stove was a box of kindlings and beside it a coal scuttle. A
heavy wooden table with leaves that expanded or reduced its dimensions stood in the middle of the floor. There were five wooden
homemade chairs which had been chipped and hacked by a variety of
knives. Against the east wall, opposite the stove, there was a couch
which sagged in the middle and had a cushion for a pillow, and above
it a shelf which contained matches, tobacco, pencils, odd fish-hooks,
bits of twine, and a tin can filled with bills and receipts. The south wall
was dominated by a window which faced the sea and on the north there
was a five-foot board which bore a variety of clothes hooks and the
burdens of each. Beneath the board there was a jumble of odd foot-
wear, mostly of rubber. There was also, on this wall, a barometer, a
map of the marine area and a shelf which held a tiny radio. The kitchen
was shared by all of us and was a buffer zone between the immaculate
order of ten other rooms and the disruptive chaos of the single room
that was my father's.

My mother ran her house as her brothers ran their boats. Everything was clean and spotless and in order. She was tall and dark and
powerfully energetic. In later years she reminded me of the women of
Thomas Hardy, particularly Eustacia Vye, in a physical way. She fed
and clothed a family of seven children, making all of the meals and
most of the clothes. She grew miraculous gardens and magnificent
flowers and raised broods of hens and ducks. She would walk miles
on berry-picking expeditions and hoist her skirts to dig for clams when
the tide was low. She was fourteen years younger than my father, whom
she had married when she was twenty-six and had been a local beauty
for a period of ten years. My mother was of the sea as were all of her
people, and her horizons were the very literal ones she scanned with
her dark and fearless eyes.

Between the kitchen clothes rack and barometer, a door opened
into my father's bedroom. It was a room of disorder and disarray. It
was as if the wind which so often clamoured about the house succeeded
in entering this single room and after whipping it into turmoil stole
quietly away to renew its knowing laughter from without.

My father's bed was against the south wall. It always looked rumpled and unmade because he lay on top of it more than he slept within any folds it might have had. Beside it, there was a little brown table. An archaic goose-necked reading light, a battered table radio, a mound of wooden matches, one or two packages of tobacco, a deck of cigarette papers and an overflowing ashtray cluttered its surface. The brown larvae of tobacco shreds and the grey flecks of ash covered both the table and the floor beneath it. The once-varnished surface of the table was disfigured by numerous black scars and gashes inflicted by the neglected burning cigarettes of many years. They had tumbled from the ashtray unnoticed and branded their statements permanently and quietly into the wood until the odour of their burning caused the snuffing out of their lives. At the bed's foot there was a single window which looked upon the sea.

Against the adjacent wall there was a battered bureau and beside it there was a closet which held his single ill-fitting serge suit, the two or three white shirts that strangled him and the square black shoes that pinched. When he took off his more friendly clothes, the heavy woollen sweaters, mitts and socks which my mother knitted for him and the woollen and doeskin shirts, he dumped them unceremoniously on a single chair. If a visitor entered the room while he was lying on the bed, he would be told to throw the clothes on the floor and take their place upon the chair.

Magazines and books covered the bureau and competed with the clothes for domination of the chair. They further overburdened the heroic little table and lay on top of the radio. They filled a baffling and unknowable cave beneath the bed, and in the corner by the bureau they spilled from the walls and grew up from the floor.

The magazines were the most conventional: *Time, Newsweek, Life, Maclean's Family Herald, Reader's Digest.* They were the result of various cut-rate subscriptions or of the gift subscriptions associated with Christmas, "the two whole years for only $3.50."

The books were more varied. There were a few hard-cover magnificents and bygone Book-of-the-Month wonders and some were Christmas or birthday gifts. The majority of them, however, were used paperbacks which came from those second-hand bookstores which advertise in the backs of magazines: "Miscellaneous Used Paperbacks 10 cents Each." At first he sent for them himself, although my mother resented the expense, but in later years they came more and more often from my sisters who had moved to the cities. Especially at first they were very weird and varied. Mickey Spillane and Ernest Haycox vied with Dostoyevsky and Faulkner, and the Penguin Poets edition of Gerard Manley Hopkins arrived in the same box as a little book on sex technique called *Getting the Most Out of Love*. The former had been assiduously annotated by a very fine hand using a very blue-inked fountain pen while the latter had been studied by someone with very large thumbs, the prints of which were still visible in the margins. At the slightest provocation it would open almost automatically to particularly graphic and well-smudged pages.

When he was not in the boat, my father spent most of his time lying on the bed in his socks, the top two buttons of his trousers undone, his discarded shirt on the ever-ready chair and the sleeves of the woolen Stanfield underwear, which he wore both summer and winter, drawn half way up to his elbows. The pillows propped up the whiteness of his head and the goose-necked lamp illuminated the pages in his hands. The cigarettes smoked and smouldered on the ashtray and on the table and the radio played constantly, sometimes low and sometimes loud. At midnight and at one, two, three and four, one could sometimes hear the radio, his occasional cough, the rustling thud of a completed book being tossed to the corner heap, or the movement necessitated by his sitting on the edge of the bed to roll the thousandth cigarette. He seemed never to sleep, only to doze, and the light shone constantly from his window to the sea.

My mother despised the room and all it stood for and she had stopped sleeping in it after I was born. She despised disorder in rooms and in houses and in hours and in lives, and she had not read a book since high school. There she had read *Ivanhoe* and considered it a colossal waste of time. Still the room remained, like a solid rock of opposition in the sparkling waters of a clear deep harbour, opening off the kitchen where we really lived our lives, with its door always open and its contents visible to all.

The daughters of the room and of the house were very beautiful. They were tall and willowy like my mother and had her fine facial features set off by the reddish copper-colored hair that had apparently once been my father's before it turned to white. All of them were very clever in school and helped my mother a great deal about the house. When they were young they sang and were very happy and very nice to me because I was the youngest and the family's only boy.

My father never approved of their playing about the wharf like the other children, and they went there only when my mother sent them on an errand. At such times they almost always overstayed, playing screaming games of tag or hide-and-seek in and about the fishing shanties, the piled traps and tubs of trawl, shouting down to the perch that swam languidly about the wharf's algae-covered piles, or jumping in and out of the boats that tugged gently at their lines. My mother was never uneasy about them at such times, and when her husband criticized her she would say, "Nothing will happen to them there," or "They could be doing worse things in worse places."

By about the ninth or tenth grade my sisters one by one discovered my father's bedroom and then the change would begin. Each would go into the room one morning when he was out. She would go with the ideal hope of imposing order or with the more practical objective of emptying the ashtray, and later she would be found spellbound by the volume in her hand. My mother's reaction was always abrupt, bordering on the angry. "Take your nose out of that trash and come and do your work," she would say, and once I saw her slap my youngest sister so hard that the print of her hand was scarletly emblazoned upon her daughter's cheek while the broken-spined paperback fluttered uselessly to the floor.

Thereafter my mother would launch a campaign against what she had discovered but could not understand. At times although she was not overly religious she would bring in God to bolster her arguments, saying, "In the next world God will see to those who waste their lives reading useless books when they should be about their work." Or without theological aid, "I would like to know how books help anyone to live a life." If my father were in, she would repeat the remarks louder than necessary, and her voice would carry into his room where he lay upon his bed. His usual reaction was to turn up the volume of the radio, although that action in itself betrayed the success of the initial thrust.

Shortly after my sisters began to read the books, they grew restless and lost interest in darning socks and baking bread, and all of them them eventually went to work as summer waitresses in the Sea Food Restaurant. The restaurant was run by a big American concern from Boston and catered to the tourists that flooded the area during July and

August. My mother despised the whole operation. She said the restaurant was not run by "our people" and "our people" did not eat there,
and that it was run by outsiders for outsiders.

"Who are these people anyway?" she would ask, tossing back her
dark hair, "and what do they, though they go about with their cameras
for a hundred years, know about the way it is here, and what do they
care about me and mine, and why should I care about them?"

She was angry that my sisters should even conceive of working in
such a place and more angry when my father made no move to prevent
it, and she was worried about herself and about her family and about
her life. Sometimes she would say softly to her sisters, "I don't know
what's the matter with my girls. It seems none of them are interested
in any of the right things." And sometimes there would be bitter savage
arguments. One afternoon I was coming in with three mackerel I'd
been given at the wharf when I heard her say, "Well I hope you'll be
satisfied when they come home knocked up and you'll have had your
way."

It was the most savage thing I'd ever heard my mother say. Not just
the words but the way she said them, and I stood there in the porch
afraid to breathe for what seemed like the years from ten to fifteen,
feeling the damp moist mackerel with their silver glassy eyes growing
clammy against my leg.

Through the angle in the screen door I saw my father who had been
walking into his room wheel around on one of his rubber-booted heels
and look at her with his blue eyes flashing like clearest ice beneath the
snow that was his hair. His usually ruddy face was drawn and grey,
reflecting the exhaustion of a man of sixty-five who had been working in those rubber boots for eleven hours on an August day, and for a
fleeting moment I wondered what I would do if he killed my mother
while I stood there in the porch with those three foolish mackerel in
my hand. Then he turned and went into his room and the radio blared
forth the next day's weather forecast and I retreated under the noise
and returned again, stamping my feet and slamming the door too loudly to signal my approach. My mother was busy at the stove when I
came in, and did not raise her head when I threw the mackerel in a pan.
As I looked into my father's room, I said, "Well how did things go in
the boat today?" and he replied, "Oh not too badly, all things con-

sidered." He was lying on his back and lighting the first cigarette and the radio was talking about the Virginia coast.

All of my sisters made good money on tips. They bought my father an electric razor which he tried to use for a while and they took out even more magazine subscriptions. They bought my mother a great many clothes of the the type she was very fond of, the wide-brimmed hats and the brocaded dresses, but she locked them all in trunks and refused to wear any of them.

On one August day my sisters prevailed upon my father to take some of their restaurant customers for an afternoon ride in the boat. The tourists with their expensive clothes and cameras and sun glasses awkwardly backed down the iron ladder at the wharf's side to where my father waited below, holding the rocking *Jenny Lynn* in snug against the wharf with one hand on the iron ladder and steadying his descending passengers with the other. They tried to look both prim and wind-blown like the girls in the Pepsi-Cola ads and did the best they could, sitting on the thwarts where the newspapers were spread to cover the splattered blood and fish entrails, crowding to one side so that they were in danger of capsizing the boat, taking the inevitable pictures or merely trailing their fingers through the water of their dreams.

All of them liked my father very much and, after he'd brought them back from their circles in the harbour, they invited him to their rented cabins which were located high on a hill overlooking the village to which they were so alien. He proceeded to get very drunk up there with the beautiful view and the strange company and the abundant liquor, and in the late afternoon he began to sing.

I was just approaching the wharf to deliver my mother's summons when he began, and the familiar yet unfamiliar voice that rolled down from the cabins made me feel as I had never felt before in my young life or perhaps as I had always felt without really knowing it, and I was ashamed yet proud, young yet old and saved yet forever lost, and there was nothing I could do to control my legs which trembled nor my eyes which wept for what they could not tell.

The tourists were equipped with tape recorders and my father sang for more than three hours. His voice boomed down the hill and bounced off the surface of the harbour, which was an unearthly blue on that hot August day, and was then reflected to the wharf and fishing shanties where it was absorbed amidst the men who were baiting their lines for the next day's haul.

He sang all the old sea chanties which had come across from the old world and by which men like him had pulled ropes for generations, and he sang the East Coast sea songs which celebrated the sealing vessels of Northumberland Strait and the long liners of the Grand Banks, and of Anticosti, Sable Island, Grand Manan, Boston Harbor, Nantucket and Block Island. Gradually he shifted to the seemingly unending Gaelic drinking songs with their twenty or more verses and inevitable refrains, and the men in the shanties smiled at the coarseness of some the verses and at the thought that the singer's immediate audience did not know what they were applauding nor recording to take back to staid old Boston. Later as the sun was setting he switched to the laments and the wild and haunting Gaelic war songs of those spattered Highland ancestors he had never seen, and when his voice ceased, the savage melancholy of three hundred years seemed to hang over the peaceful harbour and the quiet boats and the men leaning in the doorways of their shanties with their cigarettes glowing in the dusk and the women looking to the sea from their open windows with their children in their arms.

When he came home he threw the money he had earned on the kitchen table as he did with all his earnings but my mother refused to touch it and the next day he went with the rest of the men to bait his trawl in the shanties. The tourists came to the door that evening and my mother met them there and told them that her husband was not in although he was lying on the bed only a few feet away with the radio playing and the cigarette upon his lips. She stood in the doorway until they reluctantly went away.

In the winter they sent him a picture which had been taken on the day of the singing. On the back it said, "To Our Ernest Hemingway" and the "Our" was underlined. There was also an accompanying letter telling how much they had enjoyed themselves, how popular the tape was proving and explaining who Ernest Hemingway was. In a way it almost did look like one of those unshaven taken-in-Cuba pictures of Hemingway. He looked both massive and incongruous in the setting. His bulky fisherman's clothes were too big for the green and white lawn chair in which he sat, and his rubber boots seemed to take up all of the well-clipped grass square. The beach umbrella jarred with his sunburned face and because he had already been singing for some time, his lips which chapped in the winds of spring and burned in the water glare of summer had already cracked in several places, producing tiny flecks of blood at their corners and on the whiteness of his teeth. The bracelets of brass chain which he wore to protect his wrists from chafing seemed abnormally large and his broad leather belt had been slackened and his heavy shirt and underwear were open at the throat revealing an uncultivated wilderness of white chest hair bordering on the semi-controlled stubble of his neck and chin. His blue eyes had looked directly into the camera and his hair was whiter than the two tiny clouds which hung over his left shoulder. The sea was behind him and its immense blue flatness stretched out to touch the arching blueness of the sky. It seemed very far away from him or else he was so much in the foreground that he seemed too big for it.

Each year another of my sisters would read the books and work in the restaurant. Sometimes they would stay out quite late on the hot summer nights and when they came up the stairs my mother would ask them many long and involved questions which they resented and tried to avoid. Before ascending the stairs they would go into my father's room and those of us who waited above could hear them throwing his clothes off the chair before sitting on it or the squeak of the bed as they sat on its edge. Sometimes they would talk to him a long time, the murmur of their voices blending with the music of the radio into a mysterious vapour-like sound which floated softly up the stairs.

I say this again as if it all happened at once and as if all of my sisters were of identical ages and like so many lemmings going into another sea and, again, it was of course not that way at all. Yet go they did, to Boston, to Montreal, to New York with the young men they met during the summers and later married in those far-away cities. The young men were very articulate and handsome and wore fine clothes and drove expensive cars and my sisters, as I said, were very tall and beautiful with their copper-coloured hair and were tired of darning socks and baking bread.

One by one they went. My mother had each of her daughters for fifteen years, then lost them for two and finally forever. None married a fisherman. My mother never accepted any of the young men, for in her eyes they seemed always a combination of the lazy, the effeminate, the dishonest and the unknown. They never seemed to do any physical work and she could not comprehend their luxurious vacations and she did not know whence they came nor who they were. And in the end she did not really care, for they were not of her people and they were not of her sea.

I say this now with a sense of wonder at my own stupidity in think-ing I was somehow free and would go on doing well in school and playing and helping in the boat and passing into my early teens while streaks of grey began to appear in my mother's dark hair and my father's rubber boots dragged sometimes in the pebbles of the beach as he trudged home from the wharf. And there were but three of us in the house that at one time had been so loud.

Then during the winter that I was fifteen he seem to grow old and ill at once. Most of January he lay upon the bed, smoking and reading and listening to the radio while the wind howled about the house and the needle-like snow blistered off the ice-covered harbour and the doors flew out of people's hands if they did not cling to them like death.

In February when the men began overhauling their lobster traps he still did not move, and my mother and I began to knit lobster trap head-ings in the evenings. The twine was always very sharp and harsh, and blisters formed upon our thumbs and little paths of blood snaked quiet-ly down between our fingers while the seals that had drifted down from distant Labrador wept and moaned like human children on the ice-floes of the Gulf.

In the daytime my mother's brother who had been my father's partner as long as I could remember also came to work upon the gear. He was a year older than my mother and was tall and dark and the father of twelve children.

By March we were very far behind and although I began to work very hard in the evenings I knew it was not hard enough and that there were but eight weeks left before the opening of the season on May first. And I knew that my mother worried and my uncle was uneasy and that all of our very lives depended on the boat being ready with her gear and two men, by the date of May the first. And I knew then that *David Copperfield* and *The Tempest* and all of those friends I had dearly come to love must really go forever. So I bade them all good-bye.

The night after my first full day at home and after my mother had gone upstairs he called me into his room where I sat upon the chair be-side his bed. "You will go back tomorrow," he said simply.

I refused then, saying I had made my decision and was satisfied.

"That is no way to make a decision," he said, "and if you are satisfied I am not. It is best that you go back." I was almost angry then and told him as all children do that I wished he would leave me alone and stop telling me what to do.

He looked at me a long time then, lying there on the same bed on which he had fathered me those sixteen years before, fathered me his only son, out of who knew what emotions when he was already fifty-six and his hair had turned to snow. Then he swung his legs over the edge of the squeaking bed and sat facing me and looked into my own dark eyes with his of crystal blue and placed his hand upon my knee. "I am not telling you to do anything," he said softly, "only asking you."

The next morning I returned to school. As I left, my mother followed me to the porch and said, "I never thought a son of mine would choose useless books over the parents that gave him life."

In the weeks that followed he got up rather miraculously and the gear was ready and the *Jenny Lynn* was freshly painted by the last two weeks of April when the ice began to break up and the lonely screaming gulls returned to haunt the silver herring as they flashed within the sea.

On the first day of May the boats raced out as they had always done, laden down almost to the gunwales with their heavy cargoes of traps. They were almost like living things as they plunged through the waters of the spring and manoeuvred between the still floating icebergs of crystal-white and emerald green on their way to the traditional grounds that they sought out every May. And those of us who sat that day in the high school on the hill, discussing the water imagery of Tennyson, watched them as they passed back and forth beneath us until by afternoon the piles of traps which had been stacked upon the wharf were no longer visible but were spread about the bottoms of the sea. And the *Jenny Lynn* went too, all day, with my uncle tall and dark, like a latter-day Tashtego standing at the tiller with his legs wide apart and guiding her deftly between the floating pans of ice and my father in the stern standing in the same way with his hands upon the ropes that lashed the cargo to the deck. And at night my mother asked, "Well, how did things go in the boat today?"

And the spring wore on and the summer came and school ended in the third week of June and the lobster season on July first and I wished that the two things I loved so dearly did not exclude each other in a manner that was so blunt and too clear.

At the conclusion of the lobster season my uncle said he had been offered a berth on a deep sea dragger and had decided to accept. We all knew he was leaving the *Jenny Lynn* forever and that before the next lobster season he would buy a boat of his own. He was expecting another child and would be supporting fifteen people by the next spring and could not chance my father against the family that he loved.

I joined my father then for the trawling season, and he made no protest and my mother was quite happy. Through the summer we baited the tubs of trawl in the afternoon and set them at sunset and revisited them in the darkness of the early morning. The men would come tramping by our house at four A.M. and we would join them and walk with them to the wharf and be on our way before the sun rose out of the ocean where it seemed to spend the night. If I was not up they would toss pebbles to my window and I would be very embarrassed and tumble downstairs to where my father lay fully clothed atop his bed, reading his book and listening to his radio and smoking his cigarette. When I appeared he would swing off his bed and put on his boots and be instantly ready and then we would take the lunches my mother had prepared the night before and walk off toward the sea. He would make no attempt to wake me himself.

It was in many ways a good summer. There were few storms and we were out almost every day and we lost a minimum of gear and seemed to land a maximum of fish and I tanned dark and brown after the manner of my uncles.

My father did not tan — he never tanned — because of his reddish complexion, and the salt water irritated his skin as it had for sixty years. He burned and reburned over and over again and his lips still cracked so that they bled when he smiled. and his arms, especially the left, still broke out into the oozing salt-water boils as they had ever since as a child I had first watched him soaking and bathing them in a variety of ineffectual solutions. The chafe-preventing bracelets of brass linked chain that all the men wore about their wrists in early spring were his the full season and he shaved but painfully and only once a week.

And I saw then, that summer, many things that I had seen all my life as if for the first time and I thought that perhaps my father had never been intended for a fisherman either physically or mentally. At least not in the manner of my uncles; he had never really loved it. And I remembered that, one evening in his room when we were talking about *David Copperfield*, he had said that he had always wanted to go to the university and I had dismissed it then in the way one dismisses his father's saying he would like to be a tight-rope walker, and we had gone on to talk about the Peggottys and how they loved the sea.

And I thought to then to myself that there were many things wrong with all of us and all our lives and I wondered why my father, who was himself an only son, had not married before he was forty and then I wondered why he had. I even thought that perhaps he had had to marry my mother and checked the dates on the flyleaf of the Bible where I learned that my oldest sister had been born a prosaic eleven months after the marriage, and I felt myself then very dirty and debased for my lack of faith and for what I had thought and done.

And then there came into my heart a very great love for my father and I thought it was very much braver to spend a life doing what you really do not want rather than selfishly following forever your own dreams and inclinations. And I knew then that I could never leave him alone to suffer the iron-tipped harpoons which my mother would forever hurl into his soul because he was a failure as a husband and father who had retained none of his own. And I felt that I had been very small in a little secret place within me and that even the completion of high school was for me a silly shallow selfish dream.

So I told him one night very resolutely and very powerfully that I would remain with him as long as he lived and we would fish the sea together. And he made no protest but only smiled through the cigarette smoke that wreathed his bed and replied, "I hope you will remember what you have said."

The room was now so filled with books as to be almost Dickensian, but he would not allow my mother to move or change them and continued to read them, sometimes two or three a night. They came with great regularity now, and there were more hard covers, sent by my sisters who had gone so long ago and now seemed so distant and so prosperous, and sent also pictures of small red-haired grandchildren with baseball bats and dolls which he placed upon his bureau and which my mother gazed at wistfully when she thought no one would see. Red-haired grandchildren with baseball bats and dolls who would never know the sea in hatred or in love.

And so we fished through the heat of August and into the cooler days of September when the water was so clear we could almost see the bottom and the white mists rose like delicate ghosts in the early morning dawn. And one day my mother said to me, "You have given added years to his life."

And we fished on into October when it began to roughen and we could no longer risk night-sets but took our gear out each morning and returned at the first sign of the squalls; and on into November when we lost three tugs of trawl and the clear blue water turned to sullen grey and the trochoidal waves rolled rough and high and washed across our bows and decks as we ran within their troughs. We wore heavy sweaters now and the awkward rubber slickers and the heavy woollen mitts which soaked and froze into masses of ice that hung from our wrists like the limbs of gigantic monsters until we thawed them against the exhaust pipe's heat. And almost every day we would leave for home before noon, driven by the blasts of the northwest wind, coating our eyebrows with ice and freezing our eyelids closed as we leaned into a visibility that was hardly there, charting our course from the compass and the sea, running with the waves and between them but never confronting their towering might.

And I stood at the tiller now, on these homeward lunges, stood in the place and in the manner of my uncle, turning to look at my father and to shout over the roar of the engine and slop of the sea to where he stood in the stern, drenched and dripping with the snow and the salt and the spray and his bushy eyebrows caked in ice. But on November twenty-first, when it seemed we might be making the final run of the season, I turned and he was not there and I knew even in that instant that he would never be again.

On November twenty-first the waves of the grey Atlantic are very high and the waters are very cold and there are no signposts on the surface of the sea. You cannot tell where you have been five minutes before and in the squalls of snow you cannot see. And it takes longer than you would believe to check a boat that has been running before a gale and turn her ever so carefully in a wide and stupid circle, with timbers creaking and straining, back into the face of storm. And you know that it is useless and that your voice does not carry the length of the boat and that even if you knew the original spot, the relentless waves would carry such a burden perhaps a mile or so by the time you could return. And you know also, the final irony, that your father like your uncles and all the men that form your past, cannot swim a stroke.

The lobster beds off the Cape Breton coast are still very rich and now, from May to July, their offerings are packed in crates of ice, and thundered by the gigantic transports trucks, day and night, through New Glasgow, Amherst, Saint John and Bangor and Portland and into Boston where they are tossed still living into boiling pots of water, their final home.

And though the prices are higher and the competition tighter, the grounds to which the *Jenny Lynn* once went remain untouched and un-fished as they have for the last ten years. For if there are no signposts on the sea in storm there are certain ones in calm and the lobster bot-toms were distributed in calm before any of us can remember and the grounds my father fished were those his father fished before him and there were others before and before. Twice the big boats have come from forty and fifty miles, lured by the promise of the grounds, and strewn the bottom with their traps and twice they have returned to find their buoys cut adrift and their gear lost and destroyed. Twice the fisheries officer and the Mounted Police have come and asked many long and involved questions and twice they have received no answers from the men leaning in the doors of their shanties and the women standing at their windows with their children in their arms. Twice they have gone away saying: "There are no legal boundaries in the Marine area"; "No one can own the sea"; "Those grounds don't wait for anyone."

But the men and the women, with my mother dark among them, do not care for what they say, for to them the grounds are sacred and they think they wait for me.

It is not an easy thing to know that your mother lives alone on an inadequate insurance policy and that she is too proud to accept any other aid. And that she looks through her lonely window onto the ice of winter and the hot flat calm of summer and the rolling waves of fall. And that she lies awake in the early morning's darkness when the rub-ber boots of the men scrunch upon the gravel as they pass beside her house on their way down to the wharf. And she knows that the footsteps never stop, because no man goes from her house, and she alone of all the Lynns has neither son nor son-in-law that walks toward the boat that will take him to the sea. And it is not an easy thing to know that your mother looks upon the sea with love and on you with bitterness because the one has been so constant and the other so untrue.

But neither is it easy to know that your father was found on November twenty-eighth, ten miles to the north and wedged between two boulders at the base of the rock-strewn cliffs where he had been hurled and slammed so many many times. His hands were shredded ribbons as were his feet which had lost their boots to the suction of the sea, and his shoulders came apart in our hands when we tried to move him from the rocks. And the fish had eaten his testicles and the gulls had pecked out his eyes and the white-green stubble of his whiskers had continued to grow in death, like the grass on graves, upon the purple, bloated mass that was his face. There was not much left of my father, physically, as he lay there with the brass chains on his wrists and the seaweed in his hair.

JANICE KULYK KEEFER

Janice Kulyk Keefer was born in Toronto in 1952. She holds a doctorate in modern English literature from the University of Sussex, England. Her short fiction and literary criticism have appeared in many journals. Her first collection of fiction was *The Paris-Napoli Express* (Oberon ,1986). She has also published a collection of poetry, *White of the Lesser Angels* (Ragweed, 1986),a second short-story collection, *Transfigurations* (Ragweed, 1987), and a novel, *Constellations* (Random House, 1988). Her critical study of Maritime fiction, *Under Eastern Eyes*, was released by University of Toronto Press in 1987 and nominated for the Governor-General's Award for non-fiction. She is currently working on a critical study of Mavis Gallant to be published by Oxford University Press in 1989. She was a first prize-winner in the 1984 *PRISM international* Fiction Competition, and won first prize for fiction in the CBC Radio Literary Competition in both 1985 and 1986. She was a regional winner (Canada and the Caribbean) in the 1986 British Airways Commonwealth Poetry Competition.

PASSAGES

Janice Kulyk Keefer

I

At night, he dreamt of mountains: perfectly conical, with tips like ice picks aimed at the soft, grey belly of that sky which had swallowed Belle, swallowed her as a whale might some fat, small fish moving through a mess of plankton. Mountain top pricking open the sky, and riding some cosmic and placental wave, Belle, transformed by death and all the glories promised to the meek and lowly; changed into a rampaging angel come to avenge herself on him for all the things she'd never openly accused him of in forty years of marriage, but which she'd stored up inside her like some peculiarly fragile child that couldn't survive outside the womb.

Even though they slept in separate beds, Charles had been able to feel that baby kicking him from deep inside its mother's belly: as Belle put on more and more weight, he couldn't help thinking of that child inside her, growing taller and thicker, developing extra sets of ears and eyes and fingernails. What would have happened had Belle ever opened her mouth and let the child leap out her throat: made its birth

scream between them? One monstrous wail — insults, reproaches, ac-
cusations? Or would they have heard some answer to their troubles,
the child a messenger from Belle's God, telling them all would be well,
all manner of things would be well; tears dried and sins confessed as
a host of heavenly voices shouted praise from the very mountain tops?
Granite breasts swollen with ice, not milk: daggers sheathed in snow.

***

Dear Vi,

    *Bad news, I'm afraid. Belle died in her sleep last week — she was
buried yesterday morning. Funny, I never heard a thing, even though
I'm a light sleeper, as you'll perhaps remember. Doctor said it was her
heart — tricky things, you never know when they'll start acting up. I
suppose I could have been more careful with her, making sure she took
her pills, that sort of thing. But it was her weight that killed her in the
end — the doctor said. Still, it was a beautiful day to be buried: river
and sky the same clear blue, gulls like little blind angels in the air —
noisy angels — do you remember?*
    *I thought you should know, even though you two never met — life
doesn't always work out the way we plan, does it? I've sold the
Hardware Store — didn't seem much point in keeping it on, or the
house, either. I expect I'll find a nice little apartment in town — easy
to heat and clean — I won't find another housekeeper like Belle, that's
for certain. But there'll be plenty of room should you ever change your
mind and come for a visit. You know you're always welcome, as they
say.*

*fond regards
your brother, Charles*

***

He'd written the first things that had popped into his head: sealed
the envelope and mailed it off right before pick-up: he'd even watched
it being loaded into the truck and driven down the road, whether to hell
or Halifax, it didn't matter — he'd done what he had to and thought
no more about it. Once a year he wrote to Vi and she to him: Christmas

cards. "Hoping all's well." Forty years of Christmas cards with horses and sleighs, tobogganing children, snow-caked spruce. Three years ago she'd enclosed a note on black-bordered paper:

Dear Charles,

   Harry passed away last month, after a short illness. It's been hard, but I'm over the worst of it now, and keeping busy with old friends and new activities. Thank God I still have my health. As ever, Vi.

He'd written back immediately, asking her to come and stay with them, though Belle hadn't said a word when he'd told her. Both of them knew Vi would never come back — didn't need to: "Thank God I still have my money." Harry would have left her plenty. It wasn't the price of a ticket from Vancouver that would keep her away, but Belle. Forty years of Belle in the house. Now both were gone: he had his apartment over the lawyer's office, with a view of the river and low blue hills beyond. She'd like it were she to come and stay — she should come back, everyone should come back at least once to the place they were born. Come home to die — but that was morbid, there was plenty of time left, plenty of time to sort things out.

   On his way to the Post Office he stopped to lean against the railing and look out at the basin — there was a park bench behind the War Memorial: facing the water, not the street. Miss Jenner had seen to that, she'd published a letter in the local paper, saying she had no interest in counting the cars that passed or the number of candy wrappers dropped on the pavement. No, she wanted to look out at the river and if two strong men couldn't be found to turn the park bench around, then what was the world coming to? Two strong men — former students of Miss Jenner — had been found, the bench turned, and for the remaining ten years of the old woman's life she'd enjoyed the view almost as much as her victory. But Charles could never bring himself to sit down for long on Miss Jenner's bench. She'd been his English teacher — Vi's too. If Vi did come back for a visit she'd have a perfect right to sit there and count the sailboats gliding by. Vi had done what Miss Jenner had said he should do — leave home, go out into the great world, make something of yourself. Vi'd ended up as far as possible from where she'd started out. Vancouver, the West Coast, the Pacific Rim
. . . .

It made him think of an enormous circle with boats whirling round and round like a finger inside a wine glass, making the crystal ring. He'd bought Bohemian crystal, decanter and six wine glasses, for their twenty-fifth anniversary, but she'd not allowed him to fill it with anything stronger than soda water. Belle, Belle, Bible Belle, touch a drop and you'll burn in Hell. Not she — he pictured her just as she'd wished to be — in a long white gown floating over, never touching flesh that had been skimmed from her like scum from soup bones simmering. In her heaven Belle would weigh no more than a bird, would sing like a bird, notes true and high and free. *Rock of Ages/Cleft for Me/Touch my dark/Declivities.* No, not that — his mind was fuzzing over, like the lint screen in the dryer: he couldn't get the words right anymore, he couldn't remember.

Miss Jenner had been a great admirer of the early Yeats — had set them "The Rose on the Rood of Time" to memorize for the final exams — "Down by the Salley Gardens" for graduation. He'd recited it to the whole school, his parents in the front row, Vi come home to see him get his diploma. He'd thought it was "Sally," the name of a girl, until Miss Jenner had corrected him. *"It comes from the French word for willow, Charles — your sister could have told you that."* His sister had gone off to Halifax to work as a secretary, earn the money to send him through university, though she could have gone there herself, she was that smart. 100 in Maths and English without hardly cracking a book, while he'd had to sweat blood to manage a 75.

Nice girl behind the counter: the Amero's girl. "Letter for you, Mr. Spinney." He never got enough mail to warrant having one of the little metal boxes — General Delivery would do for him, and besides, he got to hear the Amero's girl calling out his name, making him feel — important, alive still. "Thanks, Alice. Give my regards to your folks when next you write. Oh, yes — of course, stupid of me, I'll be forgetting my name next. I was sorry to hear about his passing away — last year, was it? Four years ago? Yes, well, tell your mother hello when next you write." Trying to appear casual, as if he received letters like this every day, on expensive stationery, fountain pen, not ball point ink: "Mr. Charles H. Spinney, Esq./30 St. George Street,/Annapolis Royal, Nova Scotia." She forgot the postal code — figured she didn't need to use it, Annapolis being somewhat smaller than Vancouver. Mrs. V. Green. 2441 Ocean Drive, West Vancouver.

V. for Violet; H. for Henry: Charles Henry — fine and fitting name
to be inscribed on a university diploma: would she have come back for
that graduation, too? And for his wedding to Norah Hammond: Dr. and
Mrs. Philip Hammond announce the marriage of their daughter Norah
Marie to Professor Charles Henry Spinney. It was only Belle who'd
called him Charlie, down in the Salley Gardens. But "esquire" — had
Alice laughed at that? It was the first time Vi had put that on an envelope — first time she'd ever written him a letter instead of a card.
And not at Christmas but closer to Easter. Her Christmas card this year
had barely differed from the previous ones: "Hoping you're well" instead of "Hoping all's well." Had she even received his letter about
Belle — could her response have been lost in the mail? Vancouver so
far away, the end of the earth ... .

Yet here he was with her letter in his hands. He couldn't wait until
he got home, he had to open it this minute to find out — On Miss
Jenner's bench he sat down, tearing open the stiff envelope but remov-
ing the paper as carefully as if it had some rare specimen — a
wildflower or butterfly — pressed inside.

Dear Charles,

*I would have written before this but I wanted to work out the details
quite carefully. You are very kind to ask me to come and stay with you,
but of course that is out of the question.*

Of course. He looked up, over the river, to the houses on the opposite bank. Counted three white steeples, the gables of the old Hammond house, turned into a bed and breakfast these past fifteen years.
Vi had been best friends with Norah Hammond at high school, even
though Norah was two years younger, in his own class. Norah lived in
Fredericton now — she'd married a university professor. If Norah had
written asking Vi to stay, would Vi have said yes? Had she maybe come
and visited Norah, but never told him, never even taken the ferry across
to see him — only for a day, an afternoon when Belle was off at the
Tabernacle?

*My world is on the West Coast now — I simply couldn't imagine
myself in the east, even for a visit. One puts one's past behind one and
moves out. I've reached, not the end but the very rim, now — and am*

*as content as I shall ever be, with Harry gone. But I'd regret not seeing
you again, after all this time: it's unfortunate that circumstances have
prevented our meeting.*

Two hundred and twenty-three pounds of circumstances, on little
snow white feet, the only things about her that had not changed, that
had never been other than they'd seemed, that first time.

*I have a proposal, then. Why don't you come out to see me? The
house is large enough that we wouldn't get in each other's way, and it
would make a pleasant change for you. Canada's an enormous country
— you really ought to see more of it than your little corner of Nova
Scotia, you know. You could take the train out — cross the Rockies,
even stop off at Banff or Jasper for a few days. And then spend a week
here. I'm afraid any longer would be impossible right now — I have
to be away for a couple of months at my daughter's home in Colorado.
Let me know as soon as possible if this little plan suits you.*

All the best,
Vi

He put the letter in his jacket pocket. Below him the river ran, still slug-
gish with broken ice that would not melt away, though it was almost
April. Four months from now you'd never know it was the same place
— sun like a great warm hand stroking everything; fireweed growing
along the riverbank, soft pink cones that would grow anywhere, even
in burnt-out rubble. Walking those long summer evenings, under the
swallows' sickle wings, till the church bells rang eleven o'clock, playing the hymn tune to tell her she had to get home. Pink, plumed
fireweed, high enough to screen them from everything but sky and
swallows and church bells. She'd go first, smoothing her skirts, letting
him wipe the smudges from her face and hands, wipe them off with
the quivering tip of his tongue. After she'd gone he'd wait till the
quarter hour then head to the house that smelled of his mother's tal-
cum powder, his dead father's tools. His mother who couldn't read
more than the labels of the soup tins, his father who wasn't a doctor
but a carpenter, though Norah didn't mind: she would wait for him, she
said, wait until he got his degree and then marry him. But not go walking in the Salley gardens, not let him do more than shake her hand, "I
know you, Charles Spinney, I couldn't trust myself with you."

He'd ask Vi, when he got to Vancouver. "Hear from Norah Hammond at all?" Casual, as if he saw Norah every day of the week, waved to her from across the water. Nice, comfortable kind of river, this — not too wide or deep: coming from some place definite, going on to another just as settled and expected. Not like an ocean, the Pacific ocean — at least England was on the other side of the Atlantic, but where Vi lived, you'd look out and what would there be? Japan and China .... Why couldn't he remember the other ones — he'd studied them all in geography class .... Asia. Asia wasn't some place solid and definite like England — they didn't speak any kind of language you could understand there. He couldn't understand Vi having wanted to settle out on the west coast, but she'd explain it all to him when he saw her there. Long way to go, but at the end of it she'd be waiting, she would tell him everything he needed to know. No one could go all that way and not find out something important — it was a scientific fact, what did they call it? A factor of distance, that was it: the distance factor.

***

If she quizzed him about not taking the train, not taking the train because he was afraid of the mountains, he would tell her the travel agent had advised against it. "There are terrific seat sales on — it would be a shame not to take advantage of them, Mr. Spinney." He could have kissed the girl — she looked too young to be able to make all those complicated arrangements for him, but there it was — signed, sealed — what else? He'd driven in all the way to Bridgetown to collect the tickets, though she could have mailed them to him. But then he'd never have known she was pretty, as well as young. He could have kissed her, young and foolish, and his heart full of — something to rhyme with trees: ease, of course.

He walked along Main Street before driving home. Stopped in at The Elms Cafe for their daily special. Wonderful pastry on the chicken pie — Belle never could make pastry — you had to have cold hands, she'd said. Cold hands, warm heart. Belle's hands small and plump and hot, like turnovers. Belle in the bath, an enormous dumpling in too small a pot: she'd cover herself with washcloths if ever he had to come in while she were soaking on a Sunday. After church, washing off the

Blood of the Lamb. Spotless: you had to give her that. Starching his shirts just so, keeping the floors shiny as tin foil, even washing the leaves of her houseplants twice a week. But she wouldn't tolerate pets, that was the only point on which she'd ever crossed him. He'd have liked to get a puppy, train it to bring him his paper, sit by his feet in the evenings while he stroked its long, silky ears. His lease forbade pets in the building — it was too late, anyway, he wouldn't be able to walk a young dog, give it the exercise it needed.

Did Vi have a dog, he wondered? A white poodle, a miniature? Or a watchdog — she'd maybe be nervous in the house with Harry gone. She wouldn't be nervous — she'd gone off across the country just like that, hadn't she? With Harry, it's true, but he wouldn't have had a penny in his pockets after paying train fares and sandwiches and coffee. But things had worked out well for them, most likely he'd died a rich man. *The house is big enough that we wouldn't get in each other's way.* No apartment over a lawyer's office for her ....

The waitress came with his bill — he took out ten dollars, leaving too big a tip on the linoleum-topped table. This girl wasn't young or pretty: he'd no desire even to shake her hand. That girl in the travel agent's — red hair, green eyes, breasts like new-baked bread under her sweater .... Even ten years ago he would have been able to strike a smile from her, strike a spark. They'd always tell him, "You're so gentle, so careful, Charlie my darling." Stroking their hair, long and silky, my love and I, my love, till the hymn tune rang and he'd have to get home, Belle would be back from chapel: watching for him, eating a bag of sugar cookies, a whole tub of butterscotch ice cream by the time he finally walked in the door.

Drive Carefully, We Love Our Children. No sign like that in Annapolis — silly to put one up — everyone loves their children. Annapolis was full of them, he saw them every day on his walk through the fort — that tall boy walking an Irish setter, the young ones riding on cannons, firing imaginary volleys over the river, into the hills. Would there be a place to go walking in Vancouver — he needed his exercise, the doctor had warned him. If there'd been children, if he could have taken his boys out to play baseball, taken his daughters for walks with the new puppy, round and round the paths threading the green grass at the Fort, over the hills down which children went rolling, faster and faster, shrieking laughter .... *Make themselves sick,*

Belle would say, shaking her head as they walked the paths together on a Sunday afternoon, the only exercise she'd take besides cleaning house every day.

Walk together, but not arm in arm or hand in hand. Single file because Belle was so huge the two of them couldn't squeeze side by side on the path. Huge enough to be pregnant with quints, but you couldn't use that word, you were 'expecting' or 'that way', what could he do, she was 'that way' and we love our children, drive carefully, you'll make yourself sick, rolling fast and faster down the hill, shrieking and laughing. He would fly right over the mountains and never look down. Perfectly conical tips piercing the grey belly of the plane, gutting it like a mackerel, until they all fell laughing and shrieking out of the sky ....

II

Vi gave him a room from which he could see the bay: draw his curtains in the early morning and watch the freighters glide across water that looked as insubstantial as the mist suspended in the air: dampness that did not fall but insinuated itself into his hair and clothes so that after an hour's walk he felt soaked to the skin. It had rained each of the seven days he'd been in Vancouver — rain that seemed to soften his perceptions, responses, as if they were laundry soaking in a tub till the colours ran and nothing could be sorted out at all.

Vi had been cross about the weather — "this is dreadful, even for Vancouver — I can't remember when we've had such a bad stretch. But it's bound to clear tomorrow, and as soon as it does we'll head off for Squamish and Garibaldi. When I think of how we used to call them 'mountains,' back in the Valley — ridiculous, isn't it? Never mind, we'll do the Aquarium today, and there's a concert tonight at the Queen Elizabeth. We'll come back in between — you'll want to rest, and I've got some correspondence I must take care of. But I'll just run out to the shops now — get in some salmon and strawberries for supper. Won't be a minute."

She spoke just the way she wrote — as if his ears were pieces of paper she could inscribe and mail away, just as she chose — as if he'd have nothing to answer back, say to her face. He'd not recognized that face at the airport, though she had known him, straight away. "Well, my handsome brother — you've not changed so very much." But she had — not just her face, her clothes, but her voice, as well. She sounded as if she'd been born Mrs. Harold Green, and not Violet Ethel Spinney; born in a cashmere sweater and pleated skirt, gold bracelets on her wrists. *Our Vi'let's some clever. Mother, you shouldn't say "some." Real clever, then. No, mother* — Vi had learned how to talk from Miss Jenner: elocution lessons that she'd made him repeat at night, so he'd sound like the son of somebody important when he went on to university. "Down by the Salley Gardens/My love and I did meet/She met me in the something/on little snow white feet." How did it go? Feet like daisies on the grass, he'd told her; elocution: they fall for that. Fall right back on their round little heels.

He left his room as soon as he heard her car pull out from the garage. She'd be gone for half an hour at the most: he could look at the things in her house — he didn't feel right about looking when she was there. Picking up the little silver-framed photographs on her writing desk. A boy and a girl: George and Susan, she'd told him. Plastic cubes filled with pictures of their children — babies, teenagers — Susan in Colorado, married to a — doctor? George a civil engineer somewhere in — Africa? No, couldn't be Africa: what had she told him that first night? That she'd had the two children — she'd never written that on her Christmas cards. Imagine having children and not shouting it out across the continent.

His nephews and nieces, goddamnit, he had a right to know she'd had children. They were his too, even if it was a line of blood thin as thread between them. These things should be known. He would ask her for their addresses, write to them, introduce himself. Your uncle Charles. Your mother's brother, Charles Henry. *Charlie Spinney, from Royal Hardware — can get you the best deal in town on kiddies' bikes.* The one he'd bought for the boy was still in the garage when he'd sold the house: cocooned in plastic, just in case. *These things happen: better luck next time.*

This portrait on the dining room wall — Harry? It gave him a peevish sort of satisfaction to look at him at last: wall-eyed, pencil moustache, snot-grey eyes. A naval rating who hadn't bothered shipping home after the war: they'd met in Halifax, she'd said. And that was all she'd tell him — her own brother. Just the few facts she wanted him to know. And asking him nothing, as if Belle had been some enormous zero added to his life, a zero to cancel him out. "Charles? Are you ready? Good, I'll just put these things in the fridge and we can be off. I'm afraid it's raining again — I'd hoped that at least it would stay mist and we could walk in Stanley Park. It's the mountains, I'm afraid — they keep in the rain."

Crossing the Lion's Gate Bridge she gestured to what would have been mountains on a sunny day. He stared intently at the freighters chugging under the bridge — what would it cost to hop on board and sail round the world? He'd meant to do that during summer breaks at university — the big boats were always looking for crew, and he'd have worked for his keep alone, just to go off, get out. Those first few months after his marriage, waiting for the baby to be born, he'd planned it all out: he'd get a loan from the bank, get in brand-new stock, enlarge the premises. Save up for a sloop, second-hand — by the time his kid was old enough to sail with him, he'd have enough to pick one up. Have their pictures taken on board, both of them in nautical whites, gold cord, captain's hats: send it to Vi. *I'm sorry — how unfortunate.*

He was sorry when the traffic unsnarled and they got off the bridge. Vi spent a long time looking for a parking place — she didn't want the paintwork scratched. Harry had always been so careful with his cars — he'd been like a kid when he'd bought his first BMW. Charles, waiting for her to ask him what he drove but she didn't — she wouldn't ask him anything. Embarrassed when he'd told her about Belle, things going wrong. "She was so strong and healthy-looking before — you'd have thought she was built for nothing else. The baby was growing inside her tubes, instead of her —" *I'm sorry. You must be tired, Charles, why don't*—"Then it turned out there was scarring of the tubes, something — the doctor didn't explain it too well. Anyway, she couldn't have anymore, and so we — never thought of adoption, she felt it as a judgment —" *How unfortunate. Well, if you're not exhausted, Charles, I am — airports are impossible these days.*

Exhausted. Seven days he'd been here: they'd done the Art Gallery, the Museum, the St. Roche, Gastown, Chinatown, the UBC campus, seen an opera, a play, a film, gone to lectures — and now the Aquarium. Sometimes she'd get phone calls, and she'd always say, "I'm afraid I'm tied up for the present, but how kind of you to think of me, my dear." Tied up, as if they were children playing cowboys and

Indians, and he'd left her fastened to the gatepost in the garden. She'd never called him "my dear," it was always "Charles," with an invisible exclamation mark, as if she were Miss Jenner rapping him to attention, correcting his grammar and posture — checking his fingernails.

All through the Aquarium she never stopped talking, telling him about the dolphins and tropical fish, making sure he read all the posters, gathering information for which he had no more use than he did now for Belle's shoe size, her Health Plan number. They stayed long enough for the whale show, even though the seats were uncomfortable and the air so wet and heavy he thought his clothes would melt and leave him naked there. Naked in front of his sister and the trainer and the snow-white whales with their dimpled eyes and sleek, vague flesh, splashing and thumping in the cloudy water, everyone shrieking and laughing around him, rolling over and over down the hill. *Make you sick.*

He put his hankerchief up to his brow: it came back drenched with sweat. His heart lurching like one of the whales; must get your exercise, the doctor said, must take your medicine. He hadn't brought his pills, his little vial of pills. Vial, Vi — must tell her, ask her to take him out, get him away. But her eyes were fixed on the whales — she was a hundred miles away and all he could do was grip his knees and bear down against the pain hard as a fist inside him, a little embryo curled up inside the shadow place where his heart should be.

***

The day before his plane was due to leave the rain finally stopped. Vi explained to him at breakfast how they'd drive up to Garibaldi — it wasn't the best day in the world, but he couldn't leave B.C. without having seen the mountains. He'd put his cup down so hard and quick the coffee splashed over the tablecloth. Irish Linen — white: nothing but the best for her little brother. Watching her mop at the stain he remembered the way she'd scrubbed the floors at home, wearing rubber gloves so her hands wouldn't get red and rough. Like Belle's hands, up to the day she dies. He'd buried her out of town in the cemetery of the Tabernacle of the Holy Ghost: she'd have wanted to be close to her church, God knew she'd spent enough time inside it. That first year after the baby hadn't been born — she'd not set foot outside the house, and then after the minister had started coming round, she was hardly there at all, except to clean and cook. Snake-oil minister coming round, getting at her, after her — to get him too. *Jesus Christ, Belle, you mean you believe that stuff, you really believe that if I go down on my knees and pray with you, ask forgiveness, we'll get a baby out of it? Didn't you hear what the doctor said?*

"Did you hear me, Charles — we'll have to get moving."

"No." He looked into her eyes, but they weren't violets, they were crystalline, faceted, like the amethyst she wore on her finger. "I don't want to go anywhere."

"Are you all right, Charles — should I call a doctor?"

"Christ, no — why should there be anything wrong with me. I just don't want to go for a drive, I don't want to see mountains, I'm happy just to stay put and — talk."

"Talk about what, Charles?"

"Do you ever hear — I mean have you ever written — Norah Hammond?"

"Pardon? I don't understand."

"Norah. You knew her, she was your best — "

"Oh — oh yes, that prissy little girl who lived over the river. No, of course I don't write to her. Why on earth should I?"

He fiddled with the silver napkin ring, failing to stuff the crumpled napkin back inside.

"Well, if that's all you have to talk about, perhaps we can plan something for the day?"

"It's not all — I need to ask — " Dropping the ring so that it clattered, spinning on the ceramic tile. Watching till it became perfectly still before he spoke again, suddenly passionate: head clearer, words sharper than they'd ever been.

"I have to know, Vi. All kinds of things I want to know, and there's hardly any time left. Why did you ask me here, and then say nothing? Why? Thirty years, and now here we are, just like we used to be — but all that time between? What did I do that was so awful you couldn't forgive me? Marry Belle? Would you rather I'd left her — left her with a baby —"

"She didn't have the baby."

"I couldn't of known that — "

"Couldn't have, Charles — not couldn't of: couldn't have."

"Jesus Christ, Vi, what friggin' difference does it make now? Can't you say anything except what-a-wonderful-place-Vancouver-is — or correct my grammar? I want to know why you never wrote, never told me anything about yourself — your kids, your life. Don't you care? This is your brother speaking, the brother you walked out on for forty years — I needed you then, I had no one. Look, Belle's gone, she can't get in our way again."

Vi bending down, graceful, slender as a sparrow. Retrieving the napkin ring and putting it beside her plate. Then looking up at him, smiling. Pale, powdered face, always a lady's face. Suddenly he wanted to take his hand and slap her, hard; slap till the powder came off in his hands like bits of eggshell, exposing the blood and nerves beneath. His hands, lifting — and falling again as she began to speak: falling into fists clenched in his lap.

"Why are you going on about Belle, Charles? Do you really think it was Belle that made me — what did you say — walk out on you? Poor lovely, loose, unlucky Belle. She really paid for it, didn't she? Taking advantage of a dumb kid fresh out of high school — don't interrupt. You think you're the only one who took her down to the river on Friday and Saturday nights? You think it was the first time she ever got into trouble? Steady, Charles — you asked me to talk to you, and that's what I'm doing.

"It was never Belle, dear brother, little brother. It was you, being so stupid, Christ almighty you were that thick .... You still are — maybe that's why I asked you to come here, just to see if you'd learned anything over the years. Beautiful, stupid Charlie — or maybe I was the really stupid one, believing you could make it to university, get your degree. Letting Miss Jenner, may she rot in her lace and lavender Hell, letting her convince me that you were the one who ought to have the chance. I worked for four years to get you the money to start college, and what did you do? Went rolling in the clover with Belle Beeler, for God's sake. And if that weren't bad enough, marrying her; buying that rundown Hardware store no one else would touch —

"I'm sorry, Charles, sorry for both of you about the baby. But have you ever, ever stopped to consider what it was like for me? I could have taken that money and damn well sent myself through college, made something of myself. Instead I had to scrabble round for what I could get. And what I could get was Harry Green. Oh, he wasn't all bad,

Harry. And he's dead now — and I've got the children. I have just enough money to live my life exactly as I please — though the possibilities are somewhat diminished, you'll agree?

"You wanted to know why I asked you here? I don't know anymore. I suppose I wanted to prove to myself that I wasn't angry anymore, that I didn't need to hate anybody, resent anything. You said something in your letter about life never working out the way you want, the way you plan. You're right about that, at least. I've spent the whole week of your visit terrified I was going to explode at you — why else do you think I've been nattering away about Beautiful B.C., dragging you off to every tourist attraction I could find. I wasn't going to confess anything to you — but maybe it's better this way. It doesn't even matter, you'll be home tomorrow, and things will be back to where they were for both of us. Things don't work out. But we've one day left, and we might as well get through it as best we can. You don't want to drive up and see the mountains: fine — why don't I just leave you to your own devices. I have some people I should see downtown — I can drop you off wherever you like, Lighthouse Park, Stanley Park, English Bay. Charles — is that all right?"

She put her hand out to touch his arm, but he brushed her fingers as if they were flies settling on his sleeve.

"All right, then, Charles. I think it's best if I go out — you can do what you like here — there's a spare key by the telephone in the kitchen. I'll be back in time to make supper."

***

It took him less than an hour to pack, make sure he hadn't left anything under the bed, in the bathroom. At lunchtime he opened the refrigerator and stared at the remains of all the suppers they'd had together this past week. He felt helpless at the thought of putting them together into some sort of meal for himself — he'd walk the two blocks down to Marine Drive, and find a restaurant, instead. He'd spent almost nothing of the money he'd brought with him — some postcards which he'd never got round to sending to people back home. *You think you're the only one who took her down to the river on Friday and Saturday nights?* He wouldn't think about that now, he wasn't going to think about any of it, it made him dizzy: fear of heights, fear of falling —

He was out the door, down the street much too quickly for a man of his age, a man with his heart. Two blocks down to Marine Drive, and then along sidewalks filled with lilac-haired ladies towing pugs and poodles. He jutted out his chin, forced his shoulders back; tried to catch his reflection in each shop window. Distinguished: they'd told him he looked distinguished, all the giggling girls, laughing and shrieking, even though he was too old to run after them, chase them and pull them down into the fireweed. Handsome — everyone had told him how handsome he was: his mother, Vi, even Miss Jenner: *handsome is as handsome does, Charles — it'll take more than blue eyes to get you into university, my friend.*

He thought he saw Vi's car heading towards him — he ducked into the nearest door: Seashell Café. Sat down at a table near the back: ordered an omelette, toast and fruit salad, none of which he could eat. Tore the toast into little pellets with which he encircled his coffee cup. Closed his eyes and thought of the trees she'd shown him in Lighthouse Park, the day they'd driven out in the rain. Huge trees, pines were they? Rainforest like the tropical jungles he'd read about in his geography books at school. Vi had been able to tell him all the names — arbutus, he remembered arbutus …. He opened his eyes, drank the rest of his coffee: shivered. The lushness, the hugeness of the trees had repelled him, made his heart lurch, just as had the whales in the murky aquarium waters. Too big, too high — everything here was out of scale. Too much space to fill, too huge a silence to disguise with words.

Vi talking, telling him …. Cruel, unfair; she made things up just to hurt him. As if she'd suffered more than he — or Belle. He tried to stop the sound of her words coming back to him: clattered his cup on its saucer, drummed his fingers on the table, began reciting what he'd learned from Miss Jenner, graduation day in front of the whole auditorium:

> *Down by the Salley Gardens*
> *My love and I did meet*
> *She met me in the something*
> *On little snow white feet*
> *She bade me take love easy*
> *As the leaves grow on the trees*

He couldn't remember. Elocution lessons, grammar, public speaking
— Miss Jenner had said it was speech that separated man from the
animals. What then of all those silent nights with Belle? She'd talked
to the plants she washed and watered, she spoke in tongues at the Tabernacle, but with him — had he ever let her speak? Not just answer his
questions but let her tell him anything. Even when she'd come walking with him down by the river, even in the waste spaces, screened by
fireweed, pink conical tips like a whole chain of mountains round them
…. Laughing and shrieking as he'd chased her, pulled her down — and
then silence. His fingers speaking to her skin, the darkness into which
his body plunged like a car careening off a mountain ledge: "Belle, listen, hear me, somebody, anybody hear me. Things don't always work
out the way we plan."

"Did you want more coffee, sir?"

"Sure, then, why not? Nice day."

She nodded, moving away to another table, though he seemed to
be the only customer. Japanese — no bigger than a child. Pretty though
— her face made him think of piano keys, the skin so white, hair like
ebony. Fifteen, was she, seventeen? Belle had been twenty that summer: taller than this girl, but the same white skin, the same tiny feet.
Two years older than he, though you'd never have known it. By the
time she was thirty she'd looked more like those whales in the
aquarium than a woman. When had it been, at what precise moment
had she decided to make herself so monstrous he'd never so much as
rattle the lock on her bedroom door? Silent, tears coursing down her
face those times he'd forced her in the night, young and foolish but
she'd lain like a slab of marble under him, head turned away, though
the salt still stung as he tried to wipe her tears … .

"Will there be anything more, sir?"

"No. Nothing more. Miss?"

Like a bird perched on a branch, wary, rousing itself to fly away
—

"Nothing."

Leaving the café, stepping back onto the sidewalk he couldn't account to himself for the fact that he was alone. Where was Vi? What
had happened? They'd been having breakfast together, he had dropped
the silver napkin ring and it had made a noise like church bells ringing

out. She had picked it up for him, and gone off — where? And where was he? Sidewalks crammed with cut flowers in plastic pails. It would still be too cold at home for that — there'd been fresh snow the day before he left. She must be angry at him — there had been words, she had told him — He'd written a letter telling her Belle had gone, Death walking right into her room, standing over her bed, shadow like wings around her, embracing her. Angels are the birds of the soul, Miss Jenner had said, quoting — he couldn't remember who.

He should go home, but instead he took the road to the beach, walking along the concrete path and straining his eyes across the water — where was the river, the narrow, shallow river, Miss Jenner's bench? He couldn't get things into focus — while he was in the restaurant the fog had rolled in, obscuring the edges of things, making it difficult to tell where ocean began and land ended. He sat down on the log to get his bearings, and looked across the water. On one side an enormous hanging bridge, so far away, so insubstantial in the mist he couldn't believe a car could cross it. The bridge to Granville Ferry had collapsed one day, moments after a busload of school children had got across. God sees the little sparrow, God kills the little sparrow, and she had prayed to that God, cursing Charles because he wouldn't: cursing him silently, drifting in her own cloudy seas, battening there like some blind white growth, till he couldn't bear the sight of her, feel of her —

Late afternoon when he woke. Lights had gone on over the bridge — now it looked like a string of children's beads, the ones that snap together, and pull as easily apart. He stumbled to his knees, and then his feet, shaking sand and bits of bark out of his clothes, rubbing his hands over his eyes. And then opened them to see, for the first time, the mountains — soft, low, like a tired animal hunkering down, laying its head on its paws to sleep or die.

This water silent at his feet. Strange how silence makes a sound: slight shock of waves pushing to shore, like a noise heard in the night: vague, muffled, yet loud enough to wake the soundest sleeper. What Belle must have heard as she walked through the door from dreams to death. Is all suffering equal — do we each get the heaven we desire? Would Harry be banished from Vi's? Did Belle's include her Charlie-boy, standing off to the side of that chair in which she sat cradling her baby, their perfect first-born? Would he have in his heaven the Belle who'd walked with him by the river, who'd let him pull her down, silent, into the long grass, green grass, fireweed blazing the sky over their heads?

He sat back down on the log, suddenly, incomprehensibly at ease. It didn't matter what had happened at Vi's, what she'd said, what he could or couldn't remember. Air soft as milk, everything floating: buoyant and free. Under a glimmering sky he watched the freighters sail, orient-bound, their decks pricked out with lights like necklaces. They carried the dead: west to east, from dark to light. Freighters he would ride one day, passage he'd already booked. Not disappearing but dissolving — round and round the rim of unimaginable worlds.

KENT THOMPSON

Kent Thompson was born in Illinois and moved to New Brunswick in 1966 to teach in the English Department at the University of New Brunswick. He has combined a writing career with teaching at UNB since then.

He has published two collections of poetry, three novels and two collection of short stories, the most recent of which *Leaping Up, Sliding Away* (Goose Lane, 1987), shows his development of the form which has been called the "postcard story."

CORN FLAKES

Kent Thompson

We left Roy behind to look after the store. Do you think that was a mistake? So long as he doesn't drink, everything will be all right, but if he has a drink he'll decide there should be a display of Corn Flakes in the window. If he has a drink, he'll call Maisie, sure as life, and it will begin all over again. I don't want another grandchild. If he has a drink he'll have no more responsibility than water. Is that my fault? How can you discipline a kid with so much charm. "Mother," he said, "I've mended your stockings, you can stop crying now." The mess I've made of my life has cursed him. He's now 43 — and where would he be without the store? What will happen if I die? If you see the Corn Flakes in the window, stop in, won't you?

CHARLES BRUCE

Charles Bruce was born at Port Shoreham, Nova Scotia in 1906, and educated in Nova Scotia and New Brunswick. He worked as a reporter and editor for the Canadian Press for many years, much of the time in Toronto. *The Mulgrave Road*, one of four collections of his verse, won the Governor General's Award for Poetry in 1951. His other work includes the novel *The Channel Shore* and the short story collection *The Township of Time*. Charles Bruce died in 1971.

VOYAGE HOME 1910

Charles Bruce

Colin came up the companionway and hunched his shoulders against a cold and fitful wind. Northeasterly. He glanced at the sky. Dullish, with tattered rags and folds of cloud, but nothing ominous about it. If Ed McKee would tear loose from whatever petticoat held him here, they could square away, be home to Gloucester by Sunday.

He turned to cross the deck, ducked under the main boom resting in its triangles, and stood by the starboard rail, glancing absently at the snow-patched islands that ringed the harbor or Wilmot Town: Wagon Wheel, Kinsman's, Spanish Hill; and beyond that the tangle they called the Lion's Mane. Whatever petticoat, or lack of it, or whatever jug. He felt in his jacket pocket for an end of twist, and bit into it. Must be old age. He had never been one to pass judgment.

He shivered slightly, and his mind picked up memories of warmth and sunshine. A refit under the mountains of Opolu, in the *J.D.Everett*, and the sound of liquid voices. A ten-day run under daytime sunlight and the blaze of stars, west of the Keelings, and scarcely a hand to a rope.

Whatever a man could find in the huddled streets of these little down-east towns, it was not that. He spat across the rail, and raised a stained handkerchief to his lips. The big days of sail were gone. He felt no bitterness. It was handy that Gloucester and Lunenburg were still there, towns that could use the stuff a man had in him ...

The down-east towns were all right, too. Bait in the ice-pens, and a hotel room if you tired of a bunk, and men of your own kind. Obliquely, Colin sensed the fact that the palms, the color, the warmth, had always been a little strange to him. He had no quarrel with the down-east towns. It was just that Ed McKee ...

He hunched his shoulders and let them drop. He didn't have to *be* here. Should have stayed home in the room he had on Chestnut Street, waiting for spring and the new Chisholm vessel. If he hadn't picked this particular year to switch from salt-banking to seining ... South to the Virginia Capes, north to the Cape Shore, and not a decent fare in the whole of it ... Worst mackerel season in forty years.

Still, he hadn't *needed* to go freighting Newfoundland herring with Ed McKee at the season's end. All Ed had made the voyage for, he knew now, was the chance to run the *Pathfinder* into Wilmot Town on the trip back. And what he'd had in mind, urging Colin to come along, was to get a man aboard who would take charge while Ed enjoyed himself. They should have been back in Gloucester two days ago.

Home to Gloucester. The oddity of the thought engaged his mind, slightly, for a moment. Curious to be thinking *home to Gloucester* when the house he was born in was less than twenty miles away. As the crow flies, that is. A bit more if you took the steamer and the road. Ten miles, about, across the Channel's flaring mouth to Copeland. Nine or so up the road to Forester's Pond. Two and a half out the road they still called the New, though God knows when it had been first chopped out.

Well out, crawling up from the French Heads, Colin noted idly the little steamer that linked Wilmot Town and Fronsac and the railway at Copeland. And far off, the streak of unseen beaches under cloud-blurred hills.

From the corner of his eye he saw, with scant attention, a man loitering on the wharf. A man in gray sweater and jacket, cap pulled down over hooked nose, bow-legged in hip-boots folded down below the knee. Across the roadstead, under the lee of Wagon Wheel, an old plumb-stemmed Lunenburger lay at anchor. In with salt, likely, from Turks. Or maybe short of bait for winter haddocking.

Home. To a man without wife or children, these things were home. Steamy forecastles and cabins, the smell of brine, a loafer on a bare wharf, propping up a warehouse.

Still ... there was the instinct to pin the word to a place. The room on Chestnut Street. The Master Mariners.' The Cape Ann Savings Bank. And farther back in time, the gray house up the New Cut, most of the paint worn off, the last time he'd seen it, and Dave down-in-the-mouth at the way things were going.

Without much interest, he considered the possibility of a quick visit, if Ed McKee continued his activities up the hill. He glanced across at the straggling sidehill streets, their wooden houses and stores and mud-stained snow. Put Charley Fraser in charge of the vessel, take the steamer — what was her name? The *Malcolm II* — take the steamer over to Copeland at seven o'clock in the morning, go up with the mail team and back next day. One night in the house. Trouble was, you never knew, with Ed. He might come stomping down the hill an hour from now, his spree over, in a temper to get to sea. Colin had no mind to be left behind on the northside of the Channel, faced with a two-day train-ride back to Gloucester.

It didn't matter. He felt no real compulsion toward The Pond. Last letter from Clara, Dave was talking of heading West, where young Sam was. The house up the New Cut might be empty, by now. Ede was married to Phil's son; she'd be living out front on the Baillie place. Colin frowned, vaguely troubled, remembering Ede. Eighteen, last time he saw her, and married not to young Ray. That, he didn't think too much of. Hadn't when he heard about it. A relief to think that Ray was no closer to him than cousin-once-removed. A little mean, perhaps, to feel that way. Phil had been all right.

It would be nice to see Ede, though, and Clara if she was there. Clara the close-mouthed quiet one, and Ede the lively and likable. Dave's girls were A-one. Between him and them there'd been once a kind of family feeling, despite the fact that his total knowledge of them apart from a letter every second year or so, amounted to — what? A week? A day or two at a time, when Ede was four, and ten, and eighteen ... He had got the fiddle out of the parlor closet once and tuned it up

and play 'Yankee Doodle' for them, while young Sam, clowning, tried
to stepdance. You felt close to the young ones, while they were young.

But now, when he thought about it, even that sense of kinship with
the girls was fading. Must be close to two years since that last letter
form Clara, and more than three since he'd sent her a line. A postcard
from Louisbourg, where he'd run the *Penny Meadows* in for bait. He
wondered idly if Sam had taken the fiddle to Saskatchewan.

The fellow on the wharf was climbing over the rail now, tentative-
ly, glancing at Colin with half-shut eyes and then away, as if hesitant
to disturb this meditation. Colin watched him. One of those lean little
characters, you couldn't tell how old. Anything from twenty-five to
forty.

The loiterer half-nodded, crossed the deck for'ard of the mainmast,
and peered off through the passage between the mainland and Wagon
Wheel.

Colin said, "Looking for something?"

This time the half-shut eyes engaged him.

"You Col Forester?"

There was respect as well as curiosity in it, and it tickled Colin's
small streak of vanity. He was Col Forester all right. Never more than
a first mate on the trade routes of the world, but something more than
that in Gloucester and in these downeast towns. Building it up since
his first halibut trip to Baccalieu in 'ninety-eight, a doryman in the
Commodore Sampson. Salt-banking on Grand Bank, plucking halibut
from the Gully. Quero, St. Pierre, Burgeo … Fletching up off Greenland, one year. Winter haddocking off Scateri. He would never be a
Jacobs or a Harty or a Thomas or a Porper, perhaps. But there were
two or three things men thought of when the name Col Forester was
mentioned. A winter run home from Liscomb Ridges in the *Jacqueline
Parker*, with maintop gone and the jumbo rigged for a mainsail. A salt-
bank trip that stocked 380,000 pounds in less than two months, in the
old *Defiant*, back in 'o-five. Next spring he'd have the one the
Chisholm firm was building for him. Off the board of Tom McManus
and out of the yard of Tarr and James. The knockabout lines. Eighty
feet of mainmast and seventy feet of main boom.

He said, "That's me."

"Thought so."

Colin laughed. "Make you feel better?"

"Uh? — oh." The little man grinned bleakly, gestured with his hand. "Heard about you. Over across."

Colin peered at him.

"Come from the Shore, do you? What family would *you* be, now?"

"No. We're Wilmot people, Lynch. Nick Lynch. Get over to the dances in Copeland, sometimes. Or in with fish." He glanced out over the harbor basin. "Used to know a relations of yours *Ray* Forester."

Colin nodded. It was no particular recommendation. He frowned, his mind caught by something in Lynch's voice.

"*Used* to ... What's happened to him?"

Lynch squinted sidelong at him. "I was thinkin' p'raps you'd know."

"Know? ... Know what?"

"Where he's at ... How long since you been home, Capt'n?"

"Seven — eight years. What's this now, about Ray?"

"You ain't heard, then ... Well, Ray vamoosed. Close to a year ago. Went off up to Amherst. He ain't been heard tell of since."

"Amherst — ?"

"Foundry work. That's what he said. There's others there, from 'round here. But Ray — he ain't there. I thought he might ha' went to Gloucester, Boston, somewheres up that way." He cocked his head and peered at Colin. "But you ain't heard."

"No," Colin said, "I've not heard. I've not been in touch lately." He felt himself adrift and out of soundings. Why wouldn't Clara write? He could understand why Ede ... Well, his own fault. But it was irritating. Kind of demeaning, now, to be asking a stranger about the things a man should know.

He said, "Who's on the place, then? The Baillie — Ray's place."

"His wife, I guess. And her sister. The sister come out to live with her, before Dave — that'd be your brother, now, wouldn't it? — before Dave went west."

"You been over that way, lately? Hear how they're getting on?"

Lynch said, carefully, "Some of us was over to Copeland last Friday. The dance was off. Cancelled out." He hesitated. "There's sickness over there."

"Sickness? What kind of sickness?"

"Dip-*theria*."

"Where?"

"Couple of places in Copeland. Farrens, Caseys. One or two up the shore. I did hear that was one of them ... Ray's."

"Oh? You know who?"

Lynch shook his head. "I don't — well, I wasn't up the road. I *heard*, Ray's wife. Edith — that her name? I s'pose you can't tell by now. This was some days ago. There was no mention of anybody else, the sister or the young one."

Clara nursing Ede and a young one under foot. Neighbors doing the barn work, leaving the milk-pails and the split wood at the door ... Cam Sinclair, likely, and Mel Somers. Colin shook his head as if denying something. He could see it all, see it, but as a thing set off, divided from him.

It crawled through him, a sense of loss and isolation, and something close to uselessness. Cut off ... shut out ... by time and circumstance, the long, easy unrealized indifference.

Nick Lynch said, "Well, what I thought was, if you knew where Ray ... 'f he knew how things was ... "

Colin's mind came back to Wilmot Town, to the deck he stood on, to Nick Lynch.

"Maybe. But I doubt it ... "

Ray. The last time he'd seen Ray, twenty or so then, loafing around the pool hall down in Copeland. The wrong kind for the work involved in making ends meet at a place like Forester's Pond. Farm, fish, and timber, season to season. Management and thrift.

"How was he making a living? Before he left, I mean?"

Lynch grinned. "Sold some insurance. Tried fishin'. Last goin' off, I guess he borrahed most of it." There was a kind of reluctant admiration in his voice. "He's well liked."

"Borrowed — ". Colin spoke sharply: "Did he owe *you*?"

Lynch grunted. "Me? Nuthin' to speak of. He laughed, with a touch of bitterness. "I never had none. Not the kind Ray used. Lent him ten, at a time we was at Copeland, the before he left. But that's — "

Colin said, "I'll pay it."

Lynch looked up, startled.

"No — I wasn't — "

"I'll pay it," Colin said.

He turned, crossed and re-crossed the deck. Why he felt this biting inner anger he didn't know. The fact that Ray was gone had stirred in him only a kind of sadness, recognition of the visible shape of an evil hitherto foreseen but undefined. Even the knowledge of sickness in the house had shaken him more with a sense of his own aloneness, the fact that others were taking care.

But — debt. He felt the anger and was glad to feel it. Debt. This was something that only a member of the family could handle, take care of, meet. He put his hand in his pocket, took out the piece of twist and bit into it, and felt contempt for the way his mind had worked, for a minute or two, a little while ago. Divided, cut off ... hell.

Rounding the edge of Wagon Wheel, the *Malcolm II* let go a dozen passengers stirring along the rail, her fading wake slapping the hull of the *Pathfinder* as she slid past toward Helpmann's wharf. He heard, faintly, the clang of her engine-room telegraph.

Tomorrow morning. Tomorrow morning at seven. But that was fifteen hours away. And noon before the mail team started west from Copeland. He felt a restlessness and felt steady to excitement, stirring and shifting inside. A curious excitement, relaxed and sure. Something like ... It was something like the thing he'd felt at the bow oar of Long George Graham's whaleboat; and later on as a young foremast hand aboard the *Princess Beatrice*, southbound for Trinidad; and taking the *Lottie Elliot* out past Ten Pound Island for the first time.

He said, "Nick, is there anybody in Wilmot, here, that's got a gasoline boat could run me across the Channel?"

Lynch stared at him. "It's mostly sail, here, yet. And hauled up for the winter. I do' know. Maybe Steve ... "

Hunkered down in Steve Brady's mackerel boat, running beam to the slop, Colin watched the north shore for the houses. In daylight you'd be able to see them coming up, gray and white specks against the snow-patched gray-green of December fields, as the shore came out of the dulled blue of distance. But it was early dark, now, and you couldn't tell.

Have to anchor, close in, he guessed, and take the tow-flat ashore around Somers's. He had no idea now what the gap was like. Too risky. Fair sea running, but flattened out now in the lee of Miller's Point ...

He saw first, the tiny bulk of the barn. That was where he'd have to stay for a while, to keep out of quarantine. He hoped they'd left the old stove in Con Izzlie's room ... Then the house, as a light came on in the window, and small as a sprig of ground weed, the juniper at the gate. Brady cut the engine, went for'ard to drop his hook.

It came to Colin that he didn't know whether the young one was a boy or girl. He'd never thought to ask.

ANN COPELAND

Ann Copeland's stories have been published in literary periodicals in both Canada and the United States, as well as in such anthologies as *Best American Short Stories* and *Best Canadian Stories.* They have been collected in *At Peace* (Oberon, 1978); *The Back Room* (Oberon, 1979) and *Earthen Vessels* (Oberon, 1984).

After education at College of New Rochelle, Catholic University of America and Cornell University, Ann Copeland moved to Canada in 1971 and lives in Sackville, New Brunswick. She has taught or been visiting writer at several American and Canadian universities, and is presently working on another collection of short stories and a novel.

ANOTHER COUNTRY

Ann Copeland

Mother's here. It happens once a year and I dread it. I'm mesmerized by her foot, a size eleven in ragged sneakers, tracing a circle in the sand. We rest against this huge rock on the shore of Northumberland Strait and she traces that big foot in the sand. Around and around. She hates her feet.

"How long does it take the ferry to get over to the Island?" she asks as we stare out at the white dot gliding across shining blue toward the horizon.

"Forty minutes."

She used to call it Prince Edward Island, like the tourists in summer when they roll down their window to ask directions.

"I want to get back to the whole question," she says, her toe tracing.

I could almost sleep, lie down in the soft sand, brush aside seaweed and pebbles, dig a nice warm hole, and rest. Not while she's here. My mother, at 65, remains a dynamo.

"Why *doesn't* he speak, Ellie? Surely there's some medical answer. Surely doctors can offer you *something*?"

I look out at Gordie, a small five, floating in his tube.

"I've told you, Mother." I try to sound quiet and even, for I've learned any other tone backfires. She means well. She is a concerned grandmother. "There's nothing wrong with his vocal apparatus. Or his brain. Or his nerves. We've had the child tested to a faretheewell. *We have to trust.*"

I feel my own trust, now that she's been at me for three days, shaved to the thinness of that pink shell gleaming against the sand.

"Your mother," says Rob in his quieter moments, "has the affliction of most Americans. She wants instant results."

He forgets now and then that I too am American. Or was. How does one shuck off such identities? A little paper, a quiz, a book of history memorized, to say premier instead of governor, prime minister instead of president, learning not to notice the queen's picture in the post office or the omnipresent Union Jacks. To my mother I'm certainly still American.

"Ellie, if you'd just let me take him back to Boston," she is going on, her foot moving slowly to rest against the sand. "I know he'd get help there."

"I won't have him a guinea pig, Mother." Can she hear my doubt? Or does she read it as one more don't-interfere gesture? Does she guess that one comes to prefer silence to the fatigue of constant explaining? She knows only part of our efforts to coax speech from this child in every other way judged "normal." What, we wonder, *is* normal? He can throw and catch a ball better than his 14-year-old sister.

"Surely your medical bills are enormous?"

"Medicare, Mother."

"I forget that. Canada is quite socialistic, isn't it?"

She swirls in her prejudices against this country I've adopted, as if somehow the child of our loins, born in the States, might have talked on schedule and now be breaking the I.Q. record. My mother is used to bright children.

But look, he's limping toward us, one leg lifting as he walks like a lame ostrich, bright red blood dripping onto the sand.

"What happened, Gordie, what happened?" She is there in an instant, on her knees in the sand before him. "Was it out there?"

He waves a tanned arm toward the water, medium high tide right now.

"Probably jellies," I say, trying for calm. I can see a surface scratch on his leg, acquired no doubt as he raced for shore after the jellyfish got him. A circle of pink dots is beginning to appear on his chest.

He points to it. "Um, ummmmm, um ... "

His lips are tightly closed. Eloquent in his refusal to talk, he dances in the sand, pointing to his chest, waving at the sea, miming danger, hurt, fear — and above all what appears to be outrage. His blond straight hair is plastered to his high forehead and a ridge of salt lines the back of his neck. I see this as I wrap him in his towel and head him toward our blanket farther up on the beach, mother following.

Moments later, calmed, he is back in the water floating about on the big black inner tube Rob inflated for him this morning.

"Now, Ellie," Mother continues, "about Boston ... "

My mother has lived her entire life in Newton, Massachusetts. Her home — a modest colonial on a comfortable tree-lined street — she bought long after we'd grown and gone. It satisfies her. At last, after 30 years of hard work, she quit, splurged, and gave herself the setting she longed for — and deserved. She is disappointed in me, or perhaps baffled would be a better word. She tries to disguise this now, or maybe doesn't even feel it as we lie together on the motheaten car blanket, July sun warming us, waves lapping at our feet. This setting erases much. That's why I try to have her come in summer.

But she is still disappointed, and I wonder just why a mother's disappointment should be such a burden. I'll turn 40 next October. I've made my choices, certified my own identity by being sure it's not hers. Yet every now and then when she's here I catch myself recognizing a movement of hers that is also mine — the way she dries a dish or makes a bed, or just the way she sits in a chair. As if the body repeated itself throughout time, insuring that certain simple things will last — a unique poster, a way of sitting in a chair.

"Mother," I say, "I'm firm." She turns to look at me, her gold earrings catching a glitter from late afternoon sun. "If anyone takes Gordie to Boston, it will be Rob and me. There's a superb children's hospital right in Halifax. But for this summer we're letting it go, trusting that in his own good time he'll find a way to talk. He has a year before he starts grade one."

I spare her details of frustrating sessions with doctors — pediatricians, psychologists, even a neurologist. She never took her child to a birthday party, stood in the doorway watching mothers and children babbling away beneath bright balloons, prayed her child would join in, then saw him squeal and squeal but never speak, his eyes growing bright with a pleasure he wouldn't — or couldn't — name. She never felt the shame of wanting to shout into well-meant sympathy: "Here, let me show you the pictures he draws for hours each day, beautifully shaded vistas and tightly coiled imaginings of a world I could never have thought up. Could you? My two brothers and I got A's in school, talked early and well. I had never expected to feel this loss.

What's really on her mind even more than Gordie, I suspect, is her furniture.

"All right, Ellie," she says, "I believe you. But if I can do anything — " Her voice fades as she turns again, earrings aglitter, to look at the sea, this alien stretch of Atlantic, this *not* Cape Cod.

After supper we walk the beach again. Rob has taken Gordie and Sarah to the park so mother and I can have this required talk. I know what's bugging her.

I watch her big sneakered feet flatten the sand. It amazed her that in Halifax we were able to find shoes she can't get in the States. Her feet have always been a problem. When I was a child she'd walk the floor at night with cramps, trying not to waken me with her groans. That was after dad had disappeared into the blue, after she'd moved me into her room. I could hear her get up, though I never let on.

Once, when I was old enough to think the question, I was tempted to ask if they'd conceived each time he was home on leave, we three kids were so perfectly spaced — '40, '42, '44 — me, the only girl and last baby. But the subject was taboo. How explain to three small children that a man who'd distinguished himself for bravery in the war couldn't survive fatherhood, even without distinction? He walked away from it.

The evening air is warm and clear after an almost perfect day. Shiny beach grass waves on the ledge above us. The tide is in. The water would be warm after its long trip across the sand bars. We love to come down here on clear July evenings, build a fire, roast hot dogs and marshmallows, then swim. Gordie will sit by the fire, arms locked round his knees, the deep blue of his eyes glowing as he watches the flames. I sometimes think he's the happiest then, as if he, the leaping flames and lapping waves and dipping swallows share something our voices violate.

We pick our way over barnacled rocks, ignoring dead purplish jellyfish plastered against the sand. This is the season of jellies on the Strait. It has something to do with shifts of wind, though I've never quite figured it out.

"Well, have you and Rob thought about my offer?" she begins.

There is no way to be subtle about this. She can hardly say: "Well, now that you two have done your back to the earth bit and found running water to be an asset, now that you've tried raising your own food and found buying vegetables at the grocery store more to your liking, can you bring yourselves to consider my furniture?" Actually, her irony is not that acid. She believes in manners.

She must know we've thought about her letter, talked it over.

"When are you moving, Mother?"

"Early October. I haven't set the exact date. The people want my house November 1. I start paying rent on my apartment October 2. There's a lot to get rid of, cutting down from eight rooms to three."

She isn't asking for pity. My mother is a strong woman. She cuts her ties. She raised the three of us alone, working day and night to give us the childhood she thought we should have. Only when that was over did she indulge her desire for the touches of gentility she'd observed in homes of friends — a small oriental rug, a silver tea service, special China cups. Now, after so few years, she must shrink her space to three small rooms. She will obey her doctor. She wants length of life more than tea cups. But that a weak heart should so rule a life! How maddening it must be.

"There's the dining room set," she is going on, "all mahogany. We did some auctions right after the war, got good buys. And there's the drop leaf table and the wing chair, and your old bedroom suite ... I always felt you'd want it someday. Of course — "

I know what she's thinking. *I didn't think it would be this way, Ellie, 20 years later, you stuck up here in Canada living a life I don't understand, with a good man you refuse to marry.*

She says none of this. She's much too polite.

"Where would I put it, Mother? The dining room table, for example."

"You could certainly get rid of that pine thing you've got."

"That 'pine thing', Mother, represents hours of scraping and sanding. Rob found it in Cy Talbot's barn. We did it together."

She remains silent. How tough to be in her spot — visiting mother, trapped here by economy restrictions of Air Canada, forced to sustain discomfort and stress not of her choosing.

"But the value ... " She looks out to sea. Whitecaps dot the Strait and the horizon is pale orange. "There's no comparison, Ellie. You know that."

"It means something to us."

"And doesn't my furniture?"

Furniture. It bores me. I cannot convince her of this. My child is five and will not speak.

"There's the sheer expense of moving it here, Mother, even if I had a place to put it." I shoot her a glance but her sharp, rather handsome profile reveals nothing. She has remarkably few wrinkles. "If you'd asked me eight or ten years ago I probably could have used anything, but we've managed to get the place together now and — "

"Somehow, Ellie, I always thought you ... What of the children? Sarah is old enough ... "

"At the moment, Mother, Sarah cannot see beyond the end of her 14-year-old nose. In time, maybe. She'd probably like something, that's true. But all those years in between ... How do I know even where we'll be?"

She is silent a moment. "I suppose that's true."

It has taken her years to absorb that.

"Then there's always Customs ... "

Now and then she sneaks things through. She can't understand that we can have trouble. It gets complicated — one child American, not Rob's but mine, the other ours, but Canadian. We must anticipate with passports, I.D., have everything in order. Rob hates crossing the border.

"But surely they wouldn't make trouble if it was *my* furniture."

"Mother, they don't see things that way. It's American furniture being brought into the country by Canadians. We'd have to pay duty." I can't say *It would be easier after you're dead.*

"It certainly wouldn't work that way in reverse."

Stubbornly patriotic, she kicks her American sneakers against a small striped stone. "Remember when you used to collect these at the Cape?"

"Uh-huh." I remember too well. Uncle Edward lent us his cabin for two weeks each summer. We had a fire every night — Jerry and Tim fought over who would light it — and I felt it was the snuggest, safest place in the whole world.

"Yooo-hooo. *Ellie. Yooo-hooo!*"

Rob. Waving us to come back there, his arms moving frantically, saying *hurry*. His chest looks strangely pale and vulnerable in this evening light. He still has a farmer tan, even though he's given up farming and turned salesman. He's good at that, too.

We turn back and hurry over the beach toward him.

"Must be something about the children," murmurs Mother. "What could be wrong?"

He's half running toward us, still in bare feet, leaping over razor-sharp mussel shells.

"What is it? What's happened?" I call.

"Gordie's got a terrible pain. Lower right side. I wonder could it be appendicitis?"

Mother is almost ahead of us, ready to take over. I don't resent it. She's always been good in a crisis. Rob hates to see any one of us in pain. When he takes out the children's splinters it leaves him weak.

"Where is he?" she asks.

"Doubled up on the day-bed."

Inside, we find him on her bed, moaning, Sarah sitting by him holding his hand, trying to quiet him. Lately she has discovered eye shadow and her grey eyes look large and terrified.

"Show me, Gordie. Show me where." I touch his forehead lightly.

He cannot straighten his leg. A bad sign. "Did you call the ambulance, Rob?"

Mother is fussing about the child's pillow.

"It'll take them longer to get out here than it would us to get into town. I'll start the car." He is pulling on a T-shirt while mother begins looking for a blanket.

"You'll have to come with us too, Sarah," I say. "Get a sweater. No telling how long it'll be."

His moaning is low and steady. He's past crying, just quick shallow breaths against pain, as if he's afraid to breathe too deep. I hold him in the back seat, his head cradled against my jeans, while Sarah sits in front, stiff and quiet, between Mother and Rob.

The hollow at the back of Sarah's neck is speckled with salt. Her blonde hair is pulled into two clumps, each held with a yellow elastic around a pink ceramic bubble.

"Good thing this road has finally been paved," says Mother.

I remember this first time she bumped down it from the airport, her brave effort not to say "You're living *here*?" when she saw what was then a sparsely furnished cottage, her attempt to be civil to this man not even my legal husband — because what else could she count on in blood ties? A daughter, she'd always said, is different from a son. I remember her hugging Sarah and saying, "How's my only granddaughter?" Then the two of them went off down the beach kibbitzing. Five years ago. I was about to have Gordie and too sick to register much except relief that they clicked, that my mother's frustrations would not be vented on her granddaughter. She'll take Sarah back with her now, for two weeks with her father. Little enough to give. I can see in her head that other head shape, long and narrow, with flat ears. She is not pretty.

"What's that clump of wild flowers along the road?" Mother asks, above the muted groans.

"Lupin. It's all over the place." Gordie is quieter now.

"Never see it at home."

Suddenly Gordie lets out a long sigh and opens his eyes. He points a clenched fist toward his stomach. "Hurts," he whispers.

I want to shout: "Stop the car! He's spoken!" I swallow it, act as if this is all perfectly normal — *it is* — and whisper, "Show me."

He points again and I see in his opened palm dents from the pressure of his nails.

"Hurts, mommy."

I stare out at waving purple and white and pink lupen and think this simple thought: he has called me mommy. My son knows. He *will* talk.

"We'll be there soon, honey. The doctor will take care of the pain. It may be your appendix."

My mother is talking to Rob about Ronald Reagan. Sarah interrupts — a bad habit we're trying to break — to say: "But all he wants to do is start a nuclear war, Granny. He's war-crazy."

"Not really," says Mother. "He just wants us safe."

It's nearly ten o'clock. Outpatients is deserted.

Rob fishes out the medicare number and fills out papers while Gordie is wheeled away. Mother takes a straight chair beneath a picture of the queen.

"You stay with Granny," I nod to Sarah.

Doctor Wilson is new in town this year. So far we haven't had to try him. His daughter will start grade one with Gordie next fall.

The examining room feels all fluorescence, gleaming metal, and white walls. As the doctor probes, Gordie is nearly screaming. The sound held behind his tightly sealed lips is like the high cry of an infant, coming from way back in his throat. Rob has him by both arms, trying to comfort him, and hold him still.

Doctor Wilson looks up at me as he runs an expert hand across Gordie's exposed stomach. "Appendicitis. It's not always so easy to diagnose, but I'd say this is it."

Gordie has opened his lips again. "Hurt. Hurt. Hurt." He repeats the word over and over, sucking it in with his breath.

Rob looks at me from the other side of the examining table, his skin yellow in this light. We must both be thinking: *he is talking*. How odd to find hope centered in a moment of such pain.

"I'll have to call in the anaesthetist," says the doctor. "It may take him a while to get here. We'll keep Gordie sedated."

The child has stopped speaking. He breathes hard, and little beads of perspiration line his forehead. His hair, curling and damp, is plastered down. The narrow band-aid from this afternoon still crosses his fragile leg bone. I think of the surgeon's knife and start to talk.

"When will we know, Doctor?"

"The operation's not complicated. We should have him out of the woods and awake, but groggy, in four or five hours. There'll be some pain and discomfort afterward. We'll get Gordie into a room. Then I'd suggest you all go out somewhere and have a coffee. Nothing more you can do."

He lies on his side, eyes shut, hands clenched. To straighten the leg at all is now impossible. Rob's gone out to tell Sarah and Mother that I'll wait here for a little while. After that, we'll all go out. Where? I can't put my mind on that right now.

The only room available is this double. Behind the pink dividing curtain lies an old lady snoring, breathing heavy and regular, like the snorts of a rooting pig. I peeked in after the nurse left, but didn't recognize her.

Gordie's going under, I can tell. His hands are beginning to uncurl.

Just this morning, those hands drew a wonder that intrigued even my mother. Jagged mountaintops formed his horizon, colored black and very dark green. He uses fine tipped magic markers and goes through ten doodle pads a week. No trees on his mountains, no timber line, just bare peaks. One mountain gleamed white at the peak, sliver streaks running down one side. In the foreground, at the base of the silver-sided mountain, lay a perfectly round pool of brilliant blue. Somehow, even with magic markers, he found a way to make the shiny blue water suggest both surface and depth. He's good at shadows. The mountains cast shadows like jagged exposed teeth across that pure blue. Against the water, the snow-capped mountain made a point of white. In that reflection, centered in the white, he drew a boat — not from pure imagining as the mountains must have been, for he's not even been to Cape Breton — but a boat modelled on the lobster boats here at Murray Corner which we'll watch during August lobster season. The boat was perfect to the last detail, colored red instead of white, to make it show. Leaning over the side, a small dark figure hauled in something, no doubt a lobster trap. I couldn't see his catch. Too microscopic, if it was there.

Gordie ran to me with the finished picture. He was squealing with happiness and relief. I couldn't read in it any more than I saw, but perhaps I didn't need to. It was enough to hold it with him, and *look*. Our house is filled with pictures piled on bookcases, in drawers, beneath his bed. Sometimes I think if I could read them I would know him. Their beauty is undeniable.

He has Rob's ears, small and low. Now and then — I've never told her — I can see mother in him, the imperious way he waves a hand or stalks away from us when he is denied. He has a trace of the dictator — a frustration, I think, that the world will not open for him, wordless.

The air here smells thick and sharp, like a mixture of alcohol and candle wax. Just outside the door nurses are talking softly. Gordie frowns, as if some ghost prowled his dreams.

From what reservoir of pain did he extract his first word this afternoon? We thought we heard him whisper *Sarah* once in the examining room. The lips have been so firmly closed we've almost adjusted to a silent son. I didn't think much of it at first. Children can be early or late to speech. Sarah was early, but those were other days. Now she talks too much at the wrong time, not enough when you want her to.

This is the last child I will have. It is enough.

He's sleeping peacefully. The perspiration has dried on his face. Curled up in a ball, face pressed in toward the pillow, he has gone beyond pain.

I must find the others, be practical. There won't be much open at this hour of night.

We settle on *Martha's Place* out on the Trans-Canada. A truck stop just outside town, it's the only restaurant open most of the night.

We knew Martha quite well. When I was pregnant and sick with Gordie she came and helped out, her husband driving her to the shore to stay over with us for two weeks before mother came. Each morning she'd bring me a thick slab of her homemade bread slathered with strawberry jam and admonish me to eat up, feed the baby. When he was born, she sent us a hand crocheted yellow baby blanket. Just three years ago she started this small restaurant and quickly built up a clientele. Everyone in town was shocked when she died of cancer last year, a young 42. Her daughter Debbie has taken over — a tall thin round-shouldered girl with dark wavy hair and an awkward way of holding herself that is strangely disarming. There is a delicacy about her, unexpected in this small clapboard diner that smells, even now at eleven thirty, of grease and gravy. Only she and the cook are on tonight.

"Would you like just coffee? Or maybe a nice piece of homemade pie? We've blueberry, cherry, strawberry, and just a little lemon meringue left." Debbie stands by us in her light blue apron, her weight on one foot, her voice tired after a long day. Her mother couldn't have been twenty when she had her.

"Oh, heavens," says Mother, scanning the small plastic- covered menu. "I couldn't eat anything. Just coffee, thanks."

Rob is ravenous. A cheeseburger with the works.

"Would you like your coffee in a mug or a cup?" Debbie asks.

Mother is happy with a cup.

We're too spent to talk. One other table is occupied, with two drivers from the Labatt's truck out front. The patter of their French is comforting. I sit with my back to the counter and kitchen, facing past my mother right into the dark. Lights outside shine against the windows and I see the back of Mother's silvery head, Rob's and Sarah's profiles reflected in the glass.

"Could he die?" asks Sarah suddenly.

"He won't, honey." Rob's voice is tense.

"We caught it in time, Doctor Wilson said," I add. Her bangs hang down in her eyes and her skin looks pasty. She needs sleep. I long to make her feel secure but there are no easy ways. She sees her father once a year — now that, as he says, he can "relate to her." She tells me little about those trips and I've given up wanting to know.

"Used to be you panicked at appendicitis," says Rob, biting into his cheeseburger.

"Well, I must say Rob, we wouldn't have gotten any faster health service at home."

"Helen, from you that's quite a statement."

"Don't be snide. I'm just saying I was amazed at how fast it was done. Were you pleased with the doctor?"

"Absolutely."

Mother turns to me. "What did Gordie say in the back seat?" she asks.

Until this instant I never knew she took it in.

"*Hurt, hurt, hurt*. That was all. And we thought maybe we heard him say your name, Sarah, in the examining room." Should I let more out? "And ... he said mommy."

No comment.

Sarah is busy with her apple pie à la mode. The pie here is terrific. Martha used to make it all herself. When Rob started travelling with pharmaceuticals, he'd drive into town for breakfast. Martha saw that his coffee was full and hot, his eggs done right. She'd ask about me, concerned that a new mother 40 miles out of town might go mad with loneliness.

"When do you think we'll know he's okay?" asks Sarah.

"Couple more hours." The tic in Rob's left eye has started and he's trying to keep from rubbing it.

I look through the dark window — past faces, backs of heads, the reflected cash register and counter. In front of the Sleepy Time Motel across the highway three flags hang limp in the night air: New Brunswick, Canada, United States. The murmur of French covers our silence.

Mother looks haggard, as if today has emptied her life. I can't remember seeing her look quite so worn. Her cheeks are growing thinner, and when she hurries she sometimes has to stop to catch her breath. It is as though the skeleton of age is peeking through, tracing on her features a hint of what is to come. She has deserved better than two sons who live far away and don't invite her ... and this daughter.

"Your mother almost died once — or so I thought," she is saying to Sarah. "She was only 14, no 18 months, a fat healthy baby." She pauses, as if uncertain whether to go on. "We — your grandfather and I — had to rush her to emergency at Massachusetts General."

Sarah is all ears. She's never heard a word about her grandfather. I tried to explain once why Rob and I have never married. "To lay history to rest," I said. "This time it can't repeat itself." She looked baffled, and changed the subject.

"She was a great crawler," says Mother. As she talks, a flush darkens her cheeks. "She got in under the sink and opened some liquid cleaner. I was hysterical, sure she'd swallowed some."

My mother hysterical? I try to see her, a young mother, panicky, catching up the baby, calling for her husband, running to the car, stalling it in her haste. Or did he drive? Who held the baby? Maybe they took a taxi.

"Your grandfather calmed me down. He ... was good at that then."

I cannot see him. Blank. I can imagine her younger and prettier.

"We got there around midnight. They pumped her stomach. Such a little thing to go through that. Afterward, they kept her in overnight. We went out and got a coffee, or maybe it was a stiff drink. I can't remember. Probably a drink. It wasn't ... like this." She glances around the diner.

It wasn't like this.

My mother's voice is low and steady, telling her only granddaughter something she has never uttered before, at least to me.

She speaks without rancor, as though in this moment, here with us, past the crisis, warmed by coffee, she recalls not his desertion but something else I'll never know.

I look out at the limp flags, three in a row, the high yellow lights shining down on the driveway into the motel. Against that I see Mother, the back of her head as she talks to Sarah, the girl in the window listening and eating. At the same table sit two onlookers. We are faces in the window, heads, bodies, occupying some mysterious middle space between the sleeping world out there and the spotless counter behind me. A world of shadows and reflections, merging and moving, plays against the dark. Through it comes my mother's voice, low and steady. It teaches me something as she speaks to her granddaughter elaborating history, my history.

It teaches me that furniture doesn't matter, to her or to me. Not really. We can oblige her by taking a chair or two. Perhaps Gordie or Sarah will sit in it as she once did, bringing alive for an instant the trace of something long since gone. Or maybe we'll take nothing. We'll work that out.

What matters is this space we occupy now, here in the overheated diner by the side of the highway, surrounded by the smell of fries smothered in gravy, the patter of another language, the timbre of my mother's voice putting together her life, all of us held in hope for Gordie to pass beyond pain and find his voice. The voice of another generation.

Every generation is another country.

ERNEST BUCKLER

Ernest Buckler was born in the Annapolis Valley in 1908. After a brief period in Toronto, Buckler returned to live and write in the Valley, which became the setting for most of his fiction. His major work is considered to be the novel *The Mountain and the Valley*, although he also published other novels including *The Cruelest Month*, and a short story collection, *The Rebellion of Young David and Other Stories*. Ernest Buckler died in 1984.

THE CLUMSY ONE

Ernest Buckler

Did you ever strike your brother? I don't mean with a blow. Sometimes when we were children and a flash of child's anger would make a sudden blindness in my brain, I'd strike David any place my blind hands came to. I don't care about those times. He'd never strike me back; but afterward I would ask to borrow his jackknife or something. He'd know I didn't really want it to use. He'd know that when I said "thanks, Dave," the words were really for my contrition.

I didn't do it with a blow that day.

I was standing right where I'm standing now, the day I struck David. I still stand, with my hoe idle, and remember it, whenever I come to this spot in the row. It was just such a summer's day as this, with the bowing heat of the sun turning the petals of the daisies inward and wilting the leaves of the apple trees in immobile patience for the night dew. Little watermarks of heat rose from the asphalt road where the cars passed back and forth beyond the sidehill.

If David had been alongside me, it might not have happened. But they got out of the car and came across the field quietly, to surprise me.

I didn't know they were there until their voices made me start. David was at the bottom of another row, and before he came opposite us again I had time to plan it.

That was my first summer home from college. David didn't go to college, though he was the older. There was only money enough to send one of us, and there had never been any question which of us it would be. Because even as children it was I who was clumsy with anything outside the shadow world of books, and it was David who had the magic sleight for anything that could be manoeuvred with his hands. I don't know why the quick, nervous way of my mind seemed to make me the special one of the family. I could see instantly the whole route of thought that led to the proof of a geometry theorem, without having to feel it out step by step. But surely that was a poorer talent than to have the sure touch of David's fingers on the plough handles, that could turn the long shaving of greensward from one end of the field to the other without a single break.

I remember the first day *I* tried to plough. The sod would ribbon back cleanly for a bit; and then just when it seemed easy, I'd move the handles too much one way or the other, because I was thinking about it, and suddenly the whole strip of sod would flop back into the row in one long undulation. As it happened again and again, a hairspring of anger kept tightening inside me. I stopped once and tried to catch the sod with my hands; but the earth split where my hands were trying to hold it and tail of the sod went slipping back behind me.

"You're trying to plough too deep, Dan," David said.

The hairspring broke. "Oh, is that so!" I shouted. "Well, do it yourself then, if you're so smart."

I turned to leave the field. When I was in a temper, the blot of anger seemed to strike all light and breath out of the place I was standing, like a blow in the stomach.

"Danny! For God's *sake* ... " David said. Not angrily, but patiently. Because, for all his own quiet mind, he understood me so well he knew there was no sting of meaning in the words I couldn't stop.

I don't care about that time. The anger was over as soon as David spoke. I put my hand back on the plough handles. When we got to the top of the row, I looked back and said, "Now that's a pretty job, what?" and we both laughed. And then I asked him, the way the asking of help from another can be such a warming thing when anger between you has just passed, "What do I *do*, Dave — do I hold them too much this way or *that* way?"

He said, "You're ploughing a little too deep, Danny, that's all."

I let him show me then. And the next time down the furrow I tried terribly hard to keep the sod from breaking, to show David how earnestly I was trying to learn from him —

I went to college and David didn't, but I don't care about that. Maybe I always had the best of things, but it wasn't that I took them from the rest of the family, selfishly. It wasn't as if there was ever any dividing among us; our needs were met out of what we all had together, as each required. There was a sort of shy pride and a fierce shielding of me, because I was the one in the family who was weak in the flesh, but had the quick way with learning. One Christmas I got a set of books with real leather binding, while David got only a sled. But I knew that as they watched my face glow just to touch those books, the pride and wonder of knowing that one of their own family could feel a thing like that, was a better share in the books than my own possession.

It was I who got two suits the year I went to college, and David none; because I must look as good as the strangers I went among. But I don't care about that. If it had been David going away, I'd have given up my suit just as gladly. The thought that someone in the train might have the *chance* to laugh at his clothes, even though he bore their laughter quietly and without protest, would have made such a fierce hurt for him in me that I'd have given up anything I had to make his appearance equal to theirs.

I don't care about those things. But they were the things I thought about the day I struck him, just the same. I felt the shame of my action that day heavy in me, even before the others had gone; but I couldn't seem to help what I did. Sometimes there is a cruel persuasion you can't resist in the hurting of the one who understands you best, even as it hurts you more.

You see, the people who surprised me that day were some of the ones I had known at college.

I had just quarrelled with David about the distance between the potato hills. I told him he'd dropped the seed too close. He said there was no sense in wasting space. It was no more than a discussion, to him, until I shouted, "Yes, yes, yes, you're so stubborn — "

I wasn't really shouting at David. It was only the rankling at my own helplessness to hoe more than one row to his three, or to capture the knack he had of cutting the weeds and loosening the earth between the hills in a single stroke, just grazing the stalks of the plants themselves, that was speaking. The tremble of anger was still obliterating my attention when they sneaked up behind me. I never heard a sound of them until they spoke while my back was still turned.

"D'ya suppose he knows what he's doing?" Steve said.

I turned, startled. "Steve! Perry! Well .... "

"We're taking the census," Perry said, in mock seriousness. "Is your name Daniel Redmond? What is your income last year? Can you read?"

"Come on," I laughed. "Come off it."

They had the smooth city way of talking, with a bit of laughter or a glib word always ready to bridge the small pauses; the way of not having to make the meaning that ran along in their minds match the sound track at all. David's straight talk, with the silences in it a way of speech too, would have seemed stupid to them.

I didn't call David to the side of the field by the fence. And when he heard us, hoeing over in the potato rows, I talked their way too — for him to hear. David had never heard me talk like that before. I let him think that was my *real* way of talking. The way I talked when I was with my own kind. A way he could never talk to me at all.

"How's Smokey?" I was saying. "And Chuck? What's Bill Walton doing this summer? It's funny, I was just wondering this minute if Bill had ever patched up his rift with Eleanor." (That was the year we were saying "rift.")

"I don't know," Steve said. "The last I heard, she was threatening to dump the whole complicated mess on the Security Council."

"Couldn't they work it out by algebra somehow?" I said.

"Yeah," Perry said, "or logarithms?"

"Yes," I said, darting a quick smile at him, as if we were really clicking, "or logarithms."

David hesitated alongside us, making patterns on the ground with his hoe, not knowing whether he should stop or go past. They looked at him without curiosity. I didn't introduce him.

"It's a scorcher, ain't it!" David said.

"Yes, it's really hot," they said.

"Has it been hot in the city?" I said, as if accommodating the tone of my remark to the stature of his.

"Not bad," they said. "Not so far."

"We always get a good breeze here at night," David said.

There was a pause, as if the real conversation had stopped.

I had been angry with David, and I did it that day the way the city ones did it after anger. That way, you waited until others joined you and then you talked with them. Not making a point of it, as if to show the one you'd quarrelled with that he wasn't the *only* friend you had; but just easily, as if the quarrel had become quite forgotten, now that these people you could really be yourself with were there. And if the quiet one doesn't leave at once, you draw him into the conversation, as if with kindness, from time to time; but you listen to what he says with patience, and sometimes after has has spoken you let his words hang in the silence a minute before you reply, and after awhile he begins to feel like someone trying desperately to cover his large inescapable hands.

They were asking me, why didn't the three of us get some rooms together next year, and cook our own meals?

"We could send you some sauerkraut," David said. We all laughed politely at his little joke. I saw Steve's eyes catch Perry's.

"Now, Dave ... " I said tolerantly. There was quite a long silence.

"By the way," I said to Perry, "What brings you two to these hinter parts anyway?"

David stood there, with the selfconsciousness that had made it so hard for him to stop and break into our talk at first making it just as hard, once had had stopped, for him to leave.

"Well, this ain't getting my work done," he said. We let his remark lie where it fell. We didn't help him out in the establishment of anything he said.

He bent over and began to cut the weeds again, but he still could not get clean away, because it was a slow business moving up the row with his hoe. The others scarcely glanced after him. I suppose they thought he was the hired man. I still talked their ways, for him to hear. I let him believe that the glibness of my mind and theirs was a strangeness between him and people like us that he could never hope to overcome. That he wouldn't fit in with us at all. I put him outside, in the cruellest way it is possible to be put outside.

David, who once when I had cried because they wouldn't let me go to the back field for the cows with him, had felt so badly he'd gone out and broken the handle of my cart — so I'd hate him and wouldn't *want* to go ....

That's the mean, rotten way I struck my brother that day.

It wasn't the same after the others had gone that day, as it had been times before when we had quarrelled. He didn't come over and ask me what time it was or something, to break the silence. It was I who had to speak first. I took my hoe over to him and said, "Will you touch her up a little for me with the file, Dave?" But it wasn't like the times I used to borrow his knife.

He said, "Sure"; but he said it too eagerly, and he didn't ask right away about the people who had been there. I hesitated to mention them too. And then after we had both hesitated, it wasn't possible to mention them at all. It wasn't true what I had let him believe that day — that they were my own kind and he was the stranger.

And walking back to the house that night, this thing between us that neither of us could mention lay on our tongues like a weight. He was quiet, without anger or protest, at the blow. And I had shame, which confession could only add to. The consciousness of even the movement of each other's limbs was so taut in us that if our feet had happened to slip and touch on the uneven ground, we'd have been struck with awkwardness beyond description.

Have you ever *really* lain awake the whole night? I did, that one. You know how, if you bruise your finger, it's when you go to bed that it really begins to throb. It was like that with my mind. How could I ever show David it wasn't the real me who had spoken that day — I had done my act so well. You could say, "I'm sorry I struck you, I guess I lost my temper"; but you can't say you're sorry for a thing like what I'd done, without stirring up the shame fresher still. How could my mind show me the answer now, the mind my brother was always so proud of, though he couldn't speak his pride — when it was that mind which I had used as the instrument to strike him!

I wondered if he remembered, that afternoon, the casual way I'd always answered him whenever he asked me things about college. I'd never thought he really cared about knowing. Maybe he had. That was a funny part about David. I had the quicker way with the mind, and still I couldn't feel how it was with him, the way he seemed to know, with a quiet sensing, exactly how it was with me. I wondered if he'd thought that I was putting him off when he asked me those questions. I thought, look Dave, I'd tell you about college now, if you could ask me again. We'd sit all afternoon on the doorstep, pulling the timothy heads from their stalks and talking the easy way.

I wondered if he believed now that if he were in a quarrel with someone *else*, I might not take his side. (And I remembered — Oh Lord, I remembered — how David would always let me fight my own battles with kids my own size; but if any of the older ones so much as laid a finger on me he'd go into the only rages I'd ever seen him show.) I thought foolish things. I tried to console myself with the projection of foolish fictions: there was a war and David went first; because he was the strong one in the flesh and I was the one who had only the thin muscles of the mind.

But I lied to the examiners, and after awhile they took me too. I was small, but when I was angry I was as strong as the others. I was with David when he was in danger now, and so I was strong all the time. And the day David was killed I was right there, and in that last minute when all things are without falseness of any kind, he knew at last that I had been sick for what I had done to him. He knew that I wished we might change places. That the quickness of my mind would be nothing to part with, if I could save *him*. That I was never proud of it, myself, if it stood between us.

I started at the beginning again, making it happen a different way: I saw them when they got out of the car. Before they saw me. I ran down the row to where David was standing and grabbed his arm, with the anger all forgotten. "Dave," I said, "quick — there are some guys I knew at college over at the house and we don't want *them* stuck here all afternoon. Let's get out of sight in the orchard, quick .... "

Oh they *did* laugh at David. They said, "Who's your friend?"

"Who's my friend?" I said. "That's my brother. His name is David. You wouldn't know anyone like him. They made him first, out of the muscles and heart and sense — and then they had some pieces of tongue and gut left over and they added a little water and made you. They added quite a bit of water. Would you like him to come over and turn you inside out, to dry? It'd only take a couple of minutes. One to do it, and one to wash his hands afterward. Don't worry, he wouldn't laugh at you. Dave's a gentleman. He wouldn't laugh at that smooth little city-face of yours, Perry, or those little cellar-sprouts on you mind, or that rugged little necktie you're wearing, Steve."

Oh I told them so surely just why their kind wouldn't even move the needle on the scales you'd weigh David in. With such a clean cutting that they wouldn't reply, for all their glibness. They believed it of themselves all right. They were glad to get away from our field quickly. The sharp sword of my mind shone and sang doing it, and I was really proud of its quickness. And then I leaped over the rows eagerly with my hoe, to where David was standing; the song sharp in me almost to tears. The song of one who takes up the cudgel for another with whom he has himself quarrelled, with the bright telling words the other could never in the world have found for himself —

But it was too late to do it that way now. It was foolish to take it out like that on Steve and Perry. They were good enough fellows. They weren't to blame. There was no one to blame but myself. And it would never be the same between David and me again.

The next afternoon the wood saw came. I was so draggy I didn't know how I would ever work. Lift the heavy logs and carry them to the saw table, then lift and thrust, lift and thrust, lift and thrust — without a minute's respite. With the crescendo whine of the whirling saw rising so demandingly between cuts that it seemed it would shatter itself to bits if it were not immediately fed again.

I always dreaded the wood saw. But somehow David had always managed that I got a break in the work now and then, without drawing attention to my weakness. He'd call, "Danny, go get us a dipper of water?" or "Danny, go get the crosscut, will you? We may have to junk some of the big ones." (As if he hadn't left the crosscut saw in the shop purposely.) When he sensed that I was getting intolerably tired, he'd call, "Move her ahead, fuhllas, eh? We're getting too far from the pile." There'd be five minutes or so then, while the others were pushing the machine ahead, and having a smoke maybe before they started up the engine again, that I could get my wind. And somehow, without his planning it in any way that was obvious, when we all fell into our places for the first cut, David would be at the butt end of the logs, next to the saw, and I'd be at the light end, on the far side of the pile.

Stan was sawing that day when we started, Rich was throwing away the blocks, David was the next saw, Joe and App were strung along the pile, and I was at the far end. We hadn't sawed more than three or four of the first small wire birches when David threw his head back in a motion for me to come up front.

"Take it, will you?" he shouted at me, above the roar of the engine, "I gotta get a stake for the wheel. Don't cut them too long." The one who was next the saw regulated the length of the block by thrusting the stick ahead just far enough between cuts.

David got the axe and drove a stake down tight against one wheel, to stop the vibration of the machine. I expected him to change jobs with me again as soon as that was done; but when he came back he went to my place at the end of the stick and left me in his.

It was all right while we sawed the birches. They were easy to lift onto the table, and there was a kind of exhilaration in the lightning rhythm of thrust, zing, thrust, zing, thrust, zing — and the transformation of the straggling lengths of trunk into even-lengthed blocks of firewood that flew from Rich's hands and grew into a neat mound before the shop door.

But when we came the leaden pasture spruces, their weight became hostile, punishing; and the heightening scream of the saw between cuts more demanding. It seemed as if each time I lifted the butt end of one of them from the pile, it was not by strength, but by effort of will. Then I had the butt of the stick off the pile, with my heart beating very slowly now after having beaten very fast, it was as if I were dragging it to the stable with the pit of my stomach, not my arms. My arms were trembling. Each time Stan tipped the table ahead so the saw could sever the block, I relaxed and let my weight ride with it. But the next instant it was necessary (would it be really impossible this time?) to lift, thrust, again. The others held up their part of the log with hardly any consciousness of its weight. Sometimes David and App would support it at the loop of one elbow and make a mock pretence of cuffing each others' ears with their free arms. David paid no attention to me at all.

We came to the big hemlock. I looked at it, and before I touched it even, I could feel its stupid sickening weight dragging at my stomach.

"Junk it?" I shouted to Dave.

"No," Dave shouted back, "I think we can handle that one all right, can't we, fuhllas?"

I bent over and put my arms around the butt end. I lifted and lifted, but it didn't budge. The saw was waiting, screaming higher and higher, threatening to shatter itself. I lifted again, until everything went black for an instant before my eyes. I couldn't move it an inch off the ground. I straightened up, for my sight to clear. And then I noticed that the others weren't lifting at all. David was motioning them back with his arm.

It was a kind of joke. They were standing there, sort of nudging each other with their grins.

"What's the matter, Dan?" Joe shouted. "Is she nailed down?"

I couldn't even laugh it off. If you weren't brought up in the country, you can't understand what a peculiar sort of shame there is in not being able to take as heavy a hoist as the next one. It was worse still because Joe had shouted. Everything that happened that day was worse still, because everything that was said had to be shouted above the sound of the saw.

They sprang to help me, and somehow I stumbled back and dropped my end of the stick on the saw table. I glanced at David. He was grinning too. I couldn't understand it.

We had to keep turning that one — the force of the saw would die about halfway through. The second or third block, Stan motioned us to wait until the saw had got up speed again. I let my end of the stick rest on table and relaxed. I motioned to David to come up front.

"I've got sawdust in my eye," I shouted to him. I thought he'd send me into the house to wash my eyes in the eye-cup. He didn't.

"Let's see," he said. He drew my lower lid down. "There's nothing there. It must be just the sweat."

"Okay, fuhllas," Stan shouted. David bounded back to his place at the pile in a exaggerated comic rush. When he passed App, he pointed to his own eyes and sort of smiled. App caught on — the eye business was just an excuse. I couldn't understand it at all.

It got so I could only keep going by thinking about six o'clock. Six o'clock, when this would be over, must come somehow. Nothing could stop it. It got so I turned my face sidewise from the others, because it was twitching uncontrollably, like the tic of a smile that has to be held too long; and I knew it was pale as slush, despite the heat. My second strength came and went. I kept my eyes on the belt, willing it to go off the pulleys, as it had other times we'd sawed; but it didn't. It got so I could only keep going by thinking that when I absolutely *couldn't* stand it any longer, I could ask them, myself, to move the machine ahead; saving that, like a weapon.

"Move her ahead," I shouted at last.

"Move her ahead," David shouted to Stan, "Move her ahead .... "

Stan moved to shut off the engine. I took a great deep breath and relaxed.

"No," David shouted, "Don't shut her off ... unless anyone wants a puff. Anyone tired?" The others shook their heads.

"Will I shut her off?" Stan shouted again.

"No," David shouted. "This stuff's just kindling wood for us fuhllas." He rushed front, worked the stake free in a flash, lifted the tongue of the wagon and the machine was resting on, as if it were a match stick.

It wasn't a minute before the wagon was pushed ahead into place, with the saw still running. It wasn't two minutes before the wheels were chocked, the stake driven again, and we back in place for the next cut. My last weapon was gone.

It got so the pile was a looming, leaden, inimical mound of all the weight in the world. It got so the weight of the logs was there all the time in the pit of my stomach, whether I was lifting or not. My temples drew and beat.

Finally it got so I kept lifting at the log on the table, whether the saw was in cut or not, because I couldn't let go. It got so I was suspended somewhere by my arms, with the weight of my body intolerable, but unable to touch the ground with my feet. It got so my body was full of ashes. It got so my will began to tremble as uncontrollably as my arms. It got so I couldn't lift a straw. I motioned for David to come.

"I can't — " I said.

He did something that I wouldn't have believed. He turned and shouted to the others, "Dan's all in, fuhllas. We can finish that little bit all right alone, can't we? All right, Dan, you go in the house."

He needn't have shouted it out like that. He could have sent me to water the calves, or to put hay in to the cow that had been kept in the barn because this was her day.

I held my head down as I took off my leather gloves and walked to the house. But I could see the others out of the corner of my eye. Stan and Rich glanced after me, knowingly, though they hadn't caught what David said; but without much curiosity or concern. I saw David and Joe making a comic battle for each other's caps, even as they held the log. I remembered the night David had taken me on his shoulders when I stumbled on the path from camp and carried me all the rest of the way home; pretending not only to the other kids but to me too that he thought I'd broken a bone in my ankle. So that even with him I needn't have the shame of tiring before the rest. I thought, I understood now. How he must hate me now —

We didn't make much talk with the others at supper. It was on the way down from the barn, with the milk pails in our hands, that he said to me, "Did you make up your mind to live with Perry and Steve next year Dan?"

"No!" I said, as automatically as if a trigger had been pressed — before I stopped to think that this was the first time David had mentioned them. *"Those — ?"*

"You crazy old — " He called me a name as old and earthy as the land he hoed. That's what he always called me when it was a hundred per cent perfect between us.

I didn't speak, because tired as I was and so suddenly happy, I couldn't trust my voice. I understood then what had happened this afternoon: how else could he square it between him and me, between me and my conscience, than by doing something as mean to me as I had done to him? How else, since it couldn't be mentioned with words, could he show me that he'd known all the time the falseness of what I'd done, the burden of it afterward — how else, than by doing something as unmentionable to me today and letting me see, by his face now, the falseness and burden of that?

Did I say it was David who was the clumsy one with anything that couldn't be held in his hands?

LESLEY CHOYCE

Born in New Jersey in 1951 and educated at Rutgers University, Montclair State College and the City University of New York, Lesley Choyce moved to Canada in the late 1970s and settled in Porters Lake, Nova Scotia.

Lesley Choyce's poems, short stories, articles and reviews have appeared in more than 150 journals, magazines and anthologies. He is the author of eight books of poetry, fiction and non-fiction and editor and co-editor of a number of anthologies.

Choyce has won several awards for his work, and was a finalist in 1988 for the Stephen Leacock Medal for humour. Lesley Choyce has taught at thirteen colleges and universities in Canada and the U.S.; he is presently a half-time instructor at Dalhousie University and editor/publisher at Pottersfield Press.

MAJOR REPAIRS

Lesley Choyce

Mosher has three cigarettes and I have two matches. Everything is soggy. I strike one match on the book that says "Be An Accountant!", figuring that maybe this is the first step. All accountants must smoke cigarettes. This is how they get their start. A career has to begin somewhere. Mosher dips toward the flame, his black face wonderfully tense, almost cross-eyed with purpose. Shit. He snuffs it. "Damn!"

The playground noises grow louder. The wind has shifted around from the sea. Shortly the fog will start to lift. If we aren't careful Mrs. McNaugle will spot us. My turn. Mosher strikes the match, cups it desperately against the wind. I lean over and suck in hard. Got it. Third cigarette of my whole frigging life. It cuts like a gutting knife at my windpipe and I pass it to Mosher while I pound on my chest. Mosher is more cautious, takes a drag pretending to be an old hand at it. He claims to have smoked a whole pack that he found last week behind his father's pig barn. A man of experience.

I take a second assault and the smoke rifles out through my nose. My eyes are watering. I blink out the tears just in time to see Fred Hollet diving down over us in full attack sequence as Mosher and I cover our heads.

"Assholes," Hollet shouts, his perennial battle cry. I see him pounding at Mosher's ears with his knuckles. Mosher doesn't fight back. He's bigger than Asshole Hollet but if he ever had a chance to blast the sucker good, fifty guys would kick his head in before he could say Martin Luther King. All I can do is grab for Hollet's shoe. I pull it off and throw it into the trees. He stops pounding and turns slowly toward me. I'm starting to stand up. I never run but when they go for me, I always make a point of being on my feet. If I had any defense I would use it, but I don't. Instead, I heave my own glasses in another direction into some alders. My father would have a heart attack if he had to buy me new goggles again.

"Chickenshit scumbag." Hollet loops a leg around my ankles, throws me an elbow in the stomach, and I come down hard on a bare slab of bedrock. The bell rings and Hollet goes looking for his shoe.

Mosher winks. He picks up the still glowing cigarette and sucks in the smoke. Handing it to me, he brushes off the damage. I take a drag and don't cough this time. I flick the butt Hollywood fashion toward Hollet and scramble for my glasses.

Vogler's class is famously boring. It's a wonderland of daydreamers, paperclip benders, doodlers and plotters. No one knows what Vogler is doing up there, his hands in his pockets, his mouth open and speaking, his glasses dipping down to the knot on his nose. Some of us aren't even sure what class this is. Centuries are passing in Europe, endless wars, problems over religion. It passes grudgingly slow. I know, as with all history classes, Vogler will never lift us up into the twentieth century never tell me about Germany, about the Jews. Vogler's world is a monotonous progression of grey kings and queens, haughty and boring and, thankfully, dead.

Hollet is capturing flies by his seat near the window. He tears off their legs and sends them back into flight or he stalks out a spider in the cracked gyproc wall and molds it into black snot between his paws. He is thinking about some way to catch me or Mosher off guard and he will succeed. He's not creative though. It'll be the same old routine. Mosher and I will be waiting for the bus and he'll knit together a tiny mob of guys from the East Side, Harbour Hillbillies, as Mosher calls them. He'll raise his voice and scratch his stubbly red hair and say something like, "You should have seen what *The Jew* tried to sell my old man. Some kind of underwear. Like what faggots wear."

The Jew is my father. He's called The Jew because he's probably the only one within a hundred miles in any direction. Even my mother isn't Jewish. Neither am I. My father travels around the county in a big yellow step van, stopping at houses to sell stuff. He carries things you wouldn't believe. It all comes from a guy in Montreal and it's mostly stuff that people in cities never buy. Not in this century anyway. The old farmers think he's great. "Look who's here," they say to their wives on a wet, spongy, dismal spring day. "It's the Jew. Sonofabitch." Then they play a little game on him. They treat him like he's stupid. But they like him. In the end they buy a pair of gloves that will last close to three years of hard work. And they'll pay a rock bottom price. They'll say, "I bought these Jesus gloves from The Jew. I don't think Christian people can make gloves that good." But then they'll elbow the person they're talking to and laugh. This scene is played out over and over across the county.

The bell rings and Vogler's drone is drowned out by the sound of chairs scraping wood floors. Vogler is announcing the reading assignment on Hanoverian kings that no one will read.

Mosher is in the hall standing by his locker picking at a scab on his knuckle. "Whadda we gonna do, Stein?" I shrug my shoulders, polish my glasses and watch blood leak out of Mosher's knuckle. Red blood on black skin. It's uniquely colourful, like nothing I've ever seen. I'd swear my blood could never be that red, that rich. Mosher sucks it up and swallows hard. "We gotta keep taking that shit from Hollet or what?" Mosher has always been able to endure anything. This worries me that he's worried. "Like if we stay in this dump for three more years like we're supposed to we gotta play nigger and Jew to a codworm just because he thinks he's God's favourite white boy."

"I don't know." I won't remind Mosher that I go to an Anglican church.

Here comes Hollet and his two dump truck friends. "Suck my hockey puck, Stein," he barks and hammers home Mosher's locker against my hand as I'm too slow to see the inevitable coming. I can feel my fingers ring with pain and stare at the new blood on my hands. The dump trucks think it's a great comedy.

Mosher gives a blank one syllable response. "Shit."

"Yeh, you eat it for breakfast, Mosher," Hollet snaps.

"What, you haven't been on the route with me for over a year." My old man is hurt. He's trying not to show it.

"Me and Mosher have some things we'd like to do."

"Things. What is things? Your father wants a little help once in a year. So can't you put off *things*? Bring Mosher along. I'm just going down the Harbour. Maybe you two'll learn something. There's always something happening down the Harbour."

I can't say no. The reason I don't want to go is that I'll feel embarrassed if the kids see me with The Jew. And that's why I have to go. So who knows? It'll be like the United Nations. Mosher likes trucks. My father will tell the story about working in the Sydney steel mill. Mosher will crack up when he says, "I worked at the furnace with lots of neegeroes. Oh, excuse me please, I mean coloured peoples. I was just a boy. We were all sorts of coloured peoples. They stayed black. You want to see *red*, you should have seen me after my first day staring down the flames of Hell."

Mosher is about the only black person anybody around here gets a crack at. His mother and father almost never get off their farm. A few times a year the meat company from the Harbour comes and picks up a couple of truckloads of hogs. They don't hardly ever even go to stores. But they get by. Mosher's different. He wants to be everywhere in the world at once. He doesn't get rattled easily and says whatever pops into his head. My job, half the time, is to help him keep his mouth shut.

An audience is what my father loves best. He would have been in show business only nobody in Sydney was that crazy about Yiddish jokes. My mother had just run away from home in Grand Etang and at first took him for a Frenchman. When he opened his mouth, she thought he was from Mars. Since she knew he would raise the eyebrows of the Murphys, the McIvers, and her own dear McPhersons back home, she married him.

The coke ovens grew intolerable and hopes of show business gave way to business and they moved up toward the mainland where they had me. The Jew became locally famous after selling Kelson LaPierre a baseball glove. Kelson had lost two arms when his tractor turned over and was the least likely man to ever try out for the Boston Red Sox but he always wanted a baseball glove and never had the spending cash to buy one until the tractor accident brought on the compensation. But the way other folks saw the story, it was different. "Never seen somebody who could sell a no-handed man a catcher's mitt. That Jew could sell the queen a shithouse." It went on like that.

Mosher and me are wedged together up front by the engine as we wind our way toward the Harbour. My father, the comedian, has become my father, the philosopher. The subject is fear. Fear and hate.

"Fear does not exist unless we invent it for ourselves. A little caution sometimes is wise, but no fear. Also, you cannot allow yourself to hate any man. This I learned from my father the hard way. I won't tell you about Europe, you know that. But it filled my own father up with so much hatred that he would walk around spitting on the ground. He said he had to spit in order to try and get the hatred out of him. He spit so much that no one would have anything to do with him. I told people he chewed tobacco, but it was lie. You don't like lectures, I know, but there, I teached you something. Remember. Mosher, how many people do you hate?"

Mosher is silent for a minute, contemplating. "Three." He doesn't need to tell me who they were: Reilly, the guy who bought the pigs and paid good money but had no respect for his parents — once he had even pissed on the ground outside his house while his mother was present; Mrs. McNaugle who had called him out in front of the class, asking him if his family had a history of mental retardation; and Hollet, just because he was a rotten son-of-a-bitch.

"So look. You put all three of those people in your mind. You gotta close your eyes first, see." (My father closes his eyes even though we are travelling down the road at fifty miles an hour with a string of approaching cars up ahead). "Then you think about how much you hate all three."

"Got it."

My father reaches into a glove compartment and takes out a rock the size of a fist. "Now take this rock and give to it all the hate floating around in your head. Then throw it out the window. Goodbye hate. Just like that."

Mosher seems baffled but stares down at the rock.

"Good. Now roll down the window and throw. Say goodbye to those feelings."

Mosher isn't convinced but does it. "Goodbye feelings." The rock skips across the edge of a pebbled shoreline and into the shallows of the Harbour.

We all sit without speaking for a few minutes swaddled in a steady roar of the flathead six. Sometimes the old man hums along with the engine in perfect pitch with the drone. He will chant a song he learned as a boy that none of us understand. He never tells me what the words mean just like he has never tried to tell me more than I have ever asked to know about the Jews. "I know that engine like my own mind," he has bragged to my mother and me. But the truth was that he knows nothing of mechanics and rarely has the courtesy to keep the truck in good repair unless it is absolutely necessary.

We are nearing the turnoff toward the Harbour settlement when the truck begins bucking and engine coughs, violently shaking me off the seat. It jerks a few more times, then runs smoothly, then starts again. My father, being in his best philosopher form today, refuses to show annoyance in front of Mosher and me. "We better stop up at the Irving's and check it out." The Irving's is the Irving gas station and garage just up ahead. Duane Hollet owned the place and it would be Duane who would have to assess the engine problem. Duane is a thick-set man all around. He looks like he has inflated tire tubes inside his skin. One big around his stomach, smaller ones around each bicep, one around his neck, and one around his head where the hair was shaved down to nothing on the sides. Duane has a reputation for being a good mechanic, a sloppy dresser, a clam swallowing champion, and the father of one of the biggest brats to ever grow up at the Harbour.

I have the bad luck of running into Freddy when I walk into the men's room to take a leak. There he is with a scrub brush in hand and a can of Dutch Maid cleanser working away at the toilet bowl. I start to laugh and Freddy is clearly unnerved. "Sorry, I'll go out back," I tell him, wanting to avoid the situation altogether. I know that nothing would rile up a shitkicker like Hollet than to know that I had seen him in such a humiliating situation.

"And I'm saving all the cigarette butts for you, Stein, 'cause I know you'll like the extra flavour."

I gently close the door and hear Freddy kicking a bucket across the floor. In the garage, Duane is sprawled across the driver's seat with his head stuck inside the engine and his ass in the air, a thin alligator belt being pushed to the limits of endurance while fat flesh spills out around his waist.

"Crap in the goddamn carburetor. Maybe water. Maybe some other kind of horseshit. Christ, what have you been running this thing on anyway?"

"No lead. High test," my father answers. "Only the best." He is lying.

"Whatever it is, it ain't gasoline," Duane counters confidently.

"So I'm wondering what the problem is. Can you clean it out or fix it or whatever?"

"Needs a new carburetor. You're lucky you made it this far, Steinie. Did you bring any of them calendars?"

"Sure, well, yes. I had them with me to give to you anyway. Here." My father climbs into the back and hands Duane five or six, trying to keep them away from Mosher and me. "No charge."

"Shoot man, I gotta pay you something. You're in business aren't you.?"

"That's okay." My old man is clearly embarrassed and prefers to end the conversation. Instead, good old Duane cracks open the brown wrapping and hold up the calendar to my father's face. It has a breathtaking picture of a woman sitting on a bed with black satin sheets. She is surrounded by an assortment of wrenches, drills, hammers, ratchets, tire pressure gauges, and assorted tools. She's wearing a pink frilly half-slip and is naked above the waist. Bold letters above the picture state"PUSHOVER TOOL CO."

"Look at them wrenches will ya? Let me pay you for these."

"No charge." My father is clearly annoyed.

"You ain't still carrying those magazines too, are you?" Duane pushes on.

"No, I'm not. Now Mr. Hollet, would you kindly tell me what you can do for my truck?"

"Like I said. Needs a new carb. Period. Ain't nothing else'll do it. I got one if you want me to put it on. Rebuilt, but good as gold."

"How much?"

"Ninety five. I won't charge you the tax."

"Dollars?"

"I'll knock off another five for the calendars. Ninety bucks. Installed."

I grab Mosher by the sleeve and head him out behind the garage. Rather not be around for the rest. We start chucking rocks downhill into the stream out back where Freddy's old man has been dumping waste oil, used oil filters and rusted-out muffler parts for the past ten years. When Freddy comes back to dump some trash over the embankment he finds Mosher and me have a contest to see who can piss highest into the air out over the edge.

"I guess it appears a little complicated to somebody who still dirties diapers," I hear myself saying.

"You people must live like animals," Freddy hisses out, then grabs a blown-out tire and heaves it at me. I sidestep it but it catches Mosher on the side of his head and knocks him down the stoney embankment. I stand there mute for a few seconds looking to see if Mosher is hurt. He's getting up and slowly scrambling his way up the hill. "Just forget it, Stein," he's telling me only there's something about the way that Hollet keeps laughing that makes it impossible for me to give it up. I feel my legs operating all on their own, then see myself bringing my knee up hard in Hollet's groin. He doubles over and I shove him into an oily mess of engine junk. Watching him lying there, I feel the strong, invigorating taste of revenge, something strangely tangible in the back of my throat.

Mosher doesn't say anything, just walks over and helps Freddy up. "Let's forget it, Fred," he says real apologetically.

Freddy wrenches himself loose. "Frig off, loser."

Mosher and I go around front and stand by the open door of the garage. The truck is running, not perfectly, but it's running, and the exhaust is blowing up into our faces. Duane is talking to my father. My father is still worried about something — the engine doesn't sound much better than before. Maybe it was the spark plugs or a wire?

Duane is shaking his head and my father is reaching into his pocket. I can't hear what they are saying because the noise of the rough idling engine drowns them out. Freddy arrives on the scene and Duane starts to yell at him. Duane now pushes him away toward the office.

My father is starting to back his truck up out of the garage with Duane still hanging, half leaning, on the door with his hand out. Mosher and I jump in the side door and close it hard behind us. We sit on the floor in the back surrounded by piles of work clothes, gloves, tools, and farm utensils. My father guns the motor and lets off. It's idling perfectly now.

My father shoves a wad of bills into Duane's hand and Duane walks away. In the glove compartment is another rock, a lumpy, round sea-smooth piece of granite that my father takes out and cradles like an egg in his right hand. He holds it up toward his face and I see the muscles tensing in his boney wrist. Then he gently puts the rock back into the glove compartment. And laughs. "Imagine having a son who cannot walk around the building without falling into a puddle of oil." My father, the comedian.

SUSAN KERSLAKE

Susan Kerslake was born in Chicago, Illinois in 1943. She attended Montana State University and worked at Kroch's and Brentano's Chicago Bookstores before emigrating to Canada in 1966. She now lives in Halifax and works at the Izaak Walton Killam Hospital for Children.

Susan Kerslake's short stories have appeared in regional, national and international periodicals as well as in her collection *The Book of Fears* (Ragweed Press, 1984). She has also written two novels, *Middlewatch* (Oberon, 1976) and *Penumbra* (Aya Press, 1984).

DID YOU EVER ...

Susan Kerslake

Emma was old and the cold bothered her. It never had when she was a child, bare-legged, blue-elbowed, red-eared and the heat rose away from the top of her head making clouds climb in the air. Her room was a large parlour in the old house. There was another like it on the south side where sun poured in all day. She had only seen that room from the back yard. Two large windows just like hers shone when the sun hit them, stared like revelations you cannot see behind. The street windows, hers, were mirrors reflecting the fire engines, ambulances and garbage trucks. Emma hid behind the glass and saw everything. Across the street, in the rented rooms in the green house, a table was pushed against the window. People sat around the food, cigarettes and liquor on the table. She could see their arms and hands gesturing through the smoke. They weren't old enough to be sitting at home all hours of day and night. On welfare, no doubt, smoking and drinking money that could have gone to Emma so she wouldn't have to live in danger. From time to time, the woman would lean out the window to check on her children who played on the sidewalk. The children ran into Emma when she went for groceries; they didn't look where they were going; they didn't see that it was hard for her to walk on the broken sidewalk, that she might fall again. When Emma was a girl, the grocery store took phone orders and delivered to the door. A boy unpacked it. Milk came three times a week, laundry once. Now it was pizza. A man used to come with his cart to sharpen knives and scissors. There were bells on the cart like the ice cream man's that drew the children from under porches and down from trees. And everyone had money.

In the top drawer of the dresser under socks and snuggies, she hid several jewellery gift boxes. They were in rows and hid money. The change was for laundry, the bus and ice cream. She carried money in her inside pocket so if someone snatched her purse he wouldn't get much.

Emma said, "I don't want to live in a dangerous part of town."

Her social worker scolded, "But you don't have enough money to live anywhere better; lots of people have to live where they don't want to; why should you be any different; finding rooms for senior citizens isn't easy. Just be careful if you're nervous; go out when it's daylight; cross the street if you see something suspicious .... "

"But I don't know what danger looks like!" (To me everything looks dangerous. And nothing.) The whole world was safe when she was a child playing at the curb. In the summer evening, when dusk lapped like a grey-green spook in the street, she played on the edge of fear, poked sticks into it, waved shadows from under the street light. But someone was watching. The light was on in the kitchen, its glow a wave of gold across the porch, spilling down the drawbridge stairs. It was always there. She went to sleep safely, long before the lights were turned off: she had never even heard the sound of the switch. And though the great beast of night hungered for her, hung on the window sill, breathed in the night wind, she had no fear.

Before her on the table was a white bowl; it had a crack like a brain wave around the rim. When she closed her eyes she couldn't feel it. "Pure thoughts will keep you well; keep you good." Thoughts can kill. Thoughts can't kill. "Sticks and stones may break your bones, but words can never .... " Think positive. The old beast in the gall. She ran her finger round and round the rim. She used to be able to make it sing, rubbing her wet finger around and around the smooth rim; her dad taught her that while they waited at the table.

In the widest part of the summer, the sun snuck in her north windows in the late afternoon and evening. She sat as close as possible, leaning out into the sun, the sweet air. The wind came from shade and there was a tang and taste of evening.

Emma put the window down. Draughts weren't so bad in the summer; a small lap rug, her shawl shrugged up around her shoulders and the back of her neck, those tender places. Last winter she had had to put cardboard over the bottom window pane. All she could afford were thin cotton curtains. It had taken all day to find them in the bargain basement. She and two hundred others clawing through debris, the watershed of the counters upstairs, discontinued lines. Emma turned over all the synthetics, reached deep into the innards of the fourth table and found three half-curtains. "If I cut one in half, some arrangement could be made." Children's dresses, party frocks, gowns, repairs, darning, she'd done it all. The sewing basket was under the table where she could kick it out. The curtains hung on parcel string held with nails. They sighed under the crosspieces of the window. When she wanted to wash and iron them she undid the knot and slipped them off the string. But in winter she needed pieces of cardboard that could be taped over the window. It was awful, like living in a basement.

Emma turned out the lights and undressed in the thin hazard of moon looking in the window and street lights that she was sure were too weak to show the insides of her room. Even though she was used to each and every shadow gripping the floor, climbing the walls, she was uneasy and avoided stepping on the tentacles. Behind her was her own shadow, an amoeba moving without aches and pains in the watery yellow light. One day her soul would gather itself from her shape like that and mould itself anew without knobs and bumps and limp flesh.

Meanwhile, the flesh was the centre of her life. Physical needs. The irritations of bowel and gut. Tubes too small for their jobs, clotted with the body's jellies. When she was young, everything worked. That summer at sixteen, she never thought about herself except in glowing terms. All the songs were about her; the radio sang to her; she sang to herself, hanging around the kitchen counter where the spotty, sticky radio was plugged in on a short cord. The lattice of plastic over the speaker was drifted with dust and grease. "It's you, only y-o-u-u-u." "Oh, true, true," said Emma to herself, waiting for someone else to say it to her. She waited in front of the mirror, in the bath, on the front porch, standing on the corner, at the ice cream parlour, in bed. Problems arose when she thought the dreams inside were happening outside. The biggest problem of all came later when the dreams didn't come true.

It had looked like the real thing; it had felt so good, so right. As her dreams and stargazing were possible so was the future. As seen from the river bank, a rowboat, under a tree. From each other's arms. Safe. "I will keep you forever." From harm and reality. At his right hand would be success, at his left, his wife and children.

She sighed. It was so easy to remember all that now. At the time she never looked back, and struggling on her hands and knees, washing the floors, she had been unable to remember what had brought her to that, how she'd gotten there with so little fight and so little fondness. There had been a brief time, a moment, when she'd had the first child; looking with such love on that helpless child. It didn't matter that the house was a small two-room apartment over a store, looking out on the main street with nary a tree in sight. It didn't matter that he worked with one hundred men for three bosses. Theirs was the first baby ever born; the world was starting over again.

Despite the horizon, the factory spewing smoke prosperously, the small homes growing up beside the main roads, new stores, they did not exactly thrive. Soon there were two babies in the crib and there didn't seem to be room for Larry except in bed, so he stayed there when he wasn't working. Later on he would stay away. Emma would look around as if she expected him suddenly to appear. Even though he wasn't there, she'd sit at the kitchen table talking to him, haphazardly pushing empty dishes, the smell of fried meat shrunk up in her nose. In the mirror over the dresser she would look at herself. The top was cluttered; she'd had to clear a space with her elbows. And always she could hear the children breathing shallowly over the vivid, deep dreams of childhood. "I haven't dreamed for months," she'd realized, reeling between the rocky bedding of her husband and the ragged nightmares or restless sickness of the children.

What surprised her and her parents was landing on their porch, dragging the battered suitcase inside, then surrendering herself to better judgment. "What should I do, Mama?" It was horrible and wonderful at the same time. Admitting demons and doubt to the ancestral home meant their banishment. "But, Pa, Larry never talks like you do, he doesn't know anything like you do; he can't take responsibility, he doesn't ... he won't ... " Crying, comforted, scolded, secured.

A month after returning to Larry and the children, her parents died in a fire that destroyed the house as well. Because it was winter the house was tinder dry. It burned so fast the firemen could only spray rainbows helplessly over the flames in the early morning sun. The water froze in the broken windows and hardened into lumps of lava in the yard. Smoke and steam continued to sneak out. The bodies were found on the floor, encased in ice. Emma made them let her see. The coffins were opened one by one. She thought how odd they were not in the same box, a double coffin, together.

After the service, she walked out by herself to the site. The foundation was frozen in. She walked back and forth, crossed the street and even went around back, down the alley. The horizon was like a black gap in the mouth when a tooth is removed. There was so much debris she did not get a feeling of emptiness, only ruin, destruction and garbage. And anger, rubbing a rut in her soul. The sun shone on the ice; it shone through the hole where the house used to be, into her eyes.

She had a dream that the house was being painted. The paint dripped like black blood, a rainstorm of blood running down the sides of the house.

Emma sat at the table. She looked out the window to the bare street. She lay in bed next to her husband. She bathed her children. All the time she was thinking, "I shall be next. It is my turn."

Larry was out all day; a steady job for a change, but the hours were long for Emma. Things changed for the worse. Each day a few more stains on the linoleum, spots on the table, smudges on the glass. Ironing wasn't done; the tub was left dirty. Larry made the bed behind her in the morning so she wouldn't get back into it. Laughing nervously, the children told the neighbours their mother was waiting for the grim reaper. As summer came on it was possible for them to stay out later and later until dusk. When they did come in there was just time for a bath and bed.

Emma sat by the radio. She didn't know where to turn. Round and round and round in the four walls of the world. She listened carefully to the news; all the dangers out there, sniggering at the back window. Waiting for her if she went outside. By turning her chair just so, she could keep her back to the wall and watch the openings.

One hot midsummer day, she got an envelope from the County containing a legal letter, forms, two death certificates and a cheque. She and Larry opened a joint savings account. The idea was to save the money for an emergency but the next month, in the dying heat of the summer, they moved about a half-mile down the street.

The flat was three large rooms. Emma noticed right away that shadows were banished by daylight pouring in on three sides. Maybe moving was all it would take. The walls were papered with a bright print of flowers. The linoleum looked like small stones. Their old furniture looked good. Emma got out a perky yellow tablecloth and the kids picked dandelions. The main wall of windows faced south to the back alleys. Edged with sucker trees, it delighted the eye with a maze of multicoloured fences. Emma sat in the sultry sun and felt safe. Larry turned off the radio. He got Emma an armload of ladies' magazines.

Forty years later, Emma could still pull one or two of those magazines from the trunk she used for storage. There were a few things left from that time. Most didn't fit in this room. The table was shabby, chipped. A floor lamp severely tarnished. The children had confiscated most of her furniture as they moved out on their own. It was hard to say no to them. If something disastrous happened to her she wanted them to remember her fondly. Nothing had ever taken the place of her parents. She hadn't been finished with them.

The sun was gone, a last lick at the tops of the trees and it was gone. A blue-grey cloud plowed across the sky. When she looked again, the sky was black and clear. Stars began to prick through. There was plenty of time now. The slush and drip of evening across the long time before she would sleep. Evening used to mean the beginning of the time when it was too late to start anything else and she could sit with her hands cupped over the steam of tea.

Emma got up. She tucked her shawl in her bathrobe tie to keep the fringe from the coil of metal in the hot plate. At the sink she filled the small quart pan. After the time in the extended care unit, being able to do for herself was wonderful. The sink in the room was an old one. A table had been built under it for support — a good thing because she had to clutch the sides if she got a sudden pain. Sometimes she felt a little faint at the sound of the water.

Inside the pan was a watermark. It indicated the amount of water needed to make two cups of tea or dilute a half-can of soup. Emma squinted her eyes. The pan sat on the small burner. It had taken her some time to figure out how the thing worked. Each knob not only controlled its own burner but could affect the other. With no simmer, she had fashioned a coat hanger to keep the pan above the element. Things were working pretty well now. But there was no fridge. In winter she could keep a little milk on the window sill. Bread, jam, cheese whiz, sugar, cereal, all kept in the box on the floor. Occasionally she could get fresh produce in the garbage out behind the supermarket. A sympathetic grocer left the good stuff on top.

In public toilets she could unwind a bunch of paper to take home. By her door, she had a basket with toilet paper, soap, washrag, cleanser and sponge, things to take into the shared bathroom down the hall. Under her bed, Emma kept an old po. The bathroom was often locked and busy. It was often dirty. She had to clean it before she could use the facilities.

An old mirror had been left in her room. She put it above the sink and watched herself brushing her teeth, washing her face. Emma still had her teeth, well most of them anyway. She hadn't been able to afford the dentist for years, but in the convalescent home there had been a courtesy visit by a dentist. He was astonished by her mouth. Emma felt proud; he had a way of making her feel proud. The rest of her made them despair. Occasionally, if she kept quiet, there would even be the admission that they did not know what to do.

When the water started to boil, she poured it into a small teapot with one tea bag. She took a smidgen of sugar and milk when she had it. Tonight it would just be the sugar. She put the tea things on an old metal tray and went back to bed. She turned out the light so no one from the street could see in. The window was open a crack. WHenever she heard a strange noise she would lean forward heavily and walk to the window. The street was so close and dreadful.

Emma went to sleep gradually, fearfully, bit by bit. First her legs grew heavy; it would be hard to run away if someone got in. Her hands were cramped; she couldn't hit out. Then her mind woke up, alerting memories to be ready for review and revision.

Unable to educate her children for what she saw in the world at large, she found that they were, after all, admirably prepared. The streets, alleys and back lots had become their classrooms. They laughed at her. "Mother! Mother you're hopeless. Everyone is doing it ....

You're helpless. Don't you know that? Wait until the system gets you. Wait till you need something. Just wait till you're all alone." Maybe that was part of the new way. "Where did I go wrong?" But then, why was she the one who was lost while they knew where to go.

She hadn't expected the government to take care of her. She had expected her family to. The kids were smart; they got in and out of the war and back to school. Once a year she heard how optimistic they were.

Emma and Larry moved again to a smaller place in a new building. It was square. There were no window sills. The door was like a trap cut in the wall. Folded into one corner was a kitchenette.

Nowadays when getting in and out of the tub made her nervous, she gave herself a sponge bath at the sink. In the hospital she had been rubbed, buffed and powdered. Quick and easy, rolled this way and that. A sponge bath took the better part of the morning. Emma cut her own hair by grabbing fingerfuls and snipping off the ends. She didn't want anyone to mess with her. If she died in bed that couldn't be helped, but she dreaded being dependent on strangers. She hated people walking in on her when she had to expel gas.

It was still early; the streets were busy and upstairs children were having their last romp before bed. Noise distracted Emma because she couldn't hear the important sounds. She had a catalogue of irritations. From her mattress, lying on her back with both ears out she could hear the front and back doors, bathroom and next door. Upstairs, downstairs. Creaks in the floor boards. Locks. Radiator cracklings. Refrigerator motor, distant thuds on pipes, water dripping down the drain from a leaky faucet. There were dead birds in the sealed-off chimney. Their souls wailed in the flue. She heard mice in the walls, their scattering toenails. And over it all, the plunging pulse of the street, motors, wheels, horns, gears. She didn't mind the sirens of ambulances and fire engines going out to save people. Only very little children still wanted to be firemen. The kids on her block wanted to drive vans or be musicians. They wanted to make a lot of money.

Once Emma had a lot of money. Larry had died; there was an insurance policy. She had no insurance though; there was nothing left for her to leave behind. By that time it might not matter; the children were moving around a lot. One of those times they would lose her address or forget to send her theirs. It didn't matter. Emma pursed her lips. She didn't want to kiss them anyway. Her lips were tense and rigid. When Larry died she kissed him. The police leapt, trying to wipe the blood off his face. And oil. In fact there was a rainbow of blood and oil. Emma had always believed rainbows could not be photographed. She saw the rainbow on his skin but wondered why the police were trying to take a picture.

They had come to the apartment to get her.

"What do you want?"

They wanted her to go with them in the squad car because there had been an accident. On the dresser by the door was a photograph of Larry. "Are you sure this is the man?" stubborn images shouldered in her mind. It was difficult to hear the policeman talking .... Emma was giving Larry his breakfast of corn flakes, toast and coffee. She was listening to him in the shower. Getting him up in the morning. Watching him sleep on the other side of the bed. And the pinched dream she'd had last night.

As seen from the back seat of the police car, the streets seemed unreal, rushed, businesslike. Everyone looked important and official. Even the bystanders. Over there on the stretcher was Larry. They had wrapped him in a bright red wool blanket. One set of corners was folded over his face. The policeman stayed with Emma, holding her under the arm, almost pushing her off balance in the attempt to support her. She wondered what she would do when they showed Larry to her. His face should have been left uncovered so she could see it from a distance, then slowly get closer and closer, getting used to it.

They asked her where she wanted to go. For a moment she thought their apartment was gone too. She explained that the children were far away. "They won't take me," she thought. "I know they won't." Her mind shut that.

"Where do you want to go, lady?"

"To the grocery store I think." Glazed donuts, she wanted to lick the slick sugar and feel the eggy smooth caves inside the dough. Maybe her favourite checkout girl would be working. If she wasn't busy they could chat.

Everyone had a way of getting some of the insurance money. By the time the bills were paid and she moved into a bachelor flat, there was just so much to take to the bank. She would either make it or not. It was that simple and unremarkable.

Now the tea was cold; she got up and took the tray to the sink. Above her, lights from the street beat the ceiling. Voices from the street pattered in. She hated the noise of cars over the voices. From a safe place she wanted to hear kids coming home from the taverns, lovers quarrelling down the stairs and out onto the pavement; fights and secrets. Wide awake, Emma lay down in her bed. In the dark it was hard to control her thoughts. The pleasanter the memory, the more insubstantial. But the hardships were only too clear. She couldn't do anything now but wait. Cold air stirring in the bedclothes made her nervous. Changes in temperature were intolerable. The pains she'd had in childbirth, deep inside her legs and body, came back. She hated people who made her hurry; lights that changed when she was halfway across the street, kids sitting on the bus while she had to stand. Trash thrown on the sidewalk, bottles broken on stairs. She was never sure if that stain on the sidewalk was spilled pop or urine. Ketchup packets stomped on, greasy envelopes from fries. No one ate at home anymore. The street was a garbage pail.

Flowers pulled right out of the ground and left. Branches broken off trees. Grass couldn't grow. What was the use of trying to make something pleasing to the eye? People preferred smut — walls and fences obscenely marked with spray cans. Posters and signs on posts, mailboxes, storefronts. Brass and marble scratched with obscenities.

She hated the way people pushed and walked at her on the street three abreast so she had to stop or stumble off onto the grass. Kids on bikes whizzed by, endangering her. Toys, scooters, wagons, skateboards clogged the cement. Radios blaring from cars, stereos blasting from houses.

Emma waited for her heart to settle down. She hated her own helplessness. Her voice slipped down her throat, the best her legs could do was the straight and narrow. She lay immobile. the air was chilly in her lungs but it felt good. Cupping her palm over her mouth and nose, she sniffed the familiar circus of peanut butter, soap, stale cleaning cloths, bleach. Through it all she could identify the unique musk of her old body. Her skin had always been soft and smooth. Now wrinkles slid down in it. Now she could pluck folds and they would peak like beaten egg whites.

She wore a pair of white athletic socks to bed. If she moved around she knew she would warm up, but the initial effort was too great. Sometimes she wore an old blue sweater to bed. Next winter she might have to wear all her clothes. She would look fat and bloated. The smell of her body would be very strong. She would lift the neck of the garments and reassure herself. She had an inner eye for the how of her body. The doctor at the clinic could tell her nothing. "Just tell me what it means," she said to herself; though she knew the answers were deep inside and when the time was right she would know. Death was a thought. She wanted consolation that it was not a cold condition.

Outside, people were talking in the street. Lives were so complicated. She was tired. She didn't want to listen anymore, to be flung back forty years into those angers which sounded worse today, tonight, shedding violence in the air. She feared the anger would come in and kill her. A car or motorcycle would crash through the side of the house and explode in the room. "Old woman trapped and burned to death! ... " A man would break the door down escaping from the street but bringing the danger with him, capable of killing her because she was in his way. Her life would be split like water off a mill wheel, one scoop made its round and dumped. If she called out no one would come.

Old settled on her face slowly, silt from within. Her body was a dead, heavy thing discouraging the quick spirit, muddying the colours under her wings. If she had her way, the children would have done well enough to do right by her, at least to take her in. She would have done as much. There had been that period of expectation. Now that was gone.

"I don't want to live in a dangerous part of town."

If she had her way she wouldn't be alone like this in a bare, cold, dangerous firetrap of a room sharing the toilet and bathtub down the hall; she wouldn't have to tape or nail cardboard and newspaper over the cracks in the window and store a half-pint of milk on the sill, hoping it would stay fresh for morning tea. She would have a little more. And plans.

ALAN DONALDSON

Alan Donaldson was born in Alberta in 1929 and grew up in Woodstock, New Brunswick. Educated at the University of New Brunswick and the University of London, he returned to UNB in 1956 and has continued to teach in the English Department there.

Donaldson's first collection of short stories *Paradise Siding* was published by Goose Lane Editions in 1984.

PARADISE SIDING

Alan Donaldson

The day Corney and I found out we were going to work at Paradise
Siding, we asked Corney's older brother what it was like, and he
said that Paradise Siding was the beginning and end of the god damned
world. It was only years later, remembering this description one day,
that I recognized how clever it was, and by then it had come to seem
cleverer even than Corney's brother could have known.

It was the summer of 1945. Mussolini and his mistress had been
machine-gunned and hung up by their heels in Milan, Hitler and Goeb-
bels had killed themselves in Berlin, and the death camps had been
opened and their skeletons turned loose, but Japan was still fighting,
and everyone except the select few expected the war to go on for at
least another two years. So most of the able-bodied young men were
still in the armed forces, and the jobs they would have worked at were
being filled by the physically and mentally unfit, by women and middle-aged men, and in the summer by high school and university
students.

The university students got the cushy jobs, like holding rods and chains for survey crews or checking cars at the Customs, and the high school students got the shitty jobs, like working in stores, or the rough ones, like working on the highway or the railroad. Since Corney and I didn't like the shitty jobs, which didn't pay very much anyway, we looked around for one of the rough ones, and because Corney had an uncle who worked for the C.P.R., he landed himself a job on an extra-gang, and I landed one with him because the family didn't like the idea of him going so far from home without a friend.

It was difficult to understand why Paradise Siding existed at all. Perhaps back in the Nineteenth Century someone had thought for some now unimaginable reason that a town was going to grow up there, or perhaps it was merely conveniently equidistant on the railway from a number of equally improbable villages with names like McLaughlin Corner and Killarney and Jerusalem which were strung out every couple of miles along the gravel roads which ran aimlessly through the woods, leading from nowhere to nowhere.

Whatever the reason, the C.P.R. had built a two-storey, wooden station there, which was painted the same garnet colour as all the other wooden stations in Canada, and there was the long railway siding which gave the place one half of its name. There was also a house for the station master and three other houses which must have been built by people who had something to do with the railway since there didn't seem to be anything else around Paradise Siding that anyone could have worked at. At least, there hadn't been until 1940, when the Canadian Government had built a big internment camp a couple of miles away in the woods. At first, it had been used just for civilians — Canadians of dubious loyalty and enemy aliens, a lot of them Jewish, who had been shipped over by the British. Then, later on when the Allies had begun to win, German prisoners of war were interned there as well. Like most people, Corney's clever brother hadn't known about the camp, but it dominated the atmosphere of Paradise Siding, as the war dominated the atmosphere everywhere, and in the extra-gang it was second only to sex as a topic of conversation.

There were about twenty-five of us in the gang, and we lived in a couple of bunk cars which were part of a work train that was parked on the siding by the station. Like Corney and me, most of the others were teenagers, either high-school students or drop-outs from the tough coal-mining town ten miles away, but there were also three quiet married men in their forties, subsistence farmers probably, who arrived every morning in an old half-ton truck, and there were Hod and Steve, who were old enough to have been conscripted but hadn't been for reasons no one dared to ask, and there was Wilfred, who was simple-minded and who might have been any age from thirty to forty- five.

The foreman was a middle-aged man named Herb Brewer — Mr. Brewer to his face, Herb behind his back. He always wore an old, grey fedora, stained black with sweat around the band, and he was soft-spoken and not very big, but he could lift a bucket of railroad spikes with one hand that most of us could hardly lift with two, and we didn't need to be told that he wasn't someone to be crossed very often if we wanted to keep our jobs. He and a cook named Billy lived in a separate bunk car at the far end of the train from ours. Billy drank a lot, and he was an awful cook, but Herb liked him, and we only complained about him to each other.

We got up at six o'clock for breakfast, and a little after seven, we loaded up the trolleys and left for the line, where we were tramping ties. Ahead of us, railcars had spread coarse gravel along the tracks, and our job was to lift a strip with two big hand jacks and tamp the gravel under the ties with shovels so they would stay above ground for another few years.

It was a hot summer. By noon the rails and the gravel would be shimmering, making odd mirage effects when you looked along the line, and there were days when the temperature out there must have been over a hundred by mid-afternoon. In spite of the heat, most of us worked in long-sleeved shirts with collars and cuffs buttoned tight. The forest here was bad forest, not clean and dry, but full of swamps and shallow, brown-watered little lakes, and the blackflies and mosquitos came out of the trees in clouds along with the occasional deer fly that had a bite like a bee sting. So we worked in our shirts, and almost all of us rolled and smoked cigarettes to help keep the bugs off.

In the boom of wartime, there were a lot of freight trains on the line, hauling lumber and coal mostly. We would hear the warning tor-pedoes go off and let down the jacks and stand with our shovels while the train crawled through the work area. There was also one passenger train that went through every morning on its way to Fredericton. The windows would be open in the heat, and the passengers would look at us standing there, sweating and dirty. They were thinking, "My God, what a job!" and just for a minute, we were thinking, not what they were thinking, but "By God, we're young and tough. We could eat steel washers for cornflakes and old boot soles for steak, and we could dance our way through Hell in an overcoat."

We worked until five and then loaded up our tools, and the trolleys took us back to the siding. We washed and ate and then sat around outside until after dark when the bunk cars, which stood unshaded all day, began to cool down a little. This was Hod's time. Six-foot-three, over two hundred pounds, cunning-eyed, coarse, he dominated the life of the gang when Herb and the older men weren't around, and with Steve, his inseparable companion and worshipper beside him, he used to spend his evenings under a big pine tree across the tracks from the work train surrounded by a court of teenagers who listened with boundless credulity to his talk, which was all about fighting, hunting, maiming, and screwing, especially screwing in all its varieties, human, animal, and both.

I had my share of adolescent lust and curiosity, but Hod's world struck me as a place I didn't want to live in, and I used to leave Corney to listen to him and walk down the tracks to the station.

The big event of the evening in Paradise Siding was the arrival of the passenger train back from Fredericton, and some of the locals would walk two miles just to watch it come in, make its five-minute stop, and depart. Afterwards, a few of them always sat around on the benches on the platform talking, and I used to sit a little way off, reading the newspaper and listening to them. They talked about the weather and the war and the government of John B. MacNair, but mostly they talked about the internment camp. There were all sorts of stories about escapes — about tunnels and manufactured firearms and faked Canadian uniforms and about prisoners who had frozen to death in the woods or been driven insane by the blackflies before they could find there way out to a road, where they could give themselves up. There were also incredible rumours about who was being held in the camp, including one that Hitler himself had been captured and for some complicated reason was being held there in secrecy.

Only the most gullible of the locals believed stories like that, and for the boys in the gang the real fascination of the camp lay simply in the fact that a mile or so away through the woods there were hundreds of German soldiers: the enemy, alien and dangerous, who we had heard about all our lives and whom we hungered to see with a strange intensity.

We knew that some of them went out under guard to cut wood for the stoves in the camp, and whenever we were working near a crossing, we watched every army truck that went by to see if it might be filled with Germans. They never were, and one Saturday afternoon Corney and I and four of the other boys set out to walk to the camp to try to see them through the wire. After we had walked abut a mile and passed a couple of signs which said KEEP MOVING, an unmarked car pulled up beside us, and a Mountie asked us where we were going. We told him we were just going for a walk, and he told us to turn around and do our walking somewhere else.

Corney had already begun doing that anyway. Goaded by Hod's talk of easy lays, he had taken to cruising the roads looking for girls, and at first I let him talk me into going with him.

There weren't more than a dozen houses in a mile along any of the roads. They were grey and weatherbeaten, patched sometimes with metal signs for Coca Cola or Sweet Caporals or with lathe and tarpaper, and the dooryards were filled with old car bodies and bits of wagons and machinery although now and then there would be one where someone had tidied up a little and made a scruffy lawn ornamented with wooden ducks or rabbits.

In the hot evenings there were often people outside, men in overalls, women in cheap, print dresses, broods of dirty kids, a few girls, some of them frail as skeletons, the rest starch-fat and as white as bread dough, the malnourished Juliets of a perpetual depression. They seemed unimaginable to me as sexual objects, but whenever their parents weren't around, Corney would set out to play Romeo to them, throwing out smart-ass lines he had picked up from the movies. Sometimes they stared at him as if he were speaking a foreign language. Sometimes they laughed at him. Sometimes, more encouragingly, they giggled and whispered among themselves. But he never got anywhere with any of them, and I didn't want him to anyway, so after a while I gave up on it, and he found other partners to cruise with from among Hod's court of admirers.

By August 6 we had been in Paradise Siding for a month. For us, that Monday was a cloudless, windless day, the temperature in the nineties, the rails so hot you couldn't touch them with your bare hands, the forest absolutely still, exuding its scent of evergreen and its cloud of black-flies and mosquitos. We all sweated and cursed and moved no faster than we had to. Wilfred, the simple-minded one, said he wasn't feeling good and kept wandering off to sit in the shade, and Herb let him go.

We first heard of Hiroshima around noon, although it didn't as yet have a name, and by then the rescue teams would already have been digging in the ruins for hours. Herb had been back to the siding to pick up something and came back talking about a new block-buster that had been dropped on Japan. No one paid much attention. It was too hot to think of anything except how good it would be to get the hell off the line.

The truth of what happened at Hiroshima took shape very slowly as if the people who decided what other people should be allowed to know were uneasy about the success they had to announce. When I bought a paper that evening at the station, I found that the main headline was about a federal-provincial conference in Ottawa. The only reference to the bombing was a small item half way down the front page. It reported that a bomb with a force of twenty-thousand tons of TNT had been dropped on Hiroshima, which was described as an important Japanese army base. Somehow the wording contrived to make it seem as if the bomb were just the same as any other bomb, only bigger.

Even on Tuesday the bombing still wasn't the major story and the reports about it were scattered and vague although something of the truth had begun indirectly to make its way. Unobtrusively, on an inside page, there was a story which described the test explosion in New Mexico: the blinding flash brighter than the sun, the great billow of multi-coloured gasses soaring to forty-thousand feet, the huge crater in the desert, the vaporized tower.

Not many people anywhere knew enough yet to understand what any of this was about, and the news which took hold of the imagination that evening in Paradise Siding was of another event which was to give all of us in the extra gang a chance to see our Germans after all.

An hour before dusk, while I was still sitting at the station, an army truck came down the road trailing a cloud of grey dust. Army trucks went by all the time, hauling supplies for the internment camp and ferrying soldiers back and forth, but this one turned in and stopped beside the station.

The driver and a lieutenant got out of the cab and the sergeant and a dozen other soldiers off the back. The lieutenant was young, but the others were all members of the Veterans' Guard, men in their forties and fifties who had been in the First War and had been recruited for guard duties at places like the internment camp. They were in summer uniforms, their shirts dark with sweat, and they all carried Lee-Enfield rifles. The lieutenant went into the station, and the others came over into the shade of the platform.

The most talkative of the locals who lounged around the station was a man named Eldon. Like the soldiers, he was a veteran of the First War. He had been wounded in the leg and had got a small pension and had lived off that and his wife's chickens ever since. He studied the soldiers slowly out of his slits of eyes, obviously hating them for the assurance their uniforms gave them.

"What are you boys doing driving around the country this time of night?" he asked the sergeant.

"Three of the Germans ran away from a wood-cutting crew this afternoon," the sergeant said.

"What'd they want to do that for?" Eldon asked. "I thought they was sending them all home anyways."

"I don't know," the sergeant said.

He was a lean, grey-haired man, and he seemed tired and not much inclined to talk.

"Were they some of the S.S. bastards?" Eldon asked.

"No," the sergeant said. "They were all right."

"No German's all right, if you ask me," Eldon said. "They're all bastards, every one of them."

The sergeant looked at Eldon.

"Well, these ones weren't," he said, and he walked away and sat down on a bench with his rifle butt-down on the platform between his knees.

Eldon turned to one of the other soldiers.

"What'd they look like?" he asked.

"Nothing special," the soldier said. "One of them was a young guy. Didn't look more than twenty. Fair-haired. The other two were a bit older. Dark-haired. One of them was tall. They had them uniforms on with a red circle on the back and a stripe down one leg. But they've probably tore the markings off by now. They might even have got hold of some civilian clothes and put them on underneath before they left the camp."

"So what if we see them?" Eldon asked. "Can we take a shot at them?"

"You ain't got no right to shoot anybody," the sergeant said from where he was sitting on the bench. "You just stick to shooting the shit, and you won't get yourself in any trouble."

Eldon laughed. He had a mouthful of rotten teeth.

"We could say we thought they was bears," he said.

The lieutenant came out of the station and walked down the tracks to Herb's bunk car, and I followed him and told the others in the gang what I had heard. When the lieutenant had gone back to the station and loaded up his soldiers and driven away, Herb came out and told it over again and said that if we saw anyone suspicious out on the line we were to tell him and he was to get the stationmaster to phone the camp.

Since the prisoners weren't likely to come anywhere near a work crew, he said, there wasn't anything for us to get ourselves excited about. But we were already excited anyway. We were all full of the idea of war, and for six years we had watched serial movies in which kids had helped foil and capture German spies, so it wasn't long before Corney and some of the others were talking themselves into believing that the army would recruit our gang as some kind of search party like the ones the Mounties got together when someone got lost in the woods.

Hod listened to them with the superior smirk with which he listened to them always, and after he had let them run on for a while, he took over.

"Why don't we go out and look for them now," he said. "It won't be dark for a while yet. They'll be along the line waiting to get on a freight. Come on, Wilfred, we're going to catch the Germans."

"You'll be a hero," Steve said. "If we catch them, you'll be a hero and get the Victoria Cross."

So the whole gang set out with Hod out front as commander and Steve, as always, beside him. Along the side of the tracks, we picked up an assortment of crude weapons — a broken shovel handle, a few rusty railroad spikes, some fist-sized rocks — with which, I suppose, the twenty-odd of us could have mauled and beaten the three Germans to death in a fight if need be. But a deaf man could have heard us coming a mile off, and, of course, nothing happened. Half a mile down the line, people began getting tired of it and dropping out to go back to the bunk cars. I went on for a little longer than most, fascinated and afraid, and then I went back too.

That night before I went to sleep I heard trucks and jeeps going by on the road, and near dawn a freight train stopped beside us. It stayed there for a long time, panting and hissing steam, while men shouted back and forth. Then the engine heaved and spun its wheels, the clank of couplings ran past the bunk cars, and the train got under way and went off towards Fredericton, leaving behind it only the sound of a few pre-dawn birds.

The system when prisoners escaped from the camp was not to send soldiers, or anyone else, into the woods after them but simply to patrol the roads and rail lines and wait for them to come out, which they usually did after a day or two of the blackflies and mosquitos, and for the next two days out on the lines platoons of soldiers went by every hour or so. Some of them were Veterans' Guards. Some of them were conscripts and non-combatant personnel from the depot in Fredericton. A couple of platoons had Mounties with them with tracking dogs. We watched them enviously, and as we worked we kept an eye on the woods in the hope of seeing the Germans.

Back at the siding in the evenings, Eldon and the other loungers argued about what the soldiers ought to be doing and exchanged the latest rumours. The Germans had been seen in Fredericton, in Newcastle, in Moncton. Someone had seen them on a train dressed as ordinary passengers. Someone had seen them on a road dressed as Canadian soldiers. Someone had seen bodies floating in a lake in the woods.

And while all this was going on, the trickle of news about the bomb was swelling into a flood. By Wednesday, the fiction that Hiroshima was an army base had been dropped, and it had become a city in which a hundred thousand people had died in a fraction of a second. On Thursday, the bombing of Nagasaki was announced. Inside, the papers were full of background stories. There were explanations in layman's

terms of atoms, electrons, protons, and neutrons, illustrated by unin-
telligible diagrams, and there was a picture of the kind of plane that
would have carried the bomb.

There were also stories full of disquieting reassurances. One of
them proclaimed, "Anxiety re Atomic Bomb Unjustified." It was not
true, the story said, that the atomic bomb could start a chain reaction
that could destroy the world. It was not true that it could destroy the
atmosphere. It was not true that it could make the face of the earth
radio-active so that people who stayed in a bombed area would die
slowly of X-ray burns.

"It is fact," the story said, "that a huge explosion of energy creates
a little bit of this artificial radium. But that is nothing to worry about.
Because every person on the face of the earth is constantly under the
fire of radium rays. It comes naturally from the earth, the sky, and particularly from the walls of great buildings."

Down the platform Eldon had stopped talking about the escape and
was telling his well-worn stories about how the Germans had shot their
prisoners and used dum-dum bullets in the First War.

"Pity we hadn't had that bomb two or three years ago to use on
them bastards," he said.

"So long as they don't blow up the whole god damned world with
it," one of the others said, who had been reading the newspapers too.

On Friday, the three Germans still hadn't been caught, and out on the
line the patrols of soldiers were still going by. Just after noon, a platoon
we hadn't seen before stopped, and the lieutenant in charge asked Herb
a lot of questions about who we were and what we were doing and how
long we had been there.

He was a slight, sandy-haired man with a prim moustache, and he
carried a swagger stick. You could see just by looking at him that he
was an asshole, and the soldiers he had with him weren't Veterans'
Guards but half-trained conscripts from the depot in Fredericton who
had been called up before VE-Day and were now just hanging around
while someone in Ottawa tried to make up his mind what to do with
them. They were sloppy and insubordinate, and there was something
ugly and deadly about them, the way there was about Hod.

In the early afternoon, we saw this outfit coming back, not dragging along watching the edge of the woods, but marching quickly in

two lines down either side of the rails. When they got to where we were working, the lieutenant halted them. They were drenched with sweat and in an even uglier mood than when we had seen them the first time.

The lieutenant went over to Herb, and we all stopped work to listen.

There's a freight supposed to come through here in a few minutes," he said, "and I've orders to search it. Will you make sure it stops?"

"Sure," Herb said. "It'll be almost stopped anyway."

"Well, make sure it stops altogether. I'm going to search every car."

He switched his leg with his swagger stick and turned to his sergeant and got him to spread the men out along both sides of the line. Slowly, sullenly, they obeyed, and when they were in place, they stood there, sweating.

After about five minutes, we heard first one, then a second torpedo go off down the line. We let down the jacks, and the train appeared around the bend, a long freight with a lot of empty coal cars on their way back to the mines. The engineer must have been warned back at the siding because he was slowing to stop even before Herb lifted his flag. When he saw that the train was stopping anyway, the lieutenant stepped between the rails and held up his hand. Up the track, one of the soldiers farted loudly.

When the train had stopped, the lieutenant got his men re-organized into pairs, one pair on each side of a car. While one man on each side stood with a rifle ready, the other two looked under and between the cars, and climbed up to look down into them. When they had checked one car, they went on to the next car that wasn't being checked. Some cars got checked twice. Some didn't get checked at all. The lieutenant walked up and down, switching his leg with his swagger stick.

We stood leaning on our shovels, watching this chaotic operation. No one expected anything to happen.

The Germans came out near the end of the train on the side of the tracks where I was standing. They must have picked their moment because they all came out together, and they were half way to the trees before anyone saw them. Then it seemed as if everyone saw them all at once. They had only about fifty feet to run, down over the gravel slope of the rail bed and through some tall grass and saplings, and I had only a glimpse of them before they disappeared into the trees. I was conscious of three figures in shabby clothing running hard and low, one of them fair-haired, two of them dark, one of the dark ones tall, just as the soldier back at the siding had said.

The lieutenant shouted "Halt!" once before they reached the trees and once more as they disappeared. Then, sounding murderously loud in the astonished silence, there was the crack of a Lee-Enfield, and without any order from the lieutenant the soldiers on this side of the train went pouring down off the rail bed and into the woods, followed by a second wave that had climbed between the cars from the other side. Helplessly, the lieutenant and the sergeant followed along behind. From the woods came the sound of two more rifle shots.

"Come on," Hod said to Steve. "Come on, Wilfred. Come on, boys, let's go help get them."

He took off, running with long, high strides through the grass and the saplings, and Steve and Wilfred and Corney and half a dozen others went after him, Wilfred whooping and waving his arms like a child and trying to imitate Hod's high-kneed stride, which he must have thought was a special way you ran when you were chasing Germans.

"Hod, you stupid son of a bitch, come back here," Herb shouted. "Hod! Wilfred! You god damned idiot!"

They didn't pay any attention.

"Them god damned fools are going to be shooting each other in there," Herb said.

Except for the three older men, who had gathered around Herb, the rest of us ached to follow. We looked at Herb, standing with his arms folded, staring angrily from under his fedora at the trees, but even our fear of his anger wasn't enough to hold us back. We drifted in twos and threes down off the line, as if we weren't really doing what we were doing, and when we got into the trees we began to run.

Ahead of us we could hear a kind of muffled uproar — shouting, cursing, a strange whooping that must have been Wilfred, three more shots, sounding louder even at a distance than any shots I had ever heard before in my life. We crashed through the trees, dodging from side to side, ducking, trying to weave a path where we wouldn't get our faces scratched to pieces by the branches which low down in this starved, overcrowded forest were mostly brown and naked of needles. A couple of hundred yards in, the ground dropped away into a small, soggy clearing full of boot marks that were already filling with water, and we sloshed through after them rather than waste time trying to find a dry way around.

Beyond the clearing, we fought our way uphill through more scrawny evergreens and heard ahead of us, and closer now, two shots, more shouting, a single shot, then silence.

By now, our boots had begun to feel as if they were soled with lead, but we kept on running as hard as we could in order to see whatever might be left to see. Gradually the ground levelled out, and then abruptly we came out into another, much bigger clearing, this one dry with flat outcrops of rock and patches of raspberry bushes. Near the far side, the soldiers were gathered together, and the other members of the gang, towered over by Hod, were scattered around beside them. Above the trees, half a dozen crows flapped heavily, making a slow circle.

I didn't see the Germans at first, and I thought that they must have been killed, but as we got closer I recognized the two dark-haired ones in their shapeless, blue prisoners' uniforms standing in the middle of the soldiers.

Corney came running out to meet us.

"They caught two of them," he shouted. "We saw them with their hands up."

"What happened to the other one?" I asked.

"They don't know," he said. "He wasn't with them."

We made our way through the raspberry bushes and joined the others and stared at the two Germans. Their uniforms were torn, muddy, and soaked almost to the knees, and on the back and down one leg you could see the threads hanging from where they had torn off the markings. The soldier back at the siding had said that they were in their twenties, but they looked more like thirty-five or forty. They had a three-day growth of black beard, their faces were streaked with dirt and sweat, and they had been badly bitten by the flies. The taller one had a bruise and a ragged cut just above one brow that looked through the dirt as if it were still oozing blood. As we stared at them, he looked at us briefly with the sunk, indifferent look which I had seen in the eyes of prisoners of war in newsreels. The other one, broad-faced, blue-eyed, stocky and muscular-looking even in the baggy uniform, stood very straight, ignoring everyone.

The lieutenant was stationed in front of them, his feet apart, his swagger stick in his two hands behind his back.

"Sprechen Sie English?" he said.

The Germans stared across the clearing and said nothing.

"Where is your friend?" the lieutenant said. "Where did he go?"

They still said nothing, and after two more tries the lieutenant gave up and ordered the sergeant to search the clearing. While he and three of the soldiers guarded the Germans, the sergeant and the others tramped through the raspberry bushes and poked around the edge of the woods.

The two Germans watched them expressionlessly, only their eyes moving now and then.

The strangeness of their being Germans seemed to fill the clearing and make it strange too, as if our ten-minute run through the woods had brought us magically into some distant landscape of war. The boys who had gone into the woods first with Hod kept telling over and over what they had seen, embroidering it, dramatizing it, organizing the individual fragments into the collective fiction which they would later tell the friends back home who hadn't been lucky enough to be there. Even among those of us who had followed a long way behind, there was a feeling that we had somehow taken part in the capture.

"If it hadn't been for us," someone said, "they could have doubled back."

"They must have thought we were all soldiers," Corney said. "That's why they gave up. They didn't think they had a chance."

After the soldiers had spent a quarter of an hour rummaging around in the bushes, the lieutenant called them back, and we started out towards the rail line. The sergeant and two soldiers walked in front, then the two prisoners and the lieutenant, then the rest of the soldiers. We straggled along beside them, like a crowd of kids pushing along the sidewalk beside the best part of a parade. Once we got into the trees, the lieutenant's neat lines got all broken up, and he kept giving orders to the sergeant in front about where to go. Twice the tall German stumbled and fell head first through the dead boughs and was hauled to his feet again by the soldiers.

We came out onto the line a couple of hundred of yards from where we had gone in. The train had gone, and the three older men who had stayed behind had jacked the rails back up and were tamping again. Herb was sitting on a trolley. When he saw us, he got up, and the older men stopped working, and they all stood watching us. Half way there, the tall German slipped on the gravel slope of the rail bed and fell down again.

When we came up to where Herb was waiting for us, the lieutenant halted the soldiers. Herb looked at the two Germans and then at us, a look that portended trouble.

"Well, we got two of them," the lieutenant said to Herb, gesturing at the Germans with his swagger stick. He was very full of himself.

"So I see," Herb said. "The other one got away, did he?"

"For the time being," the lieutenant said. "But he won't get far."

"Nobody got shot?" Herb said.

The lieutenant's eyes narrowed, and he looked sharply at Herb.

"No," he said stiffly, "no one got shot."

Herb studied the Germans again from under the brim of the dirty fedora.

"What are you going to do with them now?" he asked.

"We'll march until we can pick up some transport," the lieutenant said, "and then we'll take them back to the camp."

"You better not march them very far," Herb said, "or they're going to drop. They been in the woods for three days."

"I know how long they've been in the woods," the lieutenant said. "But if they don't like walking, they should have thought twice before they tried to escape."

"I could load them and your boys up on the trolleys and ride them back to the siding," Herb said.

"They're going to walk," the lieutenant said angrily, his voice pitching up abruptly like the voice of an incompetent school teacher.

Behind him, the soldiers slouched and listened. Now that the excitement was over and it was obvious that the lieutenant intended to take all the credit for capturing the Germans, they had turned sullen again. Some of them had begun to smirk.

Herb shrugged.

"Well," he said, "you better give them a drink before they start."

Without waiting for the lieutenant to agree or not, he went over to the water barrel by the trolleys and filled the tin dipper we drank from. While everyone watched in silence, he brought it back and gave it to the tall German.

"This ain't very cold," he said, "but it's wet anyways."

The German looked surprised, then took the dipper and drank and passed it to the other German. He emptied it and passed it back to Herb.

"Thank you very much," he said quietly, with only a trace of an accent. "That is very kind."

The tall German made a slight bow from the waist.

The lieutenant's face flushed red above his moustache. Behind him, the soldiers smirked more broadly, and at the back one of them said something in a low voice. The lieutenant turned on them, and they straightened their faces, but not quite.

"Sergeant," the lieutenant ordered, "get them moving."

"Yes, sir," the sergeant said. "All right, then, let's march."

One of the soldiers gave the tall German a push with his rifle, and they set off down the line, the soldiers and the two Germans on one side of the tracks, the lieutenant, swinging his swagger stick, on the other.

Herb let us watch them out of sight, then turned on us.

"I'm docking every one of you the time you were gone," he said. "Now pick up your god damned shovels and get back to work."

In the three days that the soldiers had been out looking for the Germans, we had never heard anyone explain why they had escaped in the first place, but later that afternoon we got an explanation from a sergeant in charge of a patrol of Veterans' Guards. There were prisoners in the camp from parts of Germany that were now in the Russian zone of occupation, and they had heard that the Allies had agreed among themselves to return all prisoners of war to the places they had come from. There were already rumours circulating in the camp that the Russians weren't repatriating the prisoners they had taken, and the prisoners from the Russian zone were convinced that when they got home they would be shipped to Russia to be worked to death in Stalin's labour camps.

"So these three decided to run for it," the sergeant said.

"Why don't they just let them go wherever they want?" Herb asked.

"I don't know," the sergeant said. "But I don't run the god damned world any more than you do."

At five o'clock, we packed up our tools and rode the trolleys back to the siding. We got washed up — at least, those who washed got washed up — and had supper. Since the soldiers had marched off with the Germans, and especially since we had heard why they had tried to escape, no one had had very much to say. A few of us were as ashamed as the collapse of our self-esteem and our treasured boyhood simplicities would let us be. The rest, not wanting to know what they had been brought to know that afternoon about themselves and the world, transposed their shame into a confused sense of resentment, which after supper in the heat and stink of the bunk cars went hunting around for some immediate object. There was a lot of irritable snarling and jostling, and in the end two of the boys got into a fight in the narrow space between the bunks and went after each other with boots and fists until some of the others got them separated before Herb heard them and came in and fired them.

Then, when that was over, I had a row with Corney which marked the end of a friendship which had been coming apart ever since we had arrived at Paradise Siding. There was a revival meeting that night at Killarney village, and for some reason he had been trying all week to talk me into going along with him and a couple of the local toughs because Hod had told them that it was a good place to pick up girls. He had got a tin of Sheiks and a pony of cheap rye from Hod, which he had shown me in great secrecy a couple of nights before, and now he made one final pitch, talking up how easy it was going to be.

"Hod told me," he said, "that the girls get so worked up at those meetings that when they come out afterwards, they're just crazy for it. They'll get out of their pants for anyone who asks them."

"I'm not interested," I said.

"For Christ's sake, why not?"

"Because I'm not," I said. "You can go without me and have my share too."

"Well, shit on you for a friend," he said.

"Go to hell," I said.

After he was gone, I went out for a long walk by myself along another of the back roads through the woods, past weatherbeaten houses with yards full of the usual junk, past a rotting sawdust pile in a clearing where there must once have been a small sawmill, past a stinking fox farm consisting of a rusting corrugated metal shed and some wire pens in which I could see the shapes of foxes moving back and forth with the restless pace of animals crazed by captivity.

By the time I got back to the siding, it was beginning to get dark. The evening train had come and gone, but Eldon and some of his friends were still sitting on one of the benches on the platform, talking and smoking.

I collected the pages of a dismembered newspaper and sat down on another bench under a light to look through it. It was full of stories about the bomb. General Spaatz had reported that the results of the raid on Nagasaki had been good although it was difficult to check closely because of the dust that still hung in the air. Japan had begun negotiations and was expected to surrender. Corder Catchpool of the Bombing Restriction Committee in London had protested the bombings. Above yet another story about how the bomb worked, there was a photograph of a scientist standing in front of his cyclotron. He had a face as bland as the face of a small-town minister on a cover of *The Saturday Evening Post.*

Down the platform Eldon was ruminating about the bomb too, indulging his fantasies of killing everyone in the world who wasn't Eldon.

"We should use it on them god damned Russians next," he was saying. "We should wipe out them god damned communists before they get it too."

"How are they going to get it?" one of the others asked.

"Same as we did," Eldon said. "That's why we should get them first."

After a while they all got up and left, and a little while after that I saw someone walking down the tracks from the bunk cars. When he got closer, I recognized Herb by his walk and his fedora. It wasn't like him to be out walking at night. When he saw me, he came over and sat down and rolled himself a cigarette and lit it. Between puffs, I caught the smell of whiskey. He had probably been drinking in the cook car with Billy, or perhaps by himself.

Out on the road, a jeep went by, followed a few minutes later by an army truck. When it was almost out of earshot, I heard the truck slow down and shift gears. They were still looking for the third German. I thought of him out there in the dark in that rotten forest on the run from the death camps, and I wished him luck.

"Do you think they'll catch that German?" I asked Herb.

"Probably," he said.

"Did any of them ever get away?" I asked.

"I don't think so," he said. "They don't know nothing about the woods, them guys. They just wander around in circles."

"He might still get onto a freight," I said. "Or get some other clothes and hitch a ride."

"Maybe," Herb said. "But I don't see what good it'll do him. The Mounties will just pick him up somewhere else. He ain't got no papers or nothing, and he ain't going to know nobody. There ain't nowhere he can run to that I can see. Unless he runs right out of the god damned world."

ROBERT GIBBS

Robert Gibbs was born in 1930 in Saint John. He was educated at University of New Brunswick and at Cambridge, and taught school in New Brunswick before joining the English Department at UNB in 1963, where he holds the rank of professor. Since 1968, Gibbs has edited or helped to edit *The Fiddlehead.*

Gibbs' articles, reviews, poems and stories have appeared widely in Canadian magazines and journals. He has published six collections of verse, a collection of short stories, *I've Always Felt Sorry for Decimals* (Oberon, 1978) and a novel, *A Mouthorgan for Angels* (Oberon, 1984).

OH, THINK OF THE HOME
OVER THERE

Robert Gibbs

When Aunt Edie fixed her mouth that way in one straight line and went scouring at things, including Pompman and me, we knew someone was coming — and not just someone like old Bliss Copp or Hattie Sears. Uncle Earlie had phoned earlier and she'd said, "That's all I need and cleaning day too" and "you two get off those things and head straight for the tub — and no foolishness. If I find a drop on my clean floor, you'll go straight to bed with some stick. Upon my soul and body, if the Lord came, I'd have to stop and get you youn'ns fit to meet anybody." So we made a beeline, Pompman whispering, "Hey, what's gonna happen, Hutchie? Is the Lord really coming?"

Livingstone Buck wasn't exactly the Lord, but soon after the taxi drove up with him and his four big suitcases, his violin case and guitar case, his trombone and two saxophones, I guess Pompey and I about thought he was. It wasn't that he wore a peaked cap — lots of people did — most of the Catholics round our neighbourhood like Paddie Mc-

Gaughey, Jimmy Dwyer's father, and Leo Dolan, our postman — when he wasn't being a postman — wore those spotted salt- and-pepper kind that most of the rubbies around town wore too — only theirs got bent in the peak and pulled way down on their heads. Tough boys like Larry McGarrity made themselves look a lot tougher by wearing their brother's old ones backwards like baseball catchers. You could usually tell whether a kid was a protestant or a catholic by the kind of cap he wore and the way he wore it and you could tell whether it was safe to try to be friends or not by which way he had it pulled down over which eye or pushed back to let his hair show. Hattie Sears says she doesn't have to look at anything like that to tell a catholic, especially the black Irish kind. She says there's a kind of darkness in their eyes, but Aunt Edie says that's foolishness.

No, it wasn't the peaked cap, because it had hardly any peak at all and was a colour almost orange, but that was part of it. It was the minute he came through the door and saw Pompey and me at the head of the stairs and poked one finger in one cheek and screwed up the other hand into a fist and bonged himself right on the top of the head and made a noise exactly like a cork popping out of a bottle of Uncle Cameron's hop beer that Livingstone had us thinking he was somebody special. Aunt Edie, who had opened the door for him and the taxi- driver, who carried half the bags and things, stood back and kind of smiled, stiff, because she knew Livingstone didn't mean that for her. It was then he lifted his cap about three inches and as best he could with his trombone case propped against him made a little bow and said, "Mrs. Killam, I believe? I'm Livingstone Buck by the grace of our Lord. You are expecting me?" "Come in, come in, my goodness what a load you've got," was all Aunt Edie said, right then. As soon as they got everything in and up the stairs and the taxi-driver paid and Aunt Edie had motioned Livingstone to a chair in the den at the end of the hall, Pompman and I went to the upper stairs where we could see and hear, though Aunt Edie called, "Don't sit up there like dummies, come down and meet Mr. Buck. He's going to be staying with us for a few days." At that, Livingstone rolled his eyes to the side so that only the white parts were showing, woggled his Adam's apple up and down and wiggled his ears faster than a dog or anything could. Pompey and me were too impressed to laugh.

All the time he was at our house, Livingstone never said anything
— words I mean — to Pompey and me, but used a kind of sign language — which we got to understand pretty well and which we liked
because it was a secret code even though we both knew we couldn't
say anything back. (Pompey could, though, make one eyebrow go way
higher than the other and was double-jointed in his thumbs and big
toes, but he never did any of those tricks in front of Livingstone. I guess
we both knew we couldn't keep up to him.)

Livingstone had only been in Canada a few weeks. He was here to
finish High School and staying at our place over the long weekend, because he was going to take it in Fredericton and live with his aunt, but
she was away somewhere over Labour Day and so he had to wait somewhere till she got back. Livingstone's mother and father were
missionaries who knew the Pompmans and knew Pompey's and my
real mother and father before the fever got them. Aunt Edie said later
they'd let Livingstone grow right up with the Zulus and he was just
like one. The pictures I saw in lantern-slides didn't show the Zulus
looking anything like Livingstone. There were real black and he was
brown — deep brown that would never come off in winter — under
red and with bright red knobs on his cheeks. His eyes, though, were
black, just like theirs, but small and very bright like a mouse's. His
mouth was big and pushed way forward and full of very long and
strong-looking teeth — something like a horse's. But his neck was
more like a giraffe's and his Adam's apple which he could woggle up
and down just like a yo-yo stuck out quite a bit. All this is really true
because I heard Aunt Edie tell Uncle Earlie that first night before supper Livingstone looked like something out of a zoo.

"Well, you're a regular one-man band. Where did you learn to play
all those instruments?" Aunt Edie asked him when they got settled in
the den and Pompman and I were back in our favourite place halfway
up the stairs after shaking hands. "Oh, one missionary came once to
our station and left me the violin when I was just oh so high, and another
missionary came by once with the trombone and left it, and Mr. Stokles, our district supervisor, sent me one saxophone from Johannesburg
… because he'd heard I had many musical talents … and so on, as
father said, 'Livingstone was born to have a place in God's orchestra.
He provided you with ears and fingers and will have others provide
you with the instruments.' And so He did. But these I carry with me

are not my real instrument — that was the little harmonium I had to leave in the bush. Mr. Stokles had that sent up especially for me, and when I used to play, 'oh think of the home over there,' all the little Zulu children would gather round and clap their hands softly and sing, 'Koom boo li a kaya la pa ya'." And he closed his eyes and rocked his head sideways as if he were far far away and sang it in Zulu right through. We'd heard other missionaries sing in Zulu and lots of other African, but never like Livingstone. When he got to the long "La pa ya, la pa ya — a," — "Over there, over there — ere," his eyes opened but they were so far away looking and head was bent so sideways that he didn't seem to be there at all, and Pompman and I found ourselves at the bottom of the stairs and in the den without knowing we'd even moved. Aunt Edie got up and said, "You're back, you two, where did you come from? Well, I must go and get supper — you boys help Livingstone up to Grammie's room with his things." So we did, making three trips. Livingstone didn't say anything, but each time we set something down, his violin case, one of his saxophones, his trombone, he grinned and bopped himself on top and made funny clicks that seemed to come from somewhere way inside his head.

That night after supper we were all sitting in the kitchen with our chairs pushed back and Uncle Earlie was asking Livingstone things about himself. "I suppose when you finish up at Fredericton, you'll want to get back to the mission field with your folks." "You know Brother Killam, there are two kinds of music in Africa — there's the Lord's music, the missionary's music that I play on my harmonium or my trombone, or my violin or guitar, and there's what some call the Devil's music, the African's music — and well, you know Brother Killam, they tell me I can never go back to Africa because the call of that music is for my ears too, too strong. You see I lived, my brother, for nine years in an African village without white folk, without missionaries except father and mother who were very often away. Out here ... " his long fingers ran quickly from his head down over his chest ... "I'm a white man, Livingstone Buck, the missionary's son, but in here and in here ... " one long finger pointed to his head and another to his chest " ... I'm a black man — Omunu Mungo, Zulu child of Africa." Uncle Earlie and Aunt Edie kind of looked at each other just a second. Livingstone's black eyes snapped as if sparks were in them and he said, "You think the child of Africa is a child of Satan, my brother, but he is a true child of God." "I'm sure he is," said Aunt Edie pushing back her chair and starting to gather up the dishes. Pompman never took his eyes off Livingstone, though later that night in bed, he said, "Do you think Livingstone is magic, Hutchie?" "Magic! Are you crazy or something Pompey." "Is he a child of the devil?" "How could a missionary's son be a child of the devil? Don't be stupid," I said, "you're a missionary's son and so am I." "Yes, and maybe we are too," he said. "Too what? What're you talking about?" "Childs of the devil," he said, and grabbed me and started kicking under the covers with all his might. We wrestled and tumbled and choked each other with pillows until Uncle Earlie came up to the top of the stairs and hollered — only with that kind of whisper in his voice — "You two'd better settle down and get to sleep. Your Aunt Edie's coming with the stick."

Next day was Saturday and Aunt Edie took Pompman and me to town. Livingstone asked to stay in his room — he wanted to get ready for the special Zulu missionary show he was going to do next day for us kids in Sunday School. He had special costumes to sort out and masks and things. Besides he wanted to work on Aunt Edie's hassock. His eyes gleamed at breakfast time when he saw the cheese tub Uncle Earlie had brought from the market for Aunt Edie to make it out of. "What is that, if you don't mind my asking, Mr. Killam?" he said. "Why it's a cheese tub I'm going to cover with some leatherette for a hassock," said Aunt Edie. "What is a hassock?" his eyes still gleaming and him smiling at Pompey and me with a couple of clicks back in his throat. "It's just a kind of padded footstool. I got the idea from a friend of mine who makes them. They do up nice, if you get a good piece of leatherette and you have room under the lid to store things." "I have a fine piece of hide in my things. It is Zebra hide from Africa." "Oh, I wouldn't want to take that." "No, but would you let me make the hassock, my own special kind — a real African hassock — with your cheese tub?" "Well, go ahead — I'm sure Earlie can easily get another cheese tub anyway — go ahead, Livingstone — if you'd like to try it." Livingstone's large solid teeth gleamed and his tongue clicked and his eyes rolled out of sight as he bonged himself on the head for Pompey and me.

We were gone most of the day. Aunt Edie had to get Pompey and me fitted with shoes and things for school, and she had to take Pompey in to Dr. Foote to make sure his vaccination was coming along

O.K. and she had to take me to Dr. Goldstone to get my glasses
changed. So we went to the tearoom on the top floor of Manchester's
for our dinner. Pompey still wanted to ride up and down the elevator a
couple more times — kids like him think it's a lot of fun, but you get
kind of used to those things and they're not so much fun. I was looking forward to my roast pork. "You and your pork," Aunt Edie flattened her lips, "you're worse than old Milt Steeves." "Who's Milt
Steeves?" "I know who he was," Pompman piped up, "He was that old
fella grandpa used to want to give money to for working but he always
wanted pork instead." Of course, I knew too, because I'd heard the
story every time I said I liked roast pork, but I still liked to hear it again
... *"I guess I'll take a little more of that pork Charl, if you don't mind,
just another few pounds, Charl, I'd just as soon if you don't mind."
"Sure Milt, sure."* So I kicked Pompey under the table to say "shut up,
why didn't you let her tell it." But Aunt Edie didn't even have to tell
the story. Lots of times she'd just say something like "Well, I hope you
get your kite full of pork, Old Milt," or "I'm not having pork, Milt
Steeves, if that's what you're expecting." Aunt Edie had lots more
stories like that about other old fellas and lots of names that went with
them for Pompey, Uncle Earlie and me. So we got to know what she
meant when she'd say "What're you doing up this early, Father
Savage" or "I can't get you filled up can I, Clifford Herman," or "Watch
what you're doing, Sol, you'll spill that." Usually it didn't take much
asking to get her to tell me the story that went with the name, but Pompey knew them all so well, he'd often pipe up like that and spoil it.

The reason I'm telling this all now is that Livingstone got to be —
after he left — one of those names — only he was different, because
Pompman and I lived right in that story and never had to have it told
— though we still liked to hear Aunt Edie tell the ins and outs of it to
other people especially the part about Eva Ashton and the wedding,
but that's still a good ways away.

When we got back later in the afternoon, everything was quiet
upstairs. Aunt Edie went to the kitchen and started banging pots and
pans around getting supper, so it was Pompman and me that heard it
first. It was so soft and steady it was almost like breathing — like the
house breathing all through — but it was there. Pompey said to me as
if he didn't hear anything, "I wonder what Livingstone's doing." I just
said "Shh" and put my finger up to my mouth. Then we both heard it

clear as clear — a beat like you hear on the pillow when your heart's beating — only this got louder — thub, thub, thub, THUB, thub, thub, thub, THUB, — and faster — thub, thub, thub, THUB, thubba, thub, thub, THUB — and all kinds of little beats began breaking into the big beats, and soon the whole house was beating like the inside of a jungle. Pompey and I were standing both at the bottom of the hall stairs. Pompey grabbed hold of me with one hand and the banister post with the other. "What on earth?" and there was Aunt Edie wiping her hands on her apron and just saying that — "What on earth?" Well, that broke the spell and Pompey said, "It's a drum, Livingstone's got a drum," and Aunt Edie said, "A drum! That's devil music sure as you're born," and she pushed us apart and started up the stairs.

Before she got to the top, it stopped all of a sudden and there seemed to be a dead silence for about two seconds, then all the sounds the drum had pushed away came back — cars outside, water in the waterpipes knocking upstairs and suddenly the phone. Even our own breathing came back in a rush and was pushing in and out. Aunt Edie stopped when the phone rang and just then Livingstone came out carrying a big drum — almost bigger than he could carry under one arm — covered with zebra stripes with plain leather at the top and stitched criss-cross fancy all around. He smiled at Aunt Edie, his big teeth sticking right out all across, but his eyes were farther away than ever, and he didn't even see Pompey and me. "Well, Mrs. Killam, your hassock made a fine drum, but not as fine as a real Zulu one. I'm afraid I got lost in the spirit and didn't hear you call." Aunt Edie said, "Oh, there's the phone — answer it Hutchie, Pompey, one of you, and tell them I'll be there in a minute." It was only then Livingstone bonged himself on the head and rolled his eyes back and gave Pompey and me our special grin and we knew everything was O.K. as we both ran to the kitchen to get the phone.

It was Uncle Earlie and all he wanted was to remind Aunt Edie that she'd invited Miss Ashton — Eva that was — to supper tomorrow, and did she want him to pick up anything special on his way home. I ran back to tell Aunt Edie and she was laughing, thumping on the drum with both hands while Livingstone held it for her grinning all over his face and saying, "You'd make a fine Zulu, Mrs. Killam." When I hollered up the message, she stopped and almost screamed, laughing, "Heaven sakes alive, that girl."

Miss Ashton was Pompman's Sunday School teacher and I wished she'd been mine. She was the prettiest Sunday School teacher of all and she didn't have to be very pretty to be that. Mrs. McDade, my teacher, was red-faced and fat and had little white hairs on her lip and every time you told her anything she'd say, "Well I declare." Eva — that's what Aunt Edie and the other grownups called her, though we were supposed to call her just Miss Ashton, had yellow hair, lots and lots, piled up and coiled round on top of her head. Her eyes were big and neither blue nor brown, and when she smiled she did all of sudden, which made all her face light up. I know all this because Mrs. McDade's class sat right opposite hers in the opening and closing and I watched her all the time. She'd come from somewhere in the States to live with her aunt and uncle. She sang solos in the choir and had a real trained voice, Aunt Edie said. Tomorrow was the first time for her to be at our place for supper. Mrs. McDade had been there plenty of times, puffing out her cheeks and saying "I declare" at every little thing. (Aunt Edie called her old Ida and didn't know I knew what she meant). All the little kids like Pompey were crazy about Miss Ashton. She even brought them candy a couple of times, which Aunt Edie said was foolishness and spoiling them, and once she gave Pompey a couple of honeymoons — one for him and one for me — so she knew. Maybe she even saw me twisting my eyes over while we were singing "Turn, turn your eyes from evil" with the motions. Tomorrow Pompman and I had almost forgotten about with Livingstone coming and all that, but we'd been looking forward to it ever since two Sundays ago when Aunt Edie first asked her. We'd even practised "The Books of the Bible" and were all ready to sing them for her, because someone told her how we'd done them at the Sunday School concert, and she told Pompman she specially wanted to hear them. Pompman always had trouble with "Ecclesiastes" and a few of those right around there, but we had them pretty good and I could always drown him out over the rough ones and he could always remember "Zephaniah" and "Zacheriah" better than me, so it kind of balanced out.

Well, Sunday soon came and Sunday School as always. Livingstone had two big cases besides his drum and trombone and violin, so we helped him and felt pretty important walking from the streetcar. Every time we asked Livingstone what he was going to do, he just put his long finger up to his lips, made his eyes go round and round, and showed his teeth on either side of his finger in a grin. Pompey and I were quite excited. Uncle Earlie was kind of grumpy, as he usually was Sunday morning, but he helped Livingstone with one of the cases. We walked into the Sunday School hall like a small parade — Pompey in front with the violin in its case — me with the trombone — Uncle Earlie with one big suitcase and a saxophone — Livingstone with another big case and his drum. Most everyone was in their seats and Mr. Smelt, the superintendent, his face red as a beet and sweating behind his shiny glasses was dinging the little bell on the pulpit. Miss Florrie was already at the piano with her fingers all spread, as Aunt Edie would say. We were almost late and walked straight to the platform and out behind to the Bible Class room where Livingstone was to get ready for the open session. Maybe because there wouldn't be any — Bible Class that is — Uncle Earlie was so grumpy — he always said "Anything, but the Word, they'll let anything crowd that out." By the time we got everything down Miss Florrie was banging out "In the lands beyond the sea" so Pompey and I hurried back to our classes. Miss Ashton made room for Pompey right beside her and even gave me a big smile as I pushed way in opposite.

We were used to missionary shows — learning to sing in Spanish and Zulu and Eskimo — and seeing lantern slides and once real movies with elephants and everything. Aunt Edie hardly ever came. She'd say, "I know they're good people, missionaries, and I don't mind giving to them as long as I don't have to listen to them." But Livingstone was different. We knew that and all the kids knew it too as soon as he came out. He was wearing a leopard skin over a long orangey coloured gown and a mask over his face with just slits for eyes — and there was a rope round his neck with things dangling from it that looked like dried heads — though we found out later they were just gourds. He was carrying his drum. Two little kids in the beginners right down front started screaming and had to be taken out.

Livingstone didn't do anything at first but just kind of stalked around the platform with his eyes shining through the slits. Then, slowly at first — just like yesterday in the house — he began to kind of pat the drum. Then he crunched down and held the drum between his knees. Soon the whole place was throbbing just like our house — and everyone was still — though it felt like swaying back and forth and back and forth — and some of the kids did sway — I saw them out of

the corner of my eye — and I saw Miss Ashton, her mouth open a little and her eyes shining as much a Livingstone's. Then Livingstone
started singing — or chanting I guess you'd call it — with the drum
music and making those clicks with his throat as sharp as one of those
clicking frogs you get in crackerjack.

Right in the middle didn't old Amy Feltright stand up and start really swaying, and then with a kind of toss of her head didn't she pull the
comb out of her bun and shake it down loose. I hardly noticed it, though
she was sitting right on the front row not far from us, but Frankie
Demster starting pulling at my sleeve and whispering, "Hey look, hey
look at old Amy go." By this time Amy was out and had kicked off her
shoes and was doing a fantastic dance and shaking her big mop in jerks
to the drum. Nobody moved. We all kind of held our breaths but
Livingstone kept right on and seemed to be timing his thubs and tub-
badubs and thubathubbadubdubs right to old Amy. That only lasted a
little while till Mr. Smelt bustled over all red and his yellow hair sticking up straight and started to grab Amy by the arm — everyone knew
Amy was kind of funny. She and Mrs. Meikle had started their church
once down on Lombard Street and Aunt Edie said she had painted a
big red cross on her chest to prove to Mrs. Meikle the Lord wanted her
to be the preacher. She was always doing funny things and saying funny
things. Now she jerked herself free of old Smelt and shaking her hair
away from her face and blazing her eyes and pointing right at Mr. Smelt
she hollered "Whited wall, Pharisee, can't you see I'm dancing in the
spirit. Keep your hands off." But three more men from the Bible Class,
Brother Straight, Brother Wright and Brother Lawe came up and
ushered her back and out. She stopped before she left and hollered
back, "Whited walls!" Livingstone kept right on chanting and drum-
ming his big teeth sticking all out in a grin — he had taken off his mask
by this time.

When he finished at last and the whole Sunday School just snapped
back to being a Sunday School, he stepped forward. "My dear boys
and girls, that is the true music of Africa, the voice of my people. You
may have thought it was devil music as some of the white missionaries
do and that the medicine man is a child of the devil. That is not true.
The medicine man I was showing you is a good man, an African herb
man and a convert to Christianity. The music he plays is good music
— praising God — his God and our God too — for all the things he

has made. You noticed no doubt how our dear sister down here was affected by my drum. She is a true child of Africa. She wants to worship God as the Africans do — not just with her mouth but with her whole body. Now boys and girls I'm going to teach you an African song and when we sing it I want you to watch me and sing with your whole body."

Well that was just the beginning. Livingstone taught us an African song which we sang to motions but not just any old motions like "The Ravens' wings went flap flap flap" or "Climb, climb up Sunshine Mountain" but clapping one side in twos and one side in threes and swaying till we all felt again like we were right in the jungle, but our song was really just "Heavenly Sunshine." Then Livingstone took off his leopard skin and his robe and was back in his suit. He played his tin whistle, his violin, his trombone — all in one piece — "Bringing in the Sheaves" but still done kind of African. Then he showed us how a Zulu would kill a snake — acting it all out and using an old bathrobe cord with tassels for the snake. Boy, we could almost see it move. When he finished at last and Mr. Smelt went teetering and kind of wet-eyed back to the platform to thank him, all us kids started clapping. At that Livingstone started clapping too but not right with us — African clapping — and soon we were right back again doing old "Heavenly Sunshine" in Zulu, while Mr. Smelt folded and unfolded his hands and smiled a white, sickly smile over the pulpit. When he finished again, Livingstone grinned his buck-toothed grin, and Mr. Smelt jumped forwards with his hands raised for "The Lord bless thee and keep thee ..." while he had a chance. Soon there were a lot of kids milling around Livingstone and us, Pompey and me, standing there feeling kind of important with his violin case and trombone and saxophone. Just then Miss Ashton came up and held out her hand "I want to tell you how much I enjoyed your program, Mr. Buck." Livingstone took her hand kind of loose at first then gripped it hard and held on, pumping it up and down every so often but not letting go, and just staring at her and grinning out. Pompman grabbed Livingstone's coat-tail and gave a couple of yanks and blurted, "Hey, Livingstone, this is Miss Ashton and she's my teacher." I didn't want Pompey to have all the say, so I butted in, "And she's coming to our house for supper tonight." "Yes, Mr. Buck — you're staying with the Killams, are you? I expect I will be seeing you at supper." Miss Ashton blushed red and tried, you could

see, to pull her hand away but not too hard. Livingstone just held on
and pumped every so often. Then at last he raised his other hand and
patted the hand he was holding about three times and let it go. Miss
Ashton's smile just lit over her whole face. Livingstone still staring
hard and grinning all outdoors, as Aunt Edie called it, stepped back,
almost clicked his heels together and gave her a stiff little bow. It was
like watching a play or something to see the way she kind of curtsied,
then turned and went.

Then came our parade back, lined up with all of Livingstone's stuff,
Uncle Earlie coming up at the last with one of the big cases and saying,
"Move along, you fellows, you're going to miss your car, and I've got
to get back to service." Livingstone came, though he'd never stopped
grinning and staring. He never said anything to Uncle Earlie or to us,
but two or three times he said things to himself in Zulu, clicking way
back in his throat. People kind of looked at us on the steetcar, wondering I bet.

When we got home, Aunt Edie met us at the head of the stairs with
her mouth closed tight, and we knew something was up. As she reached
to help with one of the big cases, she was muttering, "With all I've got
to do today, now her!" and making a kind of funny face by screwing
up her eyes. Pompman and I both knew what that meant. Aunt Delia
— who came every once in a while down on the train from Moncton
to spend two or three days with us. Sure enough we could hear her
high, thin voice sing-songing from way up on the second landing.
"You're home, you youn'ns, and who have you got with you, the lost
tribes of Israel?" That's how she talked with no kind of sense.
Pompman and I just hollered, "Hi, Aunt Deedie."

She came flopping down the stairs, already into her slippers and
her red flowery dressing gown, which she wore most of the time around
our house. She didn't have her pipe though, because she never smoked
it at our house, at least not unless she was in the bathroom. She was
tall, taller even than Uncle Earlie, and with white hair all puffed, to
cover her bald spot Aunt Edie said. She always stood straight with her
shoulders back, and Aunt Edie said that was because she'd been to a
school for young ladies in Salisbury way back where she learned to
talk like she did so high and sing-songy and to sing which she sometimes did even higher and all warbly.

I don't think Livingstone saw her. He was still just grinning. But she saw him and stepped right up and took his hand. "Well, who've we got here, another missionary, eh? How do you do? Buck. One of the Smith's Corners Bucks? Heaven sakes alive, none of those hellions ever made a missionary, did they? Well speak up, boy, what's struck you? Haven't you ever seen an old woman in her kimono before? Oh, Edie it looks to me as if your guest is moonstruck — it must've been one of your holy floozies." And she went off into one of her warbly laughs while Livingstone sort of loosely shook her hand and mumbled, "I beg your pardon. I beg your pardon."

When we got him and all his stuff up to his room and were back down in the kitchen, Aunt Edie and Aunt Delia were right into it. "I don't know where you dig them out, but you do. Oh, he's a dilly." "I don't know what's struck him," was all Edie said. Pompman and I didn't say anything, because for once we knew and they didn't — Livingstone was struck all right — on Miss Ashton — and I don't know about Pompey but I for one knew just how he felt.

"Here, you ring-tailed snorter, let me see if this is going to go near you. Upon my soul, Edie those two imps are sprouting like toadstools, under your feet one day and up to your middle the next." Aunt Delia was knitting Pompman and me sweaters for Christmas. She always knitted us them, out of stretchy scratchy wool, too long in the arms and too short everywhere else. She always gave Aunt Edie black silk stockings and Aunt Edie always said, "That pig-headed old ninny, she knows very well I never wear black stockings. Just because she wears them herself. I've a good will to wrap them up and give them right back to her next year."

Aunt Edie by this time was busy rolling out dough for her pies and getting other things ready for the special big supper with Miss Ashton. "So you're having more company," Aunt Delia said, "Ashton did you say? What Ashton is that? I don't know that I've ever heard that name around here." "Oh, she's not from around here," Aunt Edie gave her rolling pin a flip and pressed her lips together. "Oh, she isn't, then where's she from? Africa or Zanzibar or Greenland's icy mountains or some other outlandish place?" "Boston's not all that outlandish," was all Aunt Edie said as she pinched the dough around the pie pan. Aunt Delia sitting in the kitchen rocker had her needles flying. Just then she turned to Pompey and me who were standing by the edge of the table eating the apply-skin snakes and listening. "You two, don't make your-selves sick. What are you looking so sheepish about? They're up to something, Edith, you mark my words." And she gave us a long stare, pulling her glasses down so she could look over them. Pompey, who wasn't a bit afraid of her, took an apple snake and waggled it in front of her nose and said, "Want one? They're real good, Aunt Deedie." "Get away with that thing, you'll have it all over me. Upon my word, Edie, they put me in mind of the Bateman twins, those two."

"Who are they?" I asked. Aunt Deedie settled back to rocking and knitting, rocking and knitting, and we knew she'd tell us when she was good and ready.

"You remember Sadie Bateman and how foolish she was to have twins, Edie?" she finally said. "Oh, I seem to remember something Wellington Smith used to tell." "Wellie Smith," Aunt Delia sniffed, "What did he know about anything? He had quite a hand to tell stories though — I don't know how Theresa put up with it — but he was like all those Smiths from Little Falls Brook, got everything twisted." "Her-man must have been pretty straight," said Aunt Edie, "He got to be a preacher." Aunt Delia sniffed again, this time louder, "Some preacher." Then she was quiet, rocking back and forth, her old needles just click-ety- clacking along. "Here, what are we doing talking about the Smiths when I wanted to talk about Sadie Bateman and her twins? Well she had them — two girls, about ten months apart — and she let on they were twins — dressed them just alike, took them everything together — even bought a twin go-cart for them — Posy and Pansy she called them. Of course everyone knew, except George Bateman and he was too soft to know. He'd been up in the Maine lumber woods over a year before the first one was born, and the second came about four months after he got back, but he went right along with her — Posy and Pansy, the Bateman twins, and neither of them a Bateman nor a twin."

Pompman had been over at the window running his dump-truck over the sill. He'd heard everything. "Why'd you say we was like them?" he said, almost mad. "Yeah, why Aunt Dedie, why?" I piped up, remembering. "Oh, you two — I forgot about you — but you are just like them. I never see one of you but I see the other — that's why. Do you want me to call you Posy and Pansy too?" Now Pompey was really mad. He caught hold of her old ball of wool and ran out of the kitchen unwinding it as he ran. Aunt Delia laughed — she just let go of her knitting and laughed. Then she got up and took after Pompey hollering "Here you tartar of the earth, give me that."

Just then, we heard voices on the stairs and there was Uncle Earlie coming in from meeting with Bliss Copp. They were already arguing about something in the sermon, Bliss saying something like "He needs a better concordance — that's what that young man needs," and Uncle Earlie, "Sound enough, though, in doctrine didn't you think?" By the way Bliss was puffing and grumping, Pompey and I knew he'd be there all day. Of course he'd say, "I won't stay Sister Killam since you have company." And Aunt Edie would say, "Now Bliss you're staying, so stop the foolishness." So he'd stay, sometimes till way past our bed-time, and Pompey and I would sneak out and listen at the head of the stairs, even when we knew it was just old Bliss again arguing about the ten- toed Kingdom.

Aunt Delia stopped when she saw them then burst out, "Well, if it isn't old Pharisee face, Bliss, how are you?" Bliss just grunted and reddened all the way up his bald head. His mouth corners turned down, like they did most of the time, except when he got that old big black Bible open. Aunt Edie called him the man who married an ox, I guess because Matilda his dead wife used to be fat and because once in business meeting he said, "Up there on that great day, I won't be able to say 'I married an ox and cannot come.' " Pompman and I heard that story lots of times, and we wondered why Bliss would call her an ox even if Matilda was fat, but we always laughed right along with the others.

When Bliss saw Aunt Edie come up behind Aunt Deed, he said, "Good afternoon Delia, good afternoon Edith. I won't be staying for tea but I did want to clear up something in the Word with Earlie here." Aunt Edie just clucked and said, "I'm going to bring you a lunch you can eat here in the den, and we'll be having supper about five. Of course, you'll stay — you don't call Delia company? And Livingstone — Pompey you go up and knock on his door and tell him to come down for lunch." Aunt Delia had her ball of yarn by this time and was grinning straight at Bliss while she wound her yarn on. "Do you mind the time you fell out of the crab tree trying to look in Else Tippett's bedroom?" Bliss turned even redder and twisted his mouth a little open, trying to grin I guess. "You were a pretty bird then, Bliss Copp, but you've lost your tail feathers, so you needn't try that grinny look on me."

Uncle Earlie gave Bliss a little poke and said, "Bliss has no time for that, Deedy, he's got his mind on higher things." Bliss just said, "Now now, now. Now now, now. The Day. Remember the Day. Idle words, folks, idle words." Bliss never did say much except when he got going on the Word, flipping over the pages of his Bible and spouting a mile a minute. It was then his flat mouth opened, his eyes lit up behind his horn rims, and his old gold tooth really shone.

Livingstone came downstairs with Pompey and shook hands with Bliss. He had changed his clothes and was wearing checkered brown and white bloomer pants, yellow golf socks and a yellow sweater, and instead of a necktie a red handkerchief kind of sideways on his neck like a cowboy mask. He looked real slick with his hair parted in the middle and combed down, but his eyes were still far away, even though he wiggled his ears just once at Pompey and me.

After we'd eaten and Bliss was already looking up scriptures and Uncle Earlie was listening, sort of absent-mindedly, Livingstone rolled his eyes way off from everybody, blushed, and asked, "What time is Miss Ashton to come?" "Oh, about four, she said," Aunt Edie told him, "Why, would you want to go pick her up?" "Well, would that be a courtesy, Mrs. Killam?" said Livingstone. "Any young girl that wouldn't want to be picked up by a pretty banty like you would be off her head," Aunt Delia butted in, coming up behind Aunt Edie with the teapot. "I'll call Mrs. Horsesmith, the lady she boards with, and tell her you're coming," Aunt Edie said. Suddenly Livingstone dropped his eyes and his Adam's apple bobbed up, while he said, "So kind of you, Mrs. Killam, really, I mean, so kind, but I'm not sure that I ... " "Look Livingstone, if you're that shy, take the boys along," broke in Aunt Deed, "They'll see she doesn't eat you and it'll get them out from under our feet for while. And they'd be better off anyway not listening to old Bliss here blathering about the Beast." "Yes, Livingstone, it's a lovely day," said Edie, "I'll go phone Gladys Horsesmith, and boys you'd better get your sweaters."

Soon we were going down the stairs with Livingstone, looking even slicker with his yellow cane with its gold top and his new tweed cap. Just then the bell rang and Pompey ran ahead to open the door. "Uncle Snow," he said, "Hey, here's Uncle Snow and Aunt Huldah and

Gracie and Demerchant and Lucy and Lottie." Aunt Huldah was already hugging Pompman with one arm — she was carrying Lottie over the other — and Uncle Snow had Lucy over his shoulder. "We're just passing through," he hollered up to Aunt Edie who'd come to the head of the stairs; "Hi there Hutch, hi Edie," and we all said "Hi, Hi, Uncle Snow, Hi Demerchant, Hi, Hi, Hi."

Pompey and I didn't know now whether to go with Livingstone or not. Gracie and Demerchant were just about our ages — he was his and she was mine — and we always had fun when they came. Uncle Snow was the oldest of Uncle Earlie's three brothers, Freeze and Curtis and Seymour — only Curtis who was our real father — Pompey's and mine — was dead. Aunt Delia said once, "I don't know what ever got into Lib Killam calling her boys such outlandish names. Of course, Snow and Freeze were named for the doctors who delivered them and Earlie and Curtis for their grandfathers — but Seymour — there was no call to give anyone a name like that. And you know what they used to say around Killam's Mills whenever they saw one of them coming — 'If it freezes early, we'll see more snow.' "

By the time they were all inside, poor Livingstone was almost crowded off the stairs, lifting his cap and meeting them all. Aunt Edie came to the head of the stairs and said, "Well, the likes of you — come on up, " and we knew she was planning already to let them stay for supper.

So Pompey and me, once we were clear of Gracie and Demerchant, who were staring all eyes at Livingstone — and we didn't say anything then because he was *our* secret — followed Livingstone out the door, knowing they'd all still be there when we got back. We were used to big suppers on Sundays with lots of relations and preachers. Aunt Edie used to say, "I can always plan on ten anyway on Labour Day weekend." This time she was wrong, this time there were eighteen in all — but that comes later.

Livingstone didn't say a word till we got to the foot of King, where we should have transferred to the Haymarket car. Over by the railing of the Slip with her clothesline strung between the lampposts was Millie Doherty, the woman taxi-driver. We'd seen her lots of times in her man's suit and shirt and tie and her chauffeur cap nearly sideways on her head. Right now she was hanging some frilly things on her line to blow in the breeze. Livingstone stared at her with Pompey and me, but at first he wasn't seeing. Then suddenly he popped loose and crossed over to Millie, "Is this a taxicab?" he said. "What's it look like, a fire truck?" Millie's voice was coarse and she twisted her mouth around her clothespin like a man getting ready to spit. "We'll engage it," said Livingstone. "The boys will tell you where and you're to wait for a young lady." So Pompey and I were sitting in the back of Millie Doherty's taxi where we never expected to be, because Aunt Edie said any woman that would drive a taxi and dress like a man must be a tough and probably a bootlegger.

Pompey and I sat still and waited outside Gladys Horsesmith's while Livingstone went in for Miss Ashton. Millie filled up her pipe and lit it and turned back to us with little curls of smoke rolling out the side of her mouth. "Some jimdandy limey, isn't he? He your cousin or something?" "Oh, no, " said Pompman, "Livingstone's a missionary — a half Zulu one." "A Zulu, you say. Yea, that's a good name for him. I hope he's a rich Zulu, cause he's gonna need to be if he keeps me here much longer." Just then the door of Glady's Horsesmith's house opened, held by Livingstone, and Miss Ashton all in pink came out followed by him grinning from ear to ear. Millie knocked the ashes out of her pipe and started up. Miss Ashton said, "Hello Hutchison, hello Pompman, my it's kind of you all to come and fetch me — I feel really special." Millie screwed her eyes around and her mouth too and said, "Where to?" I told her and we were soon bumping the cobbles as we dodged around street cars and through alleys taking all the shortcuts from Queen Square to Indiantown. Pompey who sat in the middle never took his eyes off Millie who handled that old car just like a man with one elbow out the window and her tongue in the side of her mouth.

When we stopped, Pompey said, "Boy, you're the best taxi-driver, Millie." And she turned quick, and gave him a fake punch and said, "Who're you calling Millie, squirt? Lookin' for a fight? I'll put a tin ear on you if you don't watch out." Livingstone was busy helping Eva out and taking her up to the door. When we were all out, he turned and smiled and, standing on the running board, handed Millie a bill — a whole dollar — and didn't wait for change. Millie slammed her door and drove off quick up Victoria Street on two wheels.

When everybody had met everybody else and all the aunts, Edie, Huldah and Delia, had gone back to the kitchen with orders for no one to bother them, Pompman and I took Gracie and Demerchant down to

show them our cave while we still had our sweaters on. "Why's he look
that way?" Gracie said stretching her neck back to where Livingstone
and Eva were still standing shaking hands with Bliss and Uncle Snow
at the top of the stairs. "Look what way," I said. "He's a Zulu, he's
magic. You shoulda seen him in Sunday School." Pompman hollered.
"He made a drum," I said "and he let me play it. He's gonna teach me
some real jungle music." Gracie and Demerchant's eyes got big and
Demerchant said, "Is he a cannibal? Does he eat real people? There's
a Chinaman lives near where we do and he eats people — somebody
caught him once tryin to steal a baby right out of the carriage." "You
made that up, Demerchant Killam. I'm telling mom, you're making up
stories again." Demerchant was scared but he wanted to keep his story
just to be even with Pompman, "I saw him. I saw him right over Mrs.
Eccles' baby, and I don't care if you tell or not."

Gracie and Demerchant both got burdocks on them and didn't want
to go any further, so we skipped the cave and walked down to the bridge
and back. Just as we got to the house, a big new car, a streamlined
Chrysler, was stopping. A big bald-headed man stuck his head out and
said, "Does Mr. Earlie Killam live around here?" When I told him yes,
he and a big, laughy woman got out and went up to the door. There
were two white-headed ladies sitting in the back. Soon Uncle Earlie
was at the door and calling Livingstone. "Look Livingstone," he said,
"your folks, Brother and Sister Merserolle." Mr. Merserolle was trying
to say something but Mrs. Merserolle wasn't giving him a chance,
"Sam MacMurchie met us in Pea Cove and said you'd got here so I
said to Garfield, 'Let's just drive back that way today and take him
right on through with us.' " Livingstone was blushing and grinning but
his eyes weren't there. Uncle Earlie was saying, "As long as you're
here come on up and have a bite with us" and Mrs. Merserolle was
saying, "But we've got the Shepherd Sisters here. We met them at the
Camp Meeting in Mars Hill and they were glad for the chance back."
Livingstone was over to the car in one leap and shaking hands and
laughing and kissing the two old ladies. He had known them, we found
out later, years and years ago when they were missionaries in Africa.
Soon we were all going upstairs and Aunt Edie was saying at the top
"Come one, come all, I'll just get the other table up." So that's how
come we had eighteen to supper and as Aunt Edie said there was plenty for everybody. "I asked old Bliss to say a short blessing and tell the

Lord maybe he'd better multiply the ham," Aunt Deed said, "And I guess he did. I never saw a leg go so far."

Aunt Edith had the double doors open and the big table pulled out as far as it could go and a smaller table set beside it for us kids. Pompman and I were sitting where we could see the big table with Lucie and Gracie and Demerchant opposite. Lottie was in the high chair pulled up by Aunt Huldah. Eva Ashton and Livingstone were right side by side and he never even waggled at us or anything. Aunt Edie and Aunt Deed waited on the table. Demerchant kept kicking Pompey under our table and Gracie whispering louder and louder "Mom-ma, mom-ma, Dermerchant's action out, Demerchant's action out."

The Shepherd Sisters sat one on each side of Eva and Livingstone and kept saying things across them like, "Isn't this a feast, Sister." Bliss was saying, "The Marriage Supper of the Lamb is post-millennial, brother," talking to Brother Merserolle, who just kept buttering hot rolls one after another and stuffing them in with his scallop and ham and stuff. Aunt Huldah and Sister Merserolle had just found out they were cousins and were both talking together "Well, she married T-Leg Lutes, you must have heard of him" "Oh, wasn't he Lindy Mitton's brother?" and "Well yes, and their daughter married a Colpitts from Colpitt's Settlement and they moved to Cross Creek." So that kept them going, while Aunt Deed and Aunt Edie just kept passing stuff and saying things like, "Now don't tell me you're not going to try my mustard pickles" or "Livingstone, you haven't eaten enough to keep a bird alive, even a lovebird." That was Aunt Delia going round the table to the kitchen and giving Pompman a twist on the ear as she passed.

Finally the pie and Maple Mousse came and the grownups began to push back their chairs and wipe their faces with their napkins except Livingstone and Eva, who just kept grinning, the both of them, and blushing, her pink and him deep red, and saying hardly anything. Just then Eva caught my eye and shook her head and said right out loud "Oh, I almost forgot everybody — we're in for a treat." Pompman knew, though I'd forgotten, and he said "I don't want to do them, do you Hutchie?" "Of course, you will, you promised," said Aunt Edie, "just as soon as I pour the tea. Eva can you play it?"

The Books of the Bible had gone right out of my head but they came back — or most of them — as soon as we got singing — though

Aunt Huldah kept saying "Sing out, sing out boys, we can hardly hear you." Eva hardly touched the keys, she played so soft and nice, and Livingstone reached into his coat and pulled out a tin whistle and played way up high and helped us over the rough ones.

When we got to Revelations and were getting back our breath, Eva smiled and said, "That's was just great, boys, I want you to promise me something right now — will you?" Pompman and I could only nod — we were still breathing hard. "I want you to sing that at my wedding." And Pompman blurted right out "You and Livingstone?" And Livingstone laughed a high funny laugh and clicked about five times in his throat, the first time he'd done anything Zulu that night.

VERONICA ROSS

Veronica Ross was born in Hanover, West Germany, but lived for
many years in Nova Scotia, the setting for much of her fiction. She has
published three collections of short stories, *Goodbye Summer* (Oberon,
1980), *Dark Secrets* (Oberon, 1983), and *Homecoming* (Oberon, 1987)
as well as a novel *Fisherwoman* (Pottersfield Press). She presently
lives in Kitchener, Ontario where she is working on a new novel.

NELS

Veronica Ross

You, Nels Tupper, climbing seaside in rubber boots, what did you think when the embryo grew in your womb? There in that ruined house, gables and cupolas cracked and splintered like bones without marrow? How did the man escape? You always gripped him with iron thighs. The child, soft female growth, dressed always in ruffles (starched) and knee socks (white) betrayed an inner warmth. Or was this stubborness? Who would know, with you? The wind attacking that treeless cliff blew your dark hair into your face. Peddling fish in the old green truck, your face showed hard irony. Sweet, they said of the child, Beth. Were you pleased?

And when the man, thirteen years later, climbed your hill, what then? *The man.* Rum nose, veined cheeks, less hair, in his awkward black suit with the jacket which was too short. What then?

You said, "Well, so you've come back, have you?"

Your hair was greying then. And a mustache was beginning on your upper lip.

He said, shuffling feet, "I just thought I'd see how you were doing."

You knew he wanted his daughter, like a dog digging up an old bone.

But the child was away, visiting a friend who had a horse. You had bought jeans for her, rose corduroy, the newest colour and style, and tied her long curls back with a pink ribbon. When she brought friends home you disappeared, but later you sat, you and she, in the kitchen for a quiet hour while she told you all. She seems like a nice girl, you'd say to her of a friend. Or: You don't want to see her again. She listened, like your father had. "You dumb crazy old drunk," you said to him, and poured his whiskey into the sea. He hung his head. Your child pressed her face against your breast. You cooked cocoa which she drank wearing pajamas warmed by you before the fire.

Was he embarrassed, the man? Gordon Harrington. A tiny man, with shanks shrunken beneath baggy unpressed trousers. He used to grin shyly, standing in your curtainless bedroom. A single light bulb burned. You flung your clothes everywhere and lay naked on the bed, hands behind your neck, watching him. The bedspread was new, ridiculous blue flowers, bought cheap. Tawdry chenille would have been better. You wanted him to be the one bright thing in the room. And when the ocean coldness of the room shrivelled limbs and raised goosebumps, you drew him to you.

You said to him, months later, "Either you want me or you don't." The boyish softness turned to stubbornness. He walked away. But you had known it was there all the time, the stubbornness. Redeemed and verified you were right then. A little man going down a cliff, escaping and proud of it. You sat with hands gripped on the table, there in your kitchen. The table oilcloth was yellow, with a round burn in the middle. Dishes draining in the sink were covered with a brown cloth, the back of a shirt. A strip of red was tied to the pump handle.

These things were your life. You would have crawled to Gordon Harrington. He was getting drunk in the tavern. Leaving, he tore his blue jacket on the hinge of the doorpost. Once, he had forgotten his jacket at your house. You took it to bed with you.

It was winter when you drove yourself to the hospital. The brakes in the truck were gone, but it was warm. There was no snow. There had been a fire in the bakery the night before. Two boys were rifling through old boards. A contraction — one of the boys stared at you as if it showed on your face. Maybe it did. In the hospital, you, strong Nels, began to cry. Let me help you, a nurse said. You pressed against her softness. You wanted then to be good and kind.

So many little things, but the world had become smaller then. The man had gone to Calgary. No one went there then. Later when the boys from home began going out west for work, and someone said, My brother he went out west, you thought, Gordon Harrington.

But when you saw him again, him with whispy hair blowing away to show white scalp, with ears sticking out, you thought, To hell with him.

You wanted him to see Beth then.

And when she came running up the hill, curls flying, face flushed, she fell as ever into the role you had given her. Beautiful, spoiled, sassy.

And very aware of the man, although she did not look at him.

"Math," she chortled. "I just can't stand it. I'm going to drop it."

"Over my dead body," you said. The mother.

"I don't care what you say." She stuck out her tongue.

"Go put some water on for tea."

"Do I have to do that again?"

"You have."

"Oh you!"

"Go on then or I'll get the stick."

"Oh sure."

You both laughed. You slapped her on the bum. "Go on then, lazy bones." And to the man you said, "Well it was nice seeing you. Bye for now."

Graciously, so graciously. For you.

Your girl looked out the window.

"Who was that?"

"No one you know. He used to live here. Funny old drunk."

The child thinks her father is dead. You have always said this. He was a good, intelligent man who died in a car crash. He had black hair and muscles. He was tall. Where is his grave? she wanted to know. In California, you said. He had no family here, you added.

He had us, the girl said.

The man, on the road, did not look back.

The child is totally yours, the best thing that ever happened to you. You would talk to yourself if you lived alone. A mad witch, feared by children. A grizzly grey old woman cackling, *Fish, fresh fish.* Or maybe you would just stay in the house and rot among rags and garbage.

He has no rights, you say. And madness is imagining the two of them together, father and daughter. You know that under her curls her ears stick out like his. Whenever you see them you think of him.

"I didn't come to make trouble," he says when he comes again.

"What then?"

"I just wanted to see how you were doing."

"Well now you see. We're doing fine, just fine."

"Does she know about me?"

"What is there to know?"

"Well I'm her —"

"You're not her father," you say.

That night you take your clothes off and look at yourself in the mirror. You are bigger. Your stomach protrudes, soft, sagging. Your thighs are white, loose. It is unused flesh, lonely, without life. You shut off the light then, get into bed, and imagine the two of them together, the man taking her away. The girl saying, I want to go with my father. In the deepest night you know the man is making a claim he is entitled to make, a claim which has nothing to do with rightness or morality, or times past. You think of your father, dead in his coffin, the year after the child was born. You didn't mean to cry, but you did. He made you angry often enough with his foul drinking and mad muttering but you never thought of leaving him. And when they lowered him into the grave, the earth seemed to tremble. Someone gripped your elbow. You remember·that, and the wind, too. What did you care then about his messes and his drinking? You only wanted you father alive and on the earth.

And so it would be with the child if she knew. Maybe she knows. In the middle of the night, you think, She knows. Her eyes dream. Sometimes they go far away from you to places you cannot visit. So it was, too, with the man when he used to smile at you. What? you asked. What do you want? He always laughed and took you in his arms, as if that explained everything.

"I saw that man," your girl says a few days later.

"What man?"

"The man who was here."

"I don't want you talking to him."

"Why not?"

"Because I said so. He's not a good man."

"Why not?"

"He used to follow little girls years ago and I don't imagine he's changed any."

"Why did he do that?"

"To lure them into the bushes."

"What for?"

"You know very well what for. Don't ask such stupid questions."

"Why did you talk to him then?"

"He saw me in the yard. I was only being polite. He always did that, pestering people. Give him an inch and he'll take a mile. He was always like that. But he won't come back."

"How come?"

"I told him not to come back."

"When did you say that?"

"A few days ago."

"So he did come back."

"He didn't stay long. I can tell you. If there's one thing I don't need it's someone like that hanging around here. And you're not to talk to him either. Don't let me catch you. What did he say to you anyway?"

She stares at you with narrowed eyes. His eyes. Regards you for a moment as if she's considering what she will say to you.

"Well? Out with it."

"He only said hello."

"And what did you say to him?"

"I didn't say anything."

"You must have said something."

"I didn't say anything."

"You must have said hello."

"I didn't even say that."

"If I find out you're lying ..."

"I'm not lying."

"You'd better not be."

"I didn't say anything. Honest."

"Next time you see him, you tell me."

"I won't talk to him."

"Still, you tell me."

"What would you do if he did bother me?"

"Call the police. What do you think? That kind of thing is against the law."

"Even if he just says hello? That's not against the law. There's nothing wrong with a person saying hello."

"With him there is. He has other things on his mind. He's evil, bad. He could kill you."

"I find that hard to believe," she says tartly, lifting her nose.

"Believe it. I know about things like that."

"What happened before?"

"They chased him out of town. He probably thinks people have forgotten but there's not a decent soul what'll have him around. I'm just thinking of your own good."

"He wouldn't hurt me."

"He would. You're not to talk to him. And you're to tell me if he comes near you. Is that clear?"

She bites her lip.

"I'm warning you."

"Just so you understand," you add. "Is it clear then?"

She nods.

"Answer me. I want to hear it, just so there's no question about it afterwards."

"It's clear."

"And if he comes near to you?"

"Then I'll tell you."

"Don't forget it."

"I won't. Honest I won't."

"You'd better not."

Standing by the window, you imagine he is watching from the bottom of the hill. He sees the woman, animated, totally oblivious to him. He stares for a long time. At last he turns away. It is raining. On the road he looks back over his shoulder. The light from the house on the hill looks like a beacon from a lighthouse. The inner life of that place, the warmth and happiness, is hidden from him. Later that night he awakens out of a troubled sleep and thinks if he hangs around the streets he will see you and the child. But you will not see him.

And so, the next day, you do not look for him in case he is watching. You're at your worst. Rubber boots, men's work pants, torn lilac sweater. Beth skips along beside you. She is not at all ashamed of you. You are going to buy her new sneakers. Beth seeks her reflection in every store window. By the drugstore you stop to light a smoke, flinging the match onto the street. "Maybe I can get socks, too," Beth says.

"I'm not a millionaire."

You buy Beth three pairs of socks and extra laces for the new blue sneakers. The laces have hearts on them. Beth springs merrily into the truck. She does not say, as she usually does, 'This old thing. Why can't we have a car like everyone else?' You spin tires. The man on the street corner watches the green truck disappear around the corner like a racing car.

But you weren't supposed to see him with the woman. Tiny, with short red hair and coral lips, she has her hand on his arm. A white sweater hangs over the shoulders like a cape. Hips away in tight black slacks and high heels. Silver earrings tangle.

Gordon Harrington doesn't see you.

Beth's early morning face is sullen, bent over cornflakes. "Don't slurp," you say. Your head aches. You hardly slept the night before. Beth had a pink bedroom in the western bungalow. You waited for mail. You found you had cancer. You broke both your legs and starved to death in the house.

"I want you to come right home after school," you tell Beth.

"But I've got volleyball."

"Never mind. You come right home."

"Why?"

"Because I said so."

"But I'm on the team. I can't miss a practice unless I'm sick."

"You heard what I said."

"But why? You don't even have a reason, do you?"

"I don't have to have a reason."

Her eyes fill with tears.

"I'll write you a note. I'll say you sprained your ankle."

"Everyone knows I don't have a sprained ankle." She is crying now.

"I know what's best for you."

"You're crazy!"

You slap her.

"You're crazy!" Beth shrieks. "Everyone knows you're crazy. Crazy, crazy, crazy!"

You grab her arm but she runs out the door.

"Come back or I'll burn your new sneakers! You better get back in the house!"

"I'll give you two seconds to get back here!"

"I'll lock you out!"

But you're screaming into the wind. Sea gulls screech. Beth's sneakers are standing by the door. You hold them and cry. You drive to the schoolyard. Beth is standing with some other girls, including Rachel Morgan, whom you said last year Beth was not to talk to. "You forgot your sneakers," you tell Beth. "You'll need them to play volleyball." "That's okay," she says. All the girls watch you walk away and you imagine yourself in some strange city schoolyard searching for your daughter just so you can say hello to her, touch her. See her.

After supper, you say, "The reason I wanted you to come straight home is because I saw that man hanging around. And yesterday the phone rang three times. When I answered it there was no one there but I could hear him breathing."

"Maybe it wasn't him."

"It was him. He's up to his old tricks. He did that before too. The phone company took out his phone."

"But he must have known I was in school."

"Why? Has he followed you to school too?"

"No," she says, shaking her head.

"You wouldn't lie to me, would you? You wouldn't lie to your own mother?"

"I never lie to you."

"Look me in the eye and say that."

She does.

"And look me in the eye and say, 'I promise not to talk to Gordon Harrington.'"

"I promise not to talk to Gordon Harrington," she parrots.

"You know I'm only thinking of your welfare."

"I know Mom. I know all that."

"We only have each other. I'd die if anything happened to you."

"Nothing's going to happen to me, Mom. Honest."

Sighing.

Yes, sighing, and is there not in that sigh something hidden, a deep stubbornness, very like that of her father, Gordon Harrington? Didn't he know all along he would not marry you? Always he kept a little bit of himself back while you opened yourself to him. Was it not as if he was in a different part of the room, watching?

And if need be, you will kill him, won't you? Lying awake in your bed, you tell yourself that no one will get the child from you, even if you have to barricade the two of you in the house. Your father's guns still hang in the unused dining room. You know how to shoot. You have killed in your life-time thirteen deer, numerous ducks and once, a wildcat which appeared suddenly in the path. It would be just as easy to kill the man, but you would prefer a show of strength. You want the child to cling to you and scream she will not leave. But you know she will not do this. No, she will cry a little as she packs her suitcase. Like him, she is selfish. But selfish or not, she is yours and no one can take her from you.

But why did you put Gordon Harrington down as the father? You do not like to remember this now, but this knowledge comes to you often, in the middle of the night.

Just as you know the reason: he is the father, no matter what anyone thought of it.

Did you think he would come back after a few months?

Did you not often check to see that the telephone was working?

Did you not ask numerous times at the post office if all the mail, every bit, had been sorted? Did you not sometimes stand in the lobby watching to see if perhaps someone else had received a letter by mistake? Did you not go to the post office on Boxing Day in case the lobby was unlocked by mistake? Mail at Christmas was slow. You had photos taken of the baby and would have sent them if you had an address, which you didn't.

Thirteen years, you think. Thirteen years.

And when he comes again, on Thursday when you have just finished cleaning fish for tomorrow's delivery you still have the fish knife in your hand. "I don't want you to come here anymore. Why don't you go back where you come from?"

"But this is where I come from," he says.

"Not anymore."

"Oh Nels," he says, sitting down.

"There's no need for you to sit. You get back up on your feet and get going."

"You wanted nothing to do with us for thirteen years," you add.

"It doesn't seem like thirteen years," he says quietly.

You could stick him with the knife. Like a pig. But you know you can't.

"Don't come crying back to me now. Go cry to your whore."

"What?"

"Your whore. I saw you with her. You're a fine one rubbing her into my nose. And then having the nerve to come here whimpering like a sick puppy."

"She's a friend of my buddy from Halifax who got killed last year. She was just passing through."

"Sure tell me another one. Not that I give a damn."

"I know you don't give a damn," he says. "You don't have to tell me that."

"So leave us alone. Go away."

He sits.

And isn't this what you want?

No?

"It's not as if I never thought of you," he says. "I never thought the kid was so big. I guess I kinda thought of her as littler."

"You leave her be. I'll kill you if you go near her."

"I don't want to make trouble."

"Why'd you come back then?"

"Got no job. Had trouble with my legs."

"To bad you didn't die."

"You sure are hard. Same as always."

"You've got a hell of a nerve. Get out of here now."

"I don't have much money but I could give you some."

"Get out get out get out," you mutter, turning away, laying the fish knife on the table. It's clean now. You know you can't pierce him with it. His heart beats beneath his shirt. His skin is warm.

"You did a good job with the kid. Beth's a good girl."

"How do you know that?"

"I can tell by talking to her." He is smiling smiling smiling —

But maybe he told lies. Or did you imagine the entire conversation? Because later everything went crazy. You were mixed up in your head.

Don't turn your head to the wall. I want to talk to you. You talk enough about it yourself but perhaps it's different when someone else wants to discuss it, or ask questions. The cell is small. Only us. I like to lean on my elbow and look at you when you talk. At first you're alive, passionate. Your eyes flash. You spring up from the bunk, you clench your fists. Once you hit the wall to make a point. But then you grow sad and stare at the ceiling, eyes large and empty. If only I had shot him, you say. I didn't mean to shoot her. But maybe your eyesight isn't what it used to be. You gave up hunting because Beth cried over dead birds.

Days when we play cards, you scratch your head and say, When I get out of here ... A cigarette hangs from the corner of your mouth. Impatiently you fling the cigarette away. When *he* comes to visit you, you return victorious. Him, you say, He brings cigarettes, warm socks. Him, you say, rocking on your haunches.

Him, him, him. I see you with the smoking gun in your hands. You say, I don't remember after that. You woke up here. *Him, him, him.* And momentarily you are not seeing bars, cement walls painted green, but rather the sea from your high cliff on a windy day when nothing has been taken away from you, when the future falls into your past. And then ... but then, you turn and go into your old house and sit there at your table in the old grey kitchen, in the silence of that room. It grows dark. At last you pace. *Him him him.*

ALDEN NOWLAN

Alden Nowlan was born in Nova Scotia in 1933. A self-educated journalist, Nowlan began his career as editor of the Hartland *Observer*, in an area of rural New Brunswick which provided settings for many of his stories and poems. He was later editor and columnist for the Saint John *Telegraph-Journal*. Nowlan's poetry has been collected in a number of volumes, one of which won the Governor-General's Award. He was also a novelist, short-story writer, essayist and playwright. Nowlan was for many years writer-in-residence at the University of New Brunswick in Fredericton, where he died in 1983.

SKIPPER

Alden Nowlan

S kipper was the youngest of the five sons of Ethel and Rupert Syver-
son. As a small boy, Skipper, like each of his brothers before him,
feared and hated his father and entered into a wordless pact of mutual
defence with his mother.

Rupert, as he himself said, was a hard man. For sixty hours in every
week, he carried deal at the sawmill, balancing the long, green boards
on a leather-padded shoulder and bearing them from the trimmer saw
to the lumber piles. Weeknights he lounged about the kitchen, slug-
gish and sullen, until nine o'clock, then went to bed. In his father's
presence, Skipper adopted his formal manners, as though before a
stranger; he walked softly and seldom spoke. In conversation with his
mother, Skipper spoke of "Rupert," never of "Father." For his part,
Rupert demanded obedience but otherwise left his son pretty much
alone. On Saturday night, like almost all of the mill hands, Rupert went
to town and came home, violently drunk, at two or three o'clock the
following morning.

When with his drinking companions, Rupert was sportive and exuberant. But when he came home drunk, he cursed his wife, called the boys brats and wished they were kittens so that he could sew them in a sack weighted down with rocks and drown them. On several occasions, he beat Ethel with his fists, and once he kicked her and sent her sprawling while Skipper stood by, screaming. Many times, he yanked Skipper out of bed in the dead of night and, on one pretext or another, flogged him with a cowhide strap. Often, if the weather was warm, Ethel led Skipper out into the night and they hid, wrapped in each other's arms, on the hillside overlooking the house until Ethel felt certain that Rupert's rage had been extinguished by sleep.

In a curiously dispassionate way, Skipper hated his father. He loathed the mill where Rupert worked himself into dumb exhaustion. He detested the men who came for his father with rum bottles hidden under their overall bibs. On numerous occasions between his sixth and fourteenth year, he vowed to his mother that never, as long as he lived, would he taste strong drink.

Ethel fostered those aspects of Skipper's character which Rupert most despised. While a little lad in cotton shorts and a polo shirt, Skipper often brought her bouquets: handfuls of violets or bunches of mayflowers or daisies. She never took such gifts for granted; they touched her deeply, like presents from a lover.

She encouraged Skipper to daydream. She had done this with his brothers before him. When he grew up, she said, he would be a clean, sober man who would wear a white shirt and a necktie to work. He would go far away from the village and, of course, his mother would accompany him. Perhaps he would never become rich — but he would be a gentleman.

Skipper listened attentively to all that she told him. She was his guide and his refuge. A snivelling brat, Rupert called him when he saw him clinging to Ethel's skirts. His daydreams were foolishness, Rupert snorted. When Skipper grew up, he would go into the mill, as his father and grandfather had done before him. He would become hard, because a man had to be hard to survive. And if there was any man in him, when Saturday came he would get drunk, because the ability to drink was one of the measures of a man.

Skipper told his mother that he would die rather than allow this to happen to him. Often, at night, Ethel slipped into his room and lay on the bed beside him, and listened to him whisper his thoughts, feelings and ambitions.

He liked to play with crayons. She bought him a watercolour set. To Rupert's vocal disgust, he spent many evenings making pictures at the kitchen table. On Ethel's infrequent visits to town, she bought him books. First, Hans Christian Andersen. Later, *Robinson Crusoe, Kidnapped* and *Treasure Island*. She rejoiced to see him run his fingers affectionately along the edges of the pages.

In Skipper, Ethel saw her last hope. His elder brothers had followed the old, brutal pattern to its conclusion. Harold, for example, had left school at fifteen to go into the mill. There he had learned to drink. At eighteen he got a girl in trouble and had to marry her. By the time he was twenty-two, they had four children. Ethel's daughter-in-law told her that now every Saturday night he came home roaring drunk like his father. The others, for whom she had once had such high and splendid hopes, were much like Harold. They were not different from any of the men who worked in the mill and lived in the village. Ethel's love for them had been soured by disappointment and hurt. Sometimes, thinking of what they had done with their lives, she almost hated them.

In the summer of his twelfth year, Skipper killed a sparrow with a sling-shot. Ethel looked upon this as an omen. To his astonishment, she wept and berated him. For several days, following this incident, she refused to speak to him.

For his fourteenth birthday, Rupert gave him a .22 calibre rifle. This gift, Ethel knew, had been inspired not by affection but by the knowledge that she would hate it. Sick at heart, she saw Skipper go hunting birds with his father. He came back dragging a partridge, a poor, bloody thing with dead, fear-crazed eyes. She could not bring herself to refuse to cook it, but she would not taste the meat. And she detested her son when she observed the gusto with which he attacked a greasy drumstick. "That Skipper's a dead shot for sure," Rupert boasted, eyeing his wife slyly. Skipper grinned, relishing his father's praise. For the first time, the man and the boy had established a bond of fellowship.

Still, she refused to believe that he would be like the others. It was not until the fall of his sixteenth year that she was for certain what the future was destined to bring.

It was Saturday night. Skipper had gone to town with the boys, something he did frequently now. Most of these boys had left school and gone into the mill. Ethel harboured a dark suspicion that they were already learning to drink. She knew that they fought with their fists and picked up strange girls. She had warned Skipper about them. "Be careful, honey," she had said. He had patted her hand, reassuringly, and she had hated the amusement she detected in his eyes.

She was waiting up for him when he got home. Rupert had not come back from town. Ethel sat in the kitchen and listened to her son's movements in the porch. He was trying to be very quiet, she knew. The knowledge that she was going to surprise him gave her a strange sensation of triumph.

"Hi, Mama," he said as he opened the kitchen door. He wore his cap at a rakish angle, like the boys who worked at the mill. There were mud-stains on the sleeves of his jacket.

"Skipper ... " She began.

"Yeah?" He continued to grin, swaying back and forth on his heels.

She got up from her chair and went over to him. She inhaled deeply, smelling his breath. Skipper laughed. "Yeah, Mama, I guess maybe I been drinking," he said.

She put her hand on his shoulders. "Skipper! You promised."

He shrugged. She had a momentary vision of him coming to her in his shorts and polo shirt, his hands filled with flowers.

"I'm a big boy now, Mama."

She returned to her chair and sat there, staring sightlessly at the floor. He shuffled his feet on the linoleum. "Look, Mama," he said. "I was talking to Bill Spence tonight."

Bill Spence was the foreman at the mill. *Don't say it,* she prayed silently. *Please don't say it.*

"He says he might be able to find a job for me."

"Yes." She would not argue. She would not try to reason with him. Already she had given up. For the fifth time, she had been defeated.

"We need the money, Mama."

"Yes."

"I didn't tell him yes and I didn't tell him no."

"No."

"Are you listening to me, Mama?"

"Yes."

He burst into laughter. "I just thought of something funny," he explained.

"What?"

"Oh, it doesn't matter. " He laughed again. "The old man really tied one on tonight. I ran into him in town. Drunk as a skunk."

In his voice, there was a strange alloy of contempt and empathy. Never before had she heard him use this tone of voice in speaking of his father.

Wearily, she rose and headed towards the stairs. "I'm going to bed now, Skipper."

"Okay, Mama. I guess I'll wait up for the old man." He threw himself into a chair at the table and lit a cigarette. For an instant, she hated him and wished that it were within her power to hurt him as he had hurt her. Then there was only the emptiness of defeat.

"You used to sit in that same chair and paint watercolours," she said.

He had not been listening. "Huh?" he said.

"Be careful of fire."

"Sure, Mama."

"Good night, Mama."

Ethel got into bed and switched off the light. In a little while she heard Rupert arrive. Then for a long time she lay in the darkness, listening to the man and his son laughing together at the other end of the house.

SOFT BODY PARTS

Susan Kerslake

There are two women at the door. The clerk thought only one was coming. "Who are you?" she asks the older one.

"I'm the mother." It is a dry crackly sound. She clears her throat.

"Which side?"

"What?"

"Who are you here for?"

"She came with me," the young woman is leaning forward; she is careful not to touch her mother.

"Oh." The clerk looks over her shoulder, but the room is empty. She'll have to wing it. "Come on in then." She leads between the chairs and large wooden tables. "I guess we have a choice," swinging her hips, her skirt, so the hem grazes the backs of the chairs. The women don't understand. She'd meant it as a little joke, to help them relax. "Let's sit here, these chairs look a little more comfortable." She sits at one end of the table like the head of the family. The mother who is as dry as a bone sits to her right. The chair is too big for her. Her clothes twist around her body; and soil and stain float on top of the slick polyester. She crosses her legs and tucks her elbows; she balances her purse on her knee and holds it with two hands. Where she bends there are tiny cracks. Now she is as small as possible.

The daughter is talking already, " … my personal truth," she is saying, and slams her bag on the table. "My turn," spreading her thighs to fill the chair. Then she sits back, arms, hands, her hair is a bluff of gel and gesture. "I am a new woman. I can talk now."

"Good for you." The clerk speaks evenly, neither cheeringly nor patronizingly. She looks up. "You are Judy Gallant?"

"I am," she smiles at her mother.

"And … ?"

"I'm the mother."

The clerk puts on her glasses. "Yes, I know. Why did you come.?"

"Her name is Harriet."

"Of course," she writes, "Harriet — ?"

"We don't have the same last name anymore," says Judy. "I've changed mine you see. It was his." She is hissing, buzzing, showing her teeth, her white fingernails. Everyone looks at her, then drops their eyes. The clerk picks up a file and taps it on the table until the papers even up.

The mother looks up into the large space above her head. It is only with a little effort that she can remember her name before it was Harriet Clayton and then she hears the bells, the bells in Clayton, how the name rang in her knees in its sounds. Oh happy girl in place of the kid who because she was in the middle was always the farthest away, not the oldest, not the next to oldest, not the baby, not the next to baby. Jerome Clayton. A go anywhere name, Jerome, Tyrone, Malone, Geronimo …

"Do you have another face mother? I'm sick of that one. I'm numb, its numbing, nothing ever shows on your face, what the hell are you thinking about, what do you ever think about?"

"I was just remembering. It's what I do best — remember —" her voice is singing a little song. "I don't walk around so good now, my bones, and my eyes are shrivelling. I've got bunions and corns and see this —" she pulls up a ridge of skin on the back of her hand.

"And I've got a pain in my —" but Judy's breath is bad, baad, baaad, it blows on her mother, it hurts; she can see that " — in my heart."

"I'm all dried up —"

"Mother —"

"I'm —"

"Mother!"

"I —"

"Stop it!" She slaps the table, "I told you it's my turn."

The mother bunches her lips and wonders how she ever accommodated such a huge creature against her little body; how she bore it; her precious burden, or was that something out of a magazine. Judy jump-jump in Mama, feet first, fist in her breast, punching bag precious burden. Bend and pluck up the diapers, precious burden, the pablum, the puke. Up to her armpits in shit and liquid green soap, precious. Who loves you?

Who loves you? Chucking Judy under the chin, so close she could have kissed her.

Mama, mama, do you? One day she'd started asking that — remember? I'd forgotten.

Mama, your fingers are cold — remember that?

I want my mother, she'd said, standing on the other side of the screen door. Perhaps she couldn't see through it, the sun beaten back by the silver wires. Who did she think was in the house? Who else smelled of soap and cigarettes in a stiff breeze.

"I just want to know one thing. Did he know my name? Hey you, get in here. What's that kiddo? Come on short stuff. You fuss-budget. Babeee." Then she speaks in a different voice, her chin cribbed in the palm of her hand, her lips limp, the words straining through her fingers. "I wonder if he knew my name. He called me — come here cherry syrup. I want you pumpkin pie. I'm coming plum pudding. My little lemon custard. I'm here plump tart. My sweet potato, creamy candy, come sing for my fruit cup, my trifle, honey bunch —"

"He had such a sweet tooth."

Judy blinks. The skin around the openings to her insides, her eyelids, nostrils, lips, is thick and pink like plasticine, molded over cracks, sculpted to guard the openings.

"I'm looking at a person I don't really know," Judy is saying. "Don't you want to hear?" She slides her fingers out on the edge of the table.

"It was so long ago."

"What was Harriet?" asks the clerk.

"Her in my house," she speaks with surprise.

Judy rolls, heaves, her bosom is up.

"She had to be born somewhere," the mother tells the clerk.

"You loved me then?"

The first time she heard that voice it struck her as a miracle. It nudged her a little, the first time, this new sound, never heard before, never imagined, not the same as she'd dreamed, not as she'd imagined it would be. Even back there in day dreams. Not much had turned out as it should have. The voice shoved; it began to take up space. It began taking up all her time. She heard it above all others, in the middle of the night, seeping in under the bathroom door, banging on the window pane from the back yard, clanging between the forks and spoons. The shrill and slap of it. Go bother your father she'd said, get out of my hair. Her lips splinter and shriek, get away from me, leave me alone.

"Daddy's girl —"

"What?"

"You always were daddy's girl."

"Can you believe she said that," blasting the clerk, "How can she say that as if it was cute?"

"Harriet, what did he say to you? Did he ever say anything that would have made you suspicious?"

"He didn't talk to me." Shaking her head, not used to talking now, and their words like cake straws poking in to see if she was undone and doughy. One morning he sat down across the breakfast table, opened his eyes wide and white with surprise and quit talking to her. She'd cut her toast into the shape of a dear little cottage, the peaked roof, a stubby chimney; she spread red jam around two windows, a door and under the eaves; it looked like a sort of serious face, but the jam melted down into a bloody mess. She scraped it off with a spoon and ate it, but it made no difference, from then on she never gained an ounce, no matter what she ate.

"It was your room, warm and gray through the lace curtains —"

"Those old lace curtains —"

" — it was your mirror on your dressing table watching me, the insides of your shoes, the quilt cloudy with your scent. The clock ticked louder and louder, the frost on the numbers glowed, things in the corners woke up and watched. I saw dust twist in the shape of the sounds I was making inside my head. 'Be Quiet!' he said. He put his fingers over my face, fingers on my eyes, on my mouth, on my nose, in my ears. They were cold and greasy ... And then it was my room, my bed where I was supposed to sleep, what did you used to say, 'safe as a bug in a rug.' My toys watched; my stuffed animals, rigid and dusty; that damn doll with the unblinking eyes, her hard heart lips– "

"I shopped all day for that doll. The one you had to have, the only one that would do."

"He didn't take me by the hand; he held me at a distance by the tips of his fingers, his thumbs stuck in the back of my neck, he plucked the bones in my shoulders, he pinched me, he stuck out his boot to catch me round the legs when I tried to go by; he bit my hair with his teeth —"

"He whopped you regular enough when you 'er small, your bare skin sounded like water being slapped —"

"He hurt me."

You were so big and noisy, the mother thinks, I couldn't stand it when you made so much noise, when you cried and —

"I was under his chest — I starting to whimper, I never cried, but he hated to hear that sound; he said, 'cover your face,' 'stuff this in your mouth.' I was so small. I couldn't see around him. I couldn't see out. I couldn't see a way out." Her face lowering into her arms which are twisted together on the table. "I couldn't do anything." She sits up straight in the chair. "Why didn't you do something. I couldn't breathe. Once I scratched him and his skin was like a stone wall in a dungeon, his sweat was cold and moldy. No no listen to this, damn you, no no, I didn't mean it," she casts her eyes up and out to the brightness in the air. There are peaks to the windows. "Was this a church?" she asks.

"No. I don't know. Why?" The clerk cocks her pen.

But the windows are tall and supple.

"All the people who should have been taking care of me —" her voice is wistful and distant, the words cloud into the small panes of glass.

"Why did you let him?" she is still looking out the windows.

"Why didn't you come to me?"

"He told me not to."

"When did you ever listen to him."

"He threatened me."

"You never left me alone ..." She could prove it! She had dark circles under her eyes, fingernails chewed to the moons, stretch marks clawing her belly, backache. Grey hair. "I lost my appetite, somewhere along the way I lost my appetite, that's why I'm so thin now. I never expected —"

"It was a secret Mama. The three of us, Papa, and me and you," she hikes and slides her fingers in the creases of her stomach.

"Not me." The mother crosses her legs. Recrosses.

"If you don't know its because you chose not to," Judy pats her breasts as if they are wide lapels.

"I never chose one thing in my whole life. Even in the beginning I took what was given me."

"You stopped wanting."

"You know I don't say what I want, or what I think!"

"What did you think Harriet?"

"I didn't think anything."

"You didn't think anything was going on?"

"I didn't think."

Judy slams the table, "You knew but you didn't think," spit by spit.

"It wasn't possible. How could it be possible?" The wood trembles.

"Had you never heard of such a thing Harriet?"

"Yes, I'd heard of it." Humming to the clerk, blinking.

"Ah! that's what you did, I remember! Now I remember how you used to blink until your eyes were more shut than open. You saw alright until you started blinking, then you only saw half of it, and pretty soon you didn't see anything at all."

But the mother had pretty pictures from glossy magazines and TV shows gleaming in scrapbooks in her brain. She turned the pages, concentrating on each; her inner eye thumbing the shine on copper bottomed pots, trips drenched in tropical promise, a treasure chest in dross, spilling bright hard stones that gleamed serenely through the sea scrub salt darkness and cold, emerging clean and whole without wear and tear, without curiosity, without dream. There were deep smouldering beverages; strawberry smooching orange slice on frothy bosoms of cream. A bubbling bath, suds, salts, bouquets of lavender and violet, steamed mirrors and chrome. She sinks into scalding water; it boils the bad. She fills her mouth with soap and shouts of joy, I can't feel it! She is someone new again, sterilized, entering landscapes white as linen, geometric as lattice, as safe as — "I never saw …" but her mouth won't close, her tongue swells on the taste of something — that something that was in the laundry, on the sheets …

"… dirty, Mama I was so dirty." She is looking at the bruises on her hands. Slowly, like a mountain of sand, she bends over the surface of the table and examines old wounds in the wood. The clerk writes nearsighted in the margin of the legal pad.

"I got out in the mornings, did you know that? That while you slept like a baby, I snuck out and walked around the block. Or down to the crossroads and back. At first it was dark outside, a deep and silent dark. There was so much space. I didn't bother it, I was small. There was plenty of room for me. I rubbed the dark on my arms, on my face, on my skin. Mine. My body. I let it grow cold. I didn't care. Cold and invisible. There was this huge space all the way to the moon, lots of room for a little girl. On nights when there was no moon, I'd look and my arms and my feet were invisible, there was just my nightgown floating loose from my body, billowing like a ghost and the ghost of a little girl inside —"

And the mother shudders and squints because she'd seen a ghost too: her best black slip and green silk shawl and spike heels and yellow feathered cloche. 'What's this? What's going on here?' The slip and silk dragging behind the little figure, her feet sunk in the toes of the shoes. 'Look Mama!' she'd said bright and delight blowing the tip of the feather, 'I'm you?'

"Now listen to this — this is what I did when I had to do something — I turned inside out!" Her hands flip over, plump fins.

Harriet remembers those fat little hands, the strength in them, the great grip on her, yanking her hair, pinching her skin, the nip blade bite of her sharp nails. But that one winter day when Judy slid next to her on the bus seat, over the crack, a bolster of flesh and devotion, nudging with the brunt of her brow. Harriet smiled in the sunshine, saw that the part in the middle of her hair was crooked, but how her hair shone anyway with a reddish gleam. A woman across the aisle was smiling at her. She sees us, like this, Harriet had thought, and thinks that's how it always is — a pretty little picture, mother and daughter. Riding on a bus. Going somewhere, perhaps shopping or to visit or an appointment. The daughter was a little tired and wriggled over to rest on the mother, how she fits inside the deep pocket shadow of the mother. The mother protects the child almost unconsciously; she knows what each whine and wiggle mean. That's what she thought, that woman sitting across the aisle; what did she know anyway?

" … and the minute the light and air hit me, I hardened —"

"Hmmm."

"You know, I got to a therapy group. From strangers I found out it wasn't my fault. Strangers know more about me than you do."

"Do they know about me?"

"Yes they do."

"My name?"

"Yes."

"Do they know where I live?"

"No — no. Who cares?"

The clerk stops doodling. "What do you think your daughter wants Harriet?"

She jiggles her shoulders; they don't work together. The clerk sees that her hands aren't the same either, disease or wear and tear, rings wobbling between her knuckles, terraces of nail polish. "Why did she want you to come here?"

"It has something to do with the court."

"Something! You've got to tell on him. I say yes. He says no. You've got to remember. You've got to say it the same as me, or — or —" her breath scuds, " — or you'll kill me again."

"I never did."

"You still don't think so? After all this? Was I so invisible?"

"I never lost sight of you."

"Am I invisible now?"

"You're —"

"You wish I were. You do don't you? You wish this weren't happening. You blame me don't you, this never would have happened if it weren't for me —"

"This person is someone I don't really know, talking to me this way, saying these things, the shame, you'd think she wasn't brought up …" There had been another person, way back then, so long ago, when her blood wasn't so drowsy. "Without you … that would be true wouldn't it …" She wonders what that would have been like; what they might have done; he might not've — She feels lightheaded.

"What are you going to do then?" Judy is punched, the words are big and heavy like black rubber boots sunk in mud.

"You want me to lie?"

"What are you afraid of Mrs. Clayton?"

"This is just the beginning mother, just the beginning —"

How odd — she had thought it to be the end, an end of sorts.

" — every day I'm getting stronger and stronger."

Me too, me too, Harriet thinks. "It would be lying for me to say those things." Her finger tips polish the golden clasp of her purse.

"Do you believe your daughter?"

"It's what she thinks —"

"It's what happened."

"I didn't see — I can't say."

"Would you say things about Judy — about her behaviour, something that would let the court know a child was in trouble and —"

"But she hasn't changed."

"He can't get you mother, it's my turn now, it's time for you to do something for me."

"You can't expect me to —"

"She can, of course she can!"

I can't stand to think of it. They can't expect me to think such things. I get sick to my stomach. I don't have to do something I can't do. If I had to do it over again? Well — what would that be like? Well? She's never gotten beyond that. See-saw, see-saw; she sees, blinks, high up high from the teeter-totter, what does she see, so small down there, little creature, who is that, who could that be, soft little doll, a shadow, a smudge, something creeping, darting, rolling around. Each time her feet touch down the ground she flexes, gets ready to push up. The air is whiter and lighter; she is a swimmer coming up from dark thick slime. She hugs the board between her legs — down there in the weeds and smooth red stones; she can barely make it out, why were the stones red as if blood had been smeared on them but they had never been washed by tears? Higher. Higher. She can barely hear someone breaking the weeds, calling softly, sweetly, "I'm coming, coming to get you ..."

She's stiff from sitting still for so long; leans forward, lifts herself a little and sashays from side to side dusting, designing a more comfortable indentation in the chair for herself.

... once I thought, she thinks, once I thought that he came to me from you or went from me to you, I can't remember just how it went, which direction. He didn't wash, he didn't wash us off, he went from one to the other, just so.

MICHAEL HENNESSEY

Michael Hennessey was born in Charlottetown in 1923 and returned there permanently in 1958, following seven years service in the Royal Canadian Navy. He is a graduate of St. Dunstan's College and St. Francis Xavier University, and retired in 1988 from his post as registrar and university secretary of the University of Prince Edward Island.

He has written seven plays for radio as well as numerous short stories for broadcast and for literary journals. Several of his stories were collected in *An Arch for the King and Other Stories* (Ragweed, 1984).

AN ARCH FOR THE KING

Michael Hennessy

I don't know when boys become aware of their fathers as human beings — as someone other than God — but for me it happened in the summer of 1939 when I was ten years old. That was the summer that King George VI and Queen Elizabeth visited Charlottetown, and, as part of the preparations to receive them, the City decided to build welcome arches, one of them directly in front of our house on Kent Street.

"What are you building, Pete?" I asked old Pete McKenna. We knew all the City workers and police officers by their first names since we lived right next door to City Hall.

"An arch for the King," Pete answered, bouncing tobacco juice off the sidewalk and all over my shoes. Pete was always doing things with tobacco juice. He'd wing one past your ear if you came close enough. He was the William Tell of tobacco juice. The brick at the fire station corner was permanently stained with tobacco juice where Pete over the years had picked off flies sitting on the side of the building.

An arch for the King! The words had a fine dignified ring to them, and I can still recall the vision I had of the arch. Our home was filled with books and magazines, and I'd seen pictures of the Marble Arch and the Arc de Triomphe, and, while I realized full well that this arch was not to be on the same magnificent scale, still I knew it would be grand. After all, it was for the King!

Three of us — my cousin Brendon, Ted Bradley and I — spent a great deal of our time that summer discussing the arch and getting ourselves excited about it. We were all the same age, and when we weren't swimming at Victoria Park or playing ball on Rochford Square or playing cowboys in Large's Livery Stable, we were watching and supervising the building of the arch.

"How are they going to join the sides together?" my cousin asked.

Ted Bradley was the one who knew about such things — or pretended to — and at times like this he would purse his lips and look wise.

"It's easy," he said. "They go out as far as they can on both sides, then they put things across — two-by-fours, likely."

Since neither my cousin nor I even knew what two-by-fours were, we just nodded our heads seriously and murmured "Uh-huh" at each other in imitation of our elders.

Old Pete loved it when the arch began to mount in the air. When he was off the ground and spitting, the place was like a total fallout area. It became an oft quoted story that the day before the King finally arrived, the City had to put a street cleaner out there at five a.m. just to clean up Pete's tobacco juice.

The arch mounted slowly. Thing were always done slowly by the City. A lot of talk was always involved, and since everyone knew everyone else, the workers and even the supervisors received numerous opinions and suggestions from people passing by. Pete enjoyed this kind of give and take and was always ready to drop his tools to talk. I think he almost regretted it when the arch got so high that he could not longer converse conveniently with passers-by. He invited his friends to climb up to talk to him and, seeing this, we began to climb on the arch without invitation.

The first time, he chased us.

"Hey, you kids, you're not supposed to be up there. Scat!"

"Aw, c'mon, Pete," I implored. "You let Pickle McCloskey up."

"That's different. He's a friend of mine. And he's big."

Bigness had to do with age. Old J.P.'s son, "Pickle," was closer to Pete's age, but he wasn't much bigger than any of us.

"But we're friends, aren't we, Pete?"

A stream of tobacco juice came flying between me and my cousin, just ticking Ted Bradley's ear.

"Good shot, Pete," I said.

His eyes flickered with pleasure.

"Yeah, well, I guess you can climb up now and again as long as it's okay with your fathers. But not before. Now get down."

It was an easy victory for all of us: for Pete, since he had made us meet a condition in order to have the privilege of climbing on the arch, and for us, since we all knew well enough how to get around our fathers.

My own method was to throw the crucial question in among a smoke screen of other questions when Father was preoccupied or busy.

"Okay, Dad," I'd say. "Here's a list of things I think I should do around the house. Just answer yes when you agree, will you?"

He'd look at me, puzzled.

"What are you up to?"

"Nothing. Okay, here we go. Cut the kindling?"

"What?"

"Just answer yes or no, okay? Cut the kindling?"

"Yes."

"Clean out the ashes?"

"Yes."

"Shovel the coal?"

"Yes."

"Go to the store for Mom?"

"Yes."

"Shine my shoes on Saturday?"

"Yes."

"Rake the lawn?"

"Yes."

"Take out the garbage?"

"Yes."

"Climb the arch?"

"Yes."

"Clean up the cellar?"

"Yes."

"Sweep the walk?"

And so on. It made no matter. I wasn't burdening myself with any responsibilities I didn't already have.

This kind of litany served two purposes: first, of course, to get permission for something you wanted; and second, to remind your father of your heavy duties in case he might be thinking of saddling you with something new. With this review fresh in his mind, he might think twice and put the new task off on a kid brother. I had one, and had found over the years that this was the most useful purpose for kid brothers.

Anyhow, the next day, there we all were cozied up to Pete on top of the arch as it began edging its way out over the street, all three of us getting in his way. We passed him tools, nails, water, scrambling up and down the frame of the arch like monkeys. With a little experience we learned regular hand and footholds and became quite cocky and secure. Pete enjoyed the service. He could have stayed up there all day with us waiting on him.

We even refused to let other kids climb up.

"We're helpers," we said. "We had to get special permission. If you want to climb up here, you have to get your father to go see the Mayor."

We just threw that last in, but Pete went along. Any more kids on the arch would have been a hindrance. We had it to ourselves. We even got in the habit of getting up early in the mornings so we'd be there at eight o'clock when Pete came to work. We took to calling one another "partner," and Pete did the same.

"Pass the hammer, partner," Pete would say.

"Okay, partner," we'd say. "Hey, partner," we'd call to one of the others below us, "pass up the hammer will you, partner." "Okay, partner. Here you are, partner." "Thanks, partner."

We "partnered" each other almost to death that summer, and now when I hear that word, I immediately find myself back in the summer of 1939, climbing on the arch.

The day the arch was joined over the centre of the street was a very special one. Pete called it "Golden Spike Day."

"What's that mean, Pete?" we asked, and he told us the story of the building of the CPR and how when East and West met and the railroad was completed, they drove the golden spike to signify the union.

Oh, how we lorded it over the other kids then.

"They joined both sides of the arch with a golden spike," we said. "Nobody saw where they placed it but us, and we're not allowed to tell."

We "golden spiked" the other kids as much as we'd "partnered" each other.

Billy Reilly said, "I asked my father about it, and he said there was no such thing as a golden spike."

We laughed at him. "That shows how much your father knows," we said.

In the end, we believed it ourselves. There never was another day like "Golden Spike Day," we told each other and anyone else who would listen. When I read years later that it was only an iron spike they used in the British Columbia mountains to complete the CPR, *that* was the story I didn't believe.

But as the summer wore on we found we were talking more and more to ourselves. We became exclusive, the envy of the other kids in the neighbourhood, and, consequently, ignored by them. But we knew we were in a superior position, so we looked on it as *us* excluding *them*. We *felt* special and therefore we *were* special.

And how we loved that arch! It didn't belong to the City in the end. It was *our* arch and we guarded it as jealously as any king his castle.

One evening I stayed up there long after Pete and the others had gone home. I was just lying there, sprawled out along the girders, enjoying myself, doing nothing, thinking big thoughts. One of the policemen, Gordon Poole, was sitting on a bench in front of City Hall, watching me.

"Time to come down for supper, Terry," he called.

I pretended I didn't hear him, and soon he was over under the arch calling up to me to come down. When I continued to disregard him, he climbed up and, after attempting to convince me to come down, he tried to pry me loose. I clung to the arch, saying nothing, not even looking at him.

My father had come out on the verandah to call me to supper and saw what was going on. Gordon looked down and saw him.

"I can't get him to let go, Frank," he called down to my father.

"Come on down, Gordon. It's all right," my father said. A few inquisitive people had gathered around, looking up, their white faces like daisies in a field.

When the policeman was on the ground, my father started up. He was a stocky, muscular man and I could see the heavy muscles in his shoulders and biceps rippling as he climbed. His head came up even with mine and I hung on tightly, expecting him to try to force me to let go. Instead, he smiled at me.

"You okay, Terry?" he asked.

"I'm fine, Dad. Look, there's nothing — "

"I know," he interrupted. "Don't mind Gordon. He just didn't think you'd be safe up here alone." He paused. "I just wanted to make sure you were feeling all right."

"Do you want me to come down?"

"Not unless you want to. You're okay here. I don't know what everybody's so excited about."

I smiled for the first time. "Neither do I," I said.

"You sure you're okay? Want a sandwich or anything?"

"I'm okay, Dad. Tell Mom I'm okay. I saw her in the window. I'll get something to eat when I come down. After a while," I added.

"Okay. Take it easy, Terry."

My father was not a touching man, but now he reached out and laid his strong hand on my head for a moment. I felt like crying. Then he climbed down and shooed the crowd away.

Father was quite contradictory in some ways. For instance, he professed to hate England and he saw no inconsistency between this and the fact that he often quoted from Kipling, an English writer and an Imperialist at that. Later, while I was still underage, he refused to let me join the Navy "to fight for England," yet he spoke admiringly of Churchill, and I remember him glued to our old radio in the parlour laughing with appreciation at the "Some chicken! Some neck!" speech, murmuring, "You tell 'em Winnie."

He was a good drinking man, which means that he drank, sometimes more than his share, but mostly with discretion. When he'd occasionally go on a toot and wind up sick in bed for a day or two, he was always full of remorse. But mostly, he was an amiable drinker. When we would come home and hear the old John McCormack 78s from the parlour, we'd be pretty sure he was into the sauce again.

"Kathleen Mavourneen," "Roses of Picardy," "I Hear You Calling Me," "Ireland, Mother Ireland," "The Harp That Once Through Tara's Halls," "The Rose of Tralee," "Believe Me, If All those Endearing Young Charms" — my God! I can hear that pure sweet tenor ringing still in my head, placing me once more in that warm, familiar-smelling house, catching the glances of my brother and sisters — the Daddy's-at-it-again look — and being aware of the malevolent stare of Aunt Gert, Father's older sister, as if his drinking were a personal insult to her; and seeing Mother acting as if nothing unusual was going on — which I found out years later was the way such situations should be handled. Detachment with love, it was called, and Mother was master of it long before any psychiatrist ever put a name on it. It was the way she learned to survive.

Soon Father would be singing along with John McCormack, his own voice mellowed by whiskey, but strong in accompaniment. Then he would get into the poetry, usually warming up with Robert Service, giving over to Yeats and Moore as his feelings rose.

He had a bit of the ham actor in him, and loved the dramatic effect he could work with Moore's lines:

Oh! Think not my spirits are always as light,
And as free from a pang as they seem to you now;
Nor expect that the heart-beaming smile of tonight
Will return with tomorrow to brighten my brow.

No: — life is a waste of wearisome hours,
Which seldom the rose of enjoyment adorns;
And the heart that is soonest awake to the flowers,
Is always the first to be touched by the thorns.

There was scarcely a dry eye among us children when Father dramatically hung his head at the end of this. We were carried away along with him.

He loved Kipling's *Barrack-Room Ballads,* and when he cut loose on such favourites as "Tommy," "Danny Deever," "Fuzzy Wuzzy" or "Gunga Din," his accent would turn any East End Cockney green with envy.

But when he was on his "Irish" kick, about the only thing he'd quote from Kipling was "The Irish Guards." I can see him standing there,

arms outstretched, imploring heaven, dark eyes flashing, nostrils di-
lated, strong voice ringing:

> *Old Days! The wild geese are flighting,*
> *Head to the storm as they faced it before!*
> *For where there are Irish there's loving and fighting,*
> *And when we stop either, it's Ireland no more!*

I think I loved him more at these tempestuous and passionate times
than at any other, because he was so openly revealing himself, allowing us to see under his skin, to see his humanity.

When I descended from the arch about twilight, I passed my older
sister, Mary, in the front hall. She just looked at me and said, "You nut."
I pointed to the framed copy of Kipling's "If" hanging on the wall, and
passed by, saying nothing. She looked after me, puzzled, then began
to study the poem.

My mother and Aunt Gert were playing cribbage in the dining room
at one corner of the big oak table that saw use only special days like
Christmas. My mother smiled at me and said, "There's a sandwich for
you in the icebox." I nodded and kept on, but not before I caught the
frown on my aunt's face. She was a mean old biddy who didn't care
much for us kids. She had been married, but her husband died in the
flu epidemic of 1918, just six weeks after they'd been married. People
used this as an explanation for her bitterness, but as kids we couldn't
accept that, and we felt that she was mean because she was selfish and
always wanted things her own way. After her husband died, she moved
back into the old family home.

It was a queer existence for my mother who never really became
the mistress of her own house. But Mother was a peacemaker and was
quite willing to let Aunt Gert have her way. Very rarely did Mother
stand up to her. When she did it usually involved one of us kids, and
then her eyes would flash and she would become a tigress. I only saw
her like this twice, but I'll never forget the experience. Each time, Aunt
Gert had the good sense to back down, making conciliatory noises at
my mother who stalked away dragging me after her. Each time she was
back inside a half-hour, putting on the kettle, calling out, "Cup of tea,
Gert?" and the two of them sat there sipping tea and chatting as if nothing had happened.

I always felt that Aunt Gert needed more of this kind of treatment. She was kind and considerate for a few days after being told off, but it was not long before she slipped back to her old arrogant, domineering self.

I was eating my sandwich and drinking a glass of milk at the kitchen table, studying the picture of the Holy Family hanging over the table and idly wondering how Joseph liked playing second fiddle in *that* family, when my sister Mary came out to the kitchen. She filled a glass with milk and sat at the other end of the table, studying me. I ignored her. Usually we got along fairly well together without much verbal communication, but there were times she got under my skin, like when she tried to get too close to me. I suspected that this was going to be one of those times.

She made a show of standing to attention beside her chair, and began to recite in a sing-song voice:

" 'If neither foes nor loving friends can hurt you,
If all men count with you but none too much;' "

I continued to chew, staring at her and saying nothing. I admired the ways she'd picked out the appropriate lines, but I'd never tell her that.

"I don't care if you don't talk," she said. "But of course I thought you might want to talk about lying up on that foolish arch all day. Are you sick or something?"

The words "foolish arch" burned into my brain and I felt myself blush. I said nothing, but she had caught sight of my high colour, and with the intuition native to children, knew immediately that she had touched a nerve. I could see it in her eyes, and I could also see that she was preparing to give me a working over, to punish me for not responding to her.

"A bunch of old sticks nailed together! How could that be attractive to anyone? A person would have to be sick to let an old pile of lumber attract him. And that phoney old green stuff they're covering it with! Trying to make it look like green leaves! Who do they think they're fooling? Junk, that's all it is — a pile of cheap junk!"

She spit out those last words. This was just too much for me. A personal attack I could take, but not an attack on the arch. I said nothing, but stood up slowly and walked down to her end of the table. I slapped her hard just once across the face. Before she dissolved into tears, I said quite distinctly, "Don't you speak to me ever again about the arch."

Two days before the arrival of the King and Queen, the finishing touches were put on the arch. The tree-green beaver-board covering the frame was trimmed and big gold lions and crowns and GRs and ERs in scroll were placed on each pillar. Across the top was printed in huge gold letters, "Greetings to Their Majesties." When the sun hit the burnished gold, it dazzled. It was truly a thing of beauty, and in the early morning light when everything was sparkling and clean it made me feel pure and close to God just to sit and stare at it.

The day of the visit itself was a disappointment. It rained, and the arch was not at its best. As members of the Queen Square School Cadet Corps, we were part of the mass of uniforms lining the parade route. We couldn't get the puttees on our legs right, and old Pete had to help us, taking great pride in laying up the edges just so with a flat kitchen knife. Our position in the parade was up near the corner, in front of Rix's grocery store and across the street from Hardy Brothers Luggage and Harness. We could see the arch, but we'd have enjoyed it more had we been directly underneath it. But we had to go where the cadet corps was stationed. At least we told ourselves that, in order to bolster our wet, sagging spirits.

The King and Queen drove by slowly in their black, shiny-wet open car, waving and smiling at everybody despite the rain, and that was that. I thought they should have been looking at the arch, but I guess they realized the arch was not at its best. Nor were the people, although they cheered and laughed and shouted, "Hi, King," and things like that, and generally made lots of noise and tried to be cheerful in the rain.

When it was over, I felt a surge of disappointment. "Is that all there is?" I thought. It was like Christmas, where you spend a whole month working yourself up to it, and then if you're not alive and aware, savouring every moment of the day, suddenly it's over and gone.

But it wasn't all gone. The arch was still there. I have the feeling that you have about your fist love. After you leave her at her house and go back to your own home, you dwell on thoughts of her, and come to look forward to those quiet moments of contemplation of her perfection before you doze off to sleep. It was that way for me with the arch. I still had the arch, and I fell asleep that night secure with the thought.

The next morning, coming out of the house, I was surprised and faintly alarmed to see Pete at the foot of the arch with his tools.

"What are you doing, Pete?" I asked.

He patted the arch fondly.

"She's gotta come down, Terry," he said.

"What?" I shouted, feeling a sinking in my stomach. "No, Pete, no. You can't do that."

He looked at me long and hard. "I'm sorry, kid," he said gently. "She's gotta go."

He took his claw-bar and began ripping at the sides.

"Pete," I wailed. "Stop!"

I threw myself on his back and began hitting him with my fists, crying, blind, lashing out, trying to hurt.

"Stop! Stop! Stop!" I cried.

He caught hold of my arms and held me.

"Terry, boy, take it easy. I have to do it. It's my job."

I was wriggling and wailing and crying, and all my carrying on brought my father out of the house. He saw immediately what the situation was. Pete held me firmly but gently.

"Frank, Frank," he said to my father. "What am I going to do?"

Pete was crying himself, although that realization only struck me days later when they told me Pete had refused to tear down the arch and had almost lost his job until my father explained the situation.

"It's all right, Pete," my father said. "I'll take him. Come with me, Terry."

He swept me up in his arms and I cried. I clung to his neck and must have almost choked him, but he said nothing until he'd carried me out to the barn, back to where the big blacks, Dolly and Daisy, were stabled. He held me for a while, sitting there on a bench, rocking slowly, saying nothing, the sweet smell of horse manure rising around us.

After a time, he told me that I was learning something about life, that often part of growing up went on when we had to do something painful such as parting from something or someone we loved.

"The arch didn't really belong to you, Terry," he said quietly. "It belonged to the people. The King is gone now, so the arch must come down. It's done its job, its usefulness is over."

"But it-it's b-b-beautiful," I sobbed.

"Yes, it's beautiful," he agreed. "And its beauty will stay with you and will live on inside you. But the arch wouldn't last forever anyway. Everything — *everybody* changes. It happens to us all. In a few years I'll be gone too, and you'll have to carry on with what you've been able to learn."

I sobbed, "You can't d-d-die."

"Oh, but I will. And then I'll go back to the dust I came from, and my soul will go back to God where *it* came from."

A ten-year-old cannot understand or accept that sort of thing, and I was no exception. they tore down the arch, of course, but I didn't watch it. I couldn't. For two days I stayed in my bedroom, listening to the hammering and ripping, the shrieking of nails being withdrawn from wood, the shouts of my playmates. Not once did I look out the window, not once. When finally I heard nothing on the third day, I looked out and everything was gone. It was as if the arch had never existed.

But I did remember that talk with my father, and when he died suddenly when I was nineteen, I was better prepared for it than I expected. And when I did not cry, people thought I was hard-hearted, and when they heard me murmur at the graveside, "Just like the arch, Dad," they thought I was crazy.

Every day now, on the way to work, I drive by the place where the arch used to stand. I duck my head through the car window and glance up. "Under the arch, Dad," I murmur. If there are people with me in the car, they say "What?" and I smile and answer without explanation, "An arch for the King." They glance at each other and raise their eyebrows. If there is only one person with me, he goes "Ummm-hmmm," and watches me out of the corner of his eye.

Once I went through this routine with my sister Mary in the car. She looked at me for a long time, then reached out and touched my arm. When I glanced at her there were tears in her eyes.

"Now I understand," she said. "At last I understand," and I believe she did.

J.J. STEINFELD

J.J. Steinfeld, a former teacher with degrees from Case Western Reserve University in Ohio and Trent University in Ontario, is a playwright and writer of fiction living in Charlottetown, Prince Edward Island. His stories have appeared in a number of Canadian literary magazines and have been collected in *The Apostate's Tattoo* (Ragweed, 1984) and *Forms of Captivity and Escape* (Thistledown Press, 1988). He has also published a novel *Our Hero in the Cradle of Confederation* (Pottersfield Press, 1987).

J.J. Steinfeld's writing won him the Norma Epstein Award in 1979, first place in Theatre Prince Edward Island's playwriting competition in 1984, 1985 and 1986, and Okanagan Short Fiction Award from "Canadian Author and Bookman" in 1984, and Pottersfield Press's 1986 Great Canadian Novella Competition.

A BEAUTIFUL WOMAN

J.J. Steinfeld

Arlene, dressed in her well-worn gardening outfit, was kneeling at the back of the house, scooping soil with her hand spade. She imagined the garden in full bloom, supplying the ingredients for the elaborate salads she enjoyed making for her family.

This year she was going to add some new seeds: parsnips, Brussels sprouts, leeks. She marvelled at the process of planting, nurturing growing, and eventually happily devouring what was once a simple seed. It was a mild afternoon and Arlene felt good. Lori, her youngest child, and the family's Saint Bernard played tug-of-war with an old shirt of her husband's, indifferent to Arlene's communing with nature.

When she heard her husband pull into the driveway, Arlene left her labour of love and walked to greet him. Rudy awkwardly slid out of the station wagon with two bouquets of flowers, a bottle of champagne, a small bow- adorned box, and his briefcase. He struggled with his load and Arlene rushed toward him, smiling at the sight of this well-organized, graceful executive reduced to a clumsy, overburdened delivery boy.

Suddenly Arlene's smile faded. She realized that Rudy had a big announcement to make — why else the gifts on an ordinary Wednesday afternoon. The armful of goodies was to cushion her, to prepare her for the next big plateau of *his* career. When he was transferred from Vancouver, her childhood home, to Calgary, it was a dozen roses and a china figurine; Calgary to Regina was chrysanthemums and a bottle of expensive perfume; Regina to Toronto had been three dozen orchids and front-row seats to a musical comedy. She recalled how miserable she was during that play while Rudy laughed loudly at every joke.

Where to now, Arlene wondered. She attempted to determine the mileage by the value of the gifts: a bottle of Dom Perignon could indicate Timbuktu! Now, after almost four years in Toronto, she was used to it here. Didn't Rudy realize she was halfway through getting her degree in English, even if it was only part-time. She had always wanted a degree in literature and was even starting to make daydreaming plans for graduate school one day. She loved the rambling old house, her expanding garden, and the older children, Eddie and Jennifer, had never attended one school for so long. She was not eager to disrupt her routine.

"I love you, darling," Rudy said, and handed his wife first the bouquet of tulips, then one of carnations. She inhaled each bouquet, the fragrances lost in her anxiety. She guessed Ottawa or Halifax, but it could be any place. Rudy's insurance company believed in keeping its employees moving. GROWTH THROUGH MOVEMENT was on all the company's brochures and stationery. Sometimes Arlene believed that her family would have more stability if Rudy worked for the Mafia. Their marriage, she helplessly thought, was destined to be a sea-to-sea extravaganza.

The dog, still holding the ragged shirt in its mouth, and Lori raced from the backyard and charged into Rudy. He reeled with good humour, regaining his balance, then leaned over and simultaneously kissed his daughter and patted Keynes. He handed Lori his briefcase to carry, her favorite task.

"You get more beautiful each day," he said to his excited daughter, her nutbrouwn pigtails jiggling with each turn of her head. His long fingers traced a loving message on her chin and soft cheeks.

"Like Mommy," Lori said, swinging her daddy's briefcase, trying to be the miniature executive.

"Exactly like Mommy," Rudy laughed with the satisfied self-assurance of a man in control of his destiny. All the components of his life and career seemed secure.

"I have something to discuss with you, Rudy," Arlene said before they had reached the kitchen door. Her blue eyes dimmed with apprehension. He paused and smiled at her, as though to say, "Don't worry, darling, I'll take care of everything." Before he announced the enforced move to Tasmania or the Arctic — the whole world needed insurance — before he boasted about the significant raise and sparkling prospects, she needed to talk to him about their oldest child. Once Jennifer came home from school and overwhelmed her father with kisses and beguiling embraces it would be too late.

"Can't it wait?" he said, giving Arlene the little box and champagne bottle. Not listening for her reaction, he lifted Lori and carried her into the sun-yellow kitchen. This kitchen is nicer than ours in Vancouver, Calgary or Regina, he had tried to console his wife, attempting in his problem-solving manner to ease the transition she had resisted. "I have a surprise myself to tell you about."

"Please," she said softly, too plaintively. She said "please" to him with a frequency that distressed her, but she couldn't break herself of the habit. It had been easier to housetrain Keynes.

"Fine, I defer to beauty," he said. That was all he deferred to, she thought. "How about a little drink to lubricate our conversation?" he added, spinning his delighted daughter, raising her even higher.

It was important that she talk to Rudy now. After supper he would retreat into his den to work and Arlene wouldn't see him again until she brought in his ten o'clock tea and Melba toast. Then another hour of work until he came to bed and read *The Financial Post* or a new book on economy. He decided when the lights would be turned off or which nights they would make love.

"Lift me to the sky, always, Daddy," Lori said joyously, touching the ceiling with a triumphant squeal. "Promise."

"Only if you stay a Munchkin, Munchkin." She giggled and Rudy spun her around even quicker until dizziness forced him to put her down. "More, more," the child begged.

"I promise tomorrow I will twirl you until we both fall down, gorgeous." Lori performed a dance of appreciation around the spacious kitchen, Keynes attempting to accompany her like a bizarre parody of

Fred Astaire and Ginger Rogers. Rudy signalled for the dancers to go play elsewhere and the duo exited.

"Well, what do you want to discuss?" he asked, taking a step toward the stove and inhaling the aromas of the cooking supper. He curiously lifted a pot lid and said, "Darling, where's my thank-you-for-the-hard-day-at-work drink?"

"Jennifer wants to enter the Miss Teen Toronto Contest," Arlene said uneasily.

"Terrific!"

"I told her no."

"No? It sounds marvellous. Like mother, like daughter."

"I was foolish in those days."

"You were a winner," he said with the enthusiasm of an exuberant hockey coach congratulating his best goal scorer.

Arlene placed her gifts on the kitchen table. She sought a few moments of solitary thought by retreating to the liquor cabinet in the dining room and mixing each of them a drink: slowly, deliberately, thoughtfully. A double. Why did such a simple decision about their daughter have to turn into a battle of wits and wills ... like everything else in their household? The earlier backyard tug-of-war flashed through her mind.

"I'll bet a year's salary *and* bonuses she wins," Rudy said as Arlene reentered the kitchen. He was beaming, obviously having further relished the thought of his teenage daughter as a beauty queen.

"I don't find beauty contests acceptable anymore," she said, handing her husband his drink, hoping he didn't notice the slight quiver in her hand.

"It merely reinforces roles," she said almost as an afterthought. As she gardened Arlene had worked out a cogent speech, all the negative arguments against beauty contests and undue stress impressionable teenagers; but the rehearsed speech dissolved in Rudy's executive presence. Even in her kitchen, he was in control. There was still soil under her fingernails and the sight momentarily comforted her. She drifted to the orderliness of her garden.

"And what is wrong with roles?" Rudy asked with the first hint of belligerence, thrusting his wife back into the kitchen reality. His body stiffened and he grew more alert, as thought he had been challenged to a duel or a gruelling game of racquetball. He removed his tie, indicating that he was ready for a real bare-knuckled, knockdown bout. Arlene strained not to feel fainthearted.

"Beauty contests shouldn't be encouraged, that's all I'm saying. It wastes an incredible amount of energy working at being beautiful. You weren't behind the scenes, Rudy."

"You're a beautiful woman," he said softly, changing his tactics.

"That's not enough anymore." Whenever she indicated depression or was plagued with a domestic problem, he responded with, "You're a beautiful woman." It was his oral medication for his wife; Arlene didn't even find the words an adequate placebo. Certainly she enjoyed being appreciated for her good looks — she was aging without panic, more pleased with her natural appearance now than in her youthful modelling days — but not as a substitute for everything else.

"I swear, darling, you're starting to sound like Betty Friedan and Gloria Steinem and those *other women*," he said. You would think he was talking about an invasion force from outer space by the way he ground out his words and grimaced, she thought.

"They are admirable women," she said sincerely, seeming to defend trusted neighbours he had maligned unnecessarily. "What's wrong with them?"

"Nothing, except there is no crime being beautiful and entering beauty contests. A girl can develop all sorts of useful skills in competition. It didn't ruin your life."

What could she answer Rudy? That as good as her life appeared to be, there was something missing. She couldn't even pinpoint what was lacking, couldn't list A, B and C for her logically minded husband. You have to define the problem precisely before you can solve it, he liked to say whenever she seemed confused or hinted at a vague irritation. Maybe if they stayed in one place she could have the feeling of rootedness and continuity she longed for. Moving about so often complicated everything for her.

"I won't allow Jennifer to enter."

"And I will," he rebutted forcefully. He stood unmoving, his gaze fixed on his wife as though he were trying to direct a laser beam to melt her stamina. She visualized Rudy as a waxwork at Madame Tussaud's — in the Chamber of Horrors section.

He always gets his way, she thought, but not this time. She clenched a fist in determination but he playfully uncurled her fingers, praising her beauty with each extended finger. He had a thousand ways to out-flank and disarm his wife.

Seeking an escape hatch, Arlene buried her concentration in the dog as it wandered back into the garden. Rudy named the dog Keynes after his favourite economist. Their first dog had been good old Adam Smith the Beagle; their next dog would probably be Galbraith or whomever else he was reading at the time. She, after much argument, got to name the cockatoo: Garbo. He never addressed the bird by its name, only as "that noisy beast." It was the present the children had selected last year for her thirty-fifth birthday.

After finishing her drink, she got two vases and haphazardly placed the flowers in them, taking out her frustrations on the inanimate objects. The impulse to throw the vases, to make a statement Rudy couldn't ignore, jolted her. Why did he force her to go to extremes? He wanted ten children, wouldn't hear of any kind of birth control for either of them, so the only way she could stop at the three children she wanted was to have a tubal ligation after Lori. He was furious when she told him of the operation. What happens if the children are in a plane crash, what do we do then, was his only response.

"Like your flowers?" he asked, attempting to appease his wife. He didn't like to see Arlene angry; it simply didn't become her. Arlene was most beautiful when serene.

"I bet you'll like what's in the box better than the flowers," he continued, annoyed that Arlene wouldn't answer him.

She looked at the wrapped gift without curiosity. She wanted to drive her fist down on the small package, the bribe. "Jennifer will be home soon. Let's resolve this. I don't want to argue in front of her," she said.

"It is resolved. Jenny can try to be a beauty queen like her mother was — and is." He gazed at his wife admiringly over the rim of the glass as he sipped his drink. Arlene felt she was parading before the judges again, unblinking eyes assessing her worth, making her dread beauty. *"And the winner is …. "*

Without warning or explanation, Rudy disappeared up the stairs and soon returned with two scrapbooks, both with singed covers. He had a conqueror's brazen, gloating smile on his face. To Arlene, at that tense moment, her handsome husband looked like an ugly stranger.

"Throw them away," she ordered, raising her voice only slightly, wanting to scream at the top of her lungs. She cursed her own ingrained self-control. "Little ladies don't shout or create a ruckus," her mother lectured after every battle Arlene had with her younger brother until she learned to deal with the vexatious brat through avoidance or silence.

"*You* never got rid of them," he accused. Why hadn't she? She had considered it for years. Twice she had even held the scrapbooks by the fireplace, had allowed the flames to lick the covers, but couldn't throw them in. The scrapbooks held the record of her various efforts in beauty contests, talent shows, amateur theatre and modelling. When she married Rudy, already pregnant with Jennifer, she had willingly given up modelling and acting. Though she never told her husband, Arlene felt more secure in the home than on any stage.

Rudy held the scrapbooks, two bombs he could detonate at any second. He opened the thicker one and began to read the caption underneath a faded photograph from an old Vancouver newspaper: "Arlene Edwards charmed the audience with her tap dancing and singing and was crowned the junior princess of the summer festival .... "

"I did it for my mother. She lived through me."

"A noble motivation," he said authoritatively. Such glib psychologicial insight she could do without. He turned several pages and resumed reading: "The vivacious young Miss Edwards includes dramatics, reading, cooking, and gardening as her leisure time activities .... "

"Please, Rudy, no more." Was she ever *really* vivacious? Weren't the first twenty years of her life one long costume ball, a masquerade that pleased her mother and broke the hearts of little boys and men?

" ... The daughter of Marsha and William Edwards has won many beauty contests in the past .... " He read randomly from the scrapbooks, confronting his wife with unwanted memories, delivering the words like an incessant meteor shower. She wished she were Annie Oakley and could shoot the scrapbooks out of Rudy's hands. She wouldn't mind if the audience applauded her marksmanship. All her former nervousness and anxiety and feelings of helplessness flooded over Arlene.

"Those beauty contests weren't beneficial for me."

"What are you missing, Arlene? Tell me."

Missing? You always dictate, never consult, she wanted to explain to her husband. She wanted to be heard, an equal voice: when they make love, where they lived ... *important* decisions.

"We're like two children on a teeter-totter and I can never decide when I go up or down. You always decide for me. I'm missing choice, Rudy," she said with growing anger.

"Choice? All right, you can have choice. Where do you want to vacation this year? It's completely your choice. The Bahamas, Miami Beach, perhaps Hawaii? Name it, darling."

"Mongolia," Arlene answered. Or Devil's Island or Alcatraz or the foot of any active volcano, she thought as her mood darkened.

"Beautiful, don't be ridiculous ... "

At last it struck her, the problem. It wasn't a question of love or lack of love, of Rudy being a good husband or a bad husband. What she wanted to change were Rudy's attitudes. His attitudes toward women. Maybe she should try to change his height or brown eyes, it might be easier. Rudy's attitudes toward women had not shifted a fraction since they fell in love during high school. Her own attitudes toward herself and being a beautiful woman had. Like her cherished seeds, she had grown, but Rudy would not acknowledge that vital growth.

"Come on, what are you missing?" he demanded to know, losing his patience. "Name something real, Arlene."

He threw the scrapbooks to the floor, then clasped his wife's hand and began to lead her around the kitchen. Keynes fled the room. Rudy pointed emphatically to each and every convenience item in the kitchen — slow cooker, sixteen-speed blender, food processor, electric fondue, on and on — then opened drawers and removed gadgets and fancy devices she rarely used. He was acting like an overzealous TV game show host leading the bewildered contestant through a mazed paradise.

"Look what you have, darling .... Your beauty has gotten you so much."

His logic confounded her. He would tell a marathon runner who had broken his legs that he had wonderful arms. What could she say to him to open his eyes? Rudy didn't — or couldn't — understand what she needed.

"Open your present," he instructed, releasing her hand. "I guarantee you'll be ecstatic."

Just then Jennifer came through the kitchen door, school books in hand, smiling radiantly. When she smiled she looked so much like her mother, Rudy thought. She kissed her father and mother, then dramatically smelled the flowers, a young Sarah Bernhardt giving an inspired performance.

"What's in the box?"

"A present for your beautiful mother. But if she doesn't want it, I'm sure I could find another beautiful girl who does."

"Have you two been arguing?" Jennifer asked. Are we that obvious, Arlene thought.

"Nothing that drastic, Jenny. Your mother has been talking to me about the beauty contest," he stated formally.

"Oh that," Jennifer said nonchalantly, waving the topic away. Rudy was certain she was attempting not to act too eager, to be the mature and sophisticated teenager. Fifteen, in her father's estimation, was an unfathomable, delightful age; she could stay this way forever if he had his way. He considered all three of his children at perfect ages. It only saddened him that there weren't more kids around the house.

Jennifer tossed her books down by the flowers and mysterious box and pulled out a mimeographed sheet of paper from a three-ring binder decorated with pictures of John Travolta and Wayne Gretzky, in a frozen face-off for her heart.

"Your mother used to worship Frankie Avalon and Elvis when she was around your age. I was hardly noticed because I couldn't sing or act. Your mother was the most beautiful home-coming queen in our school's history."

"And you were the third-string quarterback," Arlene said viciously. Caught off guard, Rudy turned angrily, poised to ward off more blows. He did have an Achilles heel, Arlene realized. Where had the words come from? They both encouraged and frightened her.

Rudy had told the children that he was a star quarterback, could have played professionally had he applied himself. If he was going to fight unfairly, so was she. He was accustomed to arguing and getting his way, working in a competitive, strenuous man's world all of his adult life. She had been competitive also, but the skills she relied on were different: an engaging smile, a heart-stopping sway, the lovely carriage; to excel and succeed had been instilled into him; into her, the belief that beauty speaks for itself was its own worthwhile end.

Arlene looked into her husband's determined eyes and thought again that he always gets his way. Even the children's names were his selections. She had wanted literary names, after the authors she enjoyed. They would be Anaïs, Brendan and Virginia had he listened to her, yet he laughed at her choices, considered them sentimental and foolish. Once, when she reminded him of her preferences, he mocked that Wynken, Blynken and Nod would be better than her choices. Arlene was reduced to triumphing through the tubal ligation and naming a cockatoo after an actress who wanted to be alone.

"I need one of your signatures," Jennifer said, holding up the sheet of paper. "Parental consent."

"I'll sign," Rudy said quickly, pulling out a pen from his shirt pocket. It was the gold pen his wife had given him for his last promotion. Now Arlene wanted to jab it into his stomach. I love him, I love him, she told herself, trying to remove the hostile emotions from her system. Why did he always need to get his way?

"Don't you want to know what you're signing?" Jennifer asked with puzzled expression on her face.

"Miss Teen Canada ... Miss Canada ... Miss World ... Miss Universe," the proud father chanted in happy singsong. It was so easy for him to imagine Jennifer as a beauty queen.

"You don't have to sign that yet. I have plenty of time to make up my mind about entering. I was thinking, maybe Mom's right."

The father and mother, totally baffled, looked at Jennifer. Suddenly Lori ran into the kitchen crying. During a half-completed somersault in the living room, she had tumbled into a coffee table and bruised her elbow. Keynes started barking, denying any responsibility for the accident. Rudy quieted the dog with a firm gesture. Arlene could never get Keynes to obey her.

Both parents moved towards the crying child and the third-string quarterback deftly scooped up his daughter and kissed the hurt better. The mother dried Lori's tear-stained cheeks as her father tightened his embrace. Arlene wanted to say, she's not a sack of potatoes, but couldn't. In her daydreams she demolished Rudy in debates and arguments and tennis matches.

Amid the confusion Eddie burst into the kitchen, a perpetual jack-in-the- box refusing to stay lidded. He was wearing an "I Love Olivia Newton- John" sweatshirt and carrying a new record album. Last month, both parents recalled, it was "I Love Linda Ronstadt." He immediately demanded centre stage. The assertive personality and impregnable confidence of his father were in clear display in the boy. Eddie, at thirteen, was already answering "a millionaire" when people asked him what he wanted to be when he grew up.

"The record was on sale," he said before his parents could accuse him of wasting his allowance.

"Who's breaking the sound barrier this time?" Rudy asked good-naturedly.

Eddie held up an album by Martha and the Muffins.

"Mmmmmmmm .... Makes me hungry. Bran or English?" The father chuckled at his own pun.

The son smiled but wasn't exactly certain what was funny. Arlene refused to change her resolute expression. Jennifer began waving her sheet of paper and Lori surveyed the family gathering from her preferred vantage point, in the air.

The timing buzzer on the stove sounded and ignited the dog's protesting bark until Arlene clicked off the knob. Lori and Eddie resumed arguing over a week-old grievance, calling each other nincompoops and creeps. The father attempted to act as referee as the mother urged him to allow the brother and sister to work things out by themselves. There seemed to be a hundred people in the kitchen, not three kids, two adults and one huge dog.

"I need your permission to try out for the boys' hockey league next season," Jennifer said into the tumult. "There's going to be a special training program this summer I don't want to miss. I want to be the first girl at our school to make a boy's team. I can do it."

The mother began to laugh, at first nervously, then without restraint; the laughter became pure and joyous. Rudy was stunned. Arlene hugged her oldest child. For an instant she thought she detected the smell of fresh vegetables in Jennifer's long blond hair.

"I'll sign, my dear," Arlene said and grabbed the pen out of her husband's hand. He put Lori down, as if she had become too heavy, and tried to grab the pen back, but Arlene would not let him have it. Now if Rudy insisted they move to Timbuktu, she would simply say no.

THE TUNING OF PERFECTION

Alistair Macleod

He thought of himself, in the middle of that April, as a man who had made it through another winter. He was seventy-eight years old and it seems best to give his exact age now, rather than trying to rely on such descriptions as "old" or "vigorous" or "younger than his years." He was seventy-eight and a tall, slim man with dark hair and brown eyes and his own teeth. He was frequently described as "neat" because he always appeared clean-shaven and the clothes he wore were clean and in order. He wore suspenders instead of a belt because he felt they kept his trousers "in line" instead of allowing them to sag sloppily down his waist, revealing too much of his shirt. And when he went out in public, he always wore shoes. In cold or muddy weather, he wore overshoes or rubbers or what he called "overboots" — the rubber kind with the zippers in the front, to protect his shoes. He never wore the more common rubber boots in public — although, of course, he owned

them and kept them neatly on a piece of clean cardboard in a corner of
his porch.

He lived alone near the top of the mountain in a house which he
himself had built when he was a much younger man. There had once
been another house in the same clearing, and the hollow of its cellar
was still visible as well as a few of the moss-covered stones which had
formed its early foundation. This "ex-house" had been built by his
great-grandfather shortly after he had come from the Isle of Skye and
it was still referred to as "the first house" or sometimes as "the old
house," although it was no longer there. No one was really sure why
his great-grandfather had built the house so high up on the mountain,
especially when one considered that he had been granted a great deal
of land and there were more accessible spots upon it where one might
build a house. Some thought that since he was a lumberman he had
wanted to start on top of the mountain and log his way down. Others
thought that because of the violence he had left in Scotland he wanted
to be inaccessible in the new world and wanted to be able to see any
potential enemies before they could see him. Others thought that he
had merely wanted to be alone, while another group maintained that
he had built it for the view. All of the reasons became confused and in-
termingled with the passing of the generations and the distancing of
the man from Skye. Perhaps the theory of the view proved the most
enduring because although the man from Skye and the house he built
were no longer visible, the view still was. And it was truly spectacular.
One could see for miles along the floor of the valley and over the tops
of the smaller mountains and when one looked to the west there was
the sea. There it was possible to see the various fishing boats of summer and the sealing ships of winter and the lines of Prince Edward
Island and the flat shapes of the Magdalen Islands and, more to the
east, the purple mass of Newfoundland.

The paved road or the "main road" which ran along the valley floor
was five miles by automobile from his house, although it was not really that far if one walked and took various short cuts: paths and
footbridges over the various tumbling brooks and creeks that spilled
down the mountain's side. Once there had been a great deal of traffic
on such paths, people on foot and people with horses, but over the years
as more and more people obtained automobiles, the paths fell into dis-
use and became overgrown, and the bridges which were washed away

by the spring freshets were no longer replaced very regularly or very well.

The section of winding road that led to his house and ended in his yard had been a bone of contention for many years, as had some of the other sections as well. Most of the people of the upper reaches of the mountain were his relatives and they were all on sections of the land granted to the man from Skye. Some of the road was "public" and therefore eligible to be maintained by the Department of Highways. Other sections of it, including his, were "private" so they were not maintained at all by government but only by the people living along them. As he lived a mile above the "second last" or the "second" house — depending upon which way you were counting — he did not receive visits from the grader or the gravel truck, or the snow plough in the winter. It was generally assumed that the Department of Highways was secretly glad that it did not have to send its men or equipment up the twisting switchbacks and around the hairpin turns which skirted the treacherous gullies containing the wrecks of rolled and abandoned cars. The Department of Highways was not that fussy about the slightly lower reaches of the road either and there were always various petitions being circulated, demanding "better service for the tax dollar." Still, whenever the issue of making a "private" section of the road "public" was raised, there were always counter-petitions that circulated and used phrases like "keeping the land of our fathers *ours*." Three miles down the mountain, though (or two miles up), there was a nice wide "turn around" for the school bus, and up to and including that spot the road was maintained as well as any other of its kind.

He did not mind living alone up on the mountain, saying that he got great television reception, which was of course true — although it was a relatively new justification. There was no television when he built the house in the two years prior to 1927 and when he was filled with the fever of his approaching marriage. Even then, people wondered why he was "going up the mountain" while many of the others were coming down, but he paid them little mind, working at it in determined perfection in the company of his twin brother and getting the others only when it was absolutely necessary: for the raising of the roof beams and the fitting of the gables.

He and his wife had been the same age and were almost consumed by one another while they were still quite young. Neither had ever had another boyfriend or girlfriend but he had told her they would not marry until he had completed the house. He wanted the house so that they could be "alone together" as soon as they were married, rather than moving in with in-laws or relatives for a while, as was frequently the custom of the time. So he had worked at it determinedly and desperately, anticipating the time when he could end "his life" and begin "their lives."

He and his twin brother had built it in "the old way," which meant making their own plans and cutting all the logs themselves and "snigging" them out with their horses and setting up their own saw mill and planing mill. And deciding also to use wooden pegs in the roof timbers instead of nails; so that the house would move in the mountain's winds — like a ship — move but not capsize, move yet still return.

In the summer before the marriage, his wife-to-be had worked as hard as he, carrying lumber and swinging a hammer; and when her father suggested she was doing too much masculine work, she had replied, "I am doing what I want to do. I am doing it for us."

During the building of their house, they often sang together and the language of their singing was Gaelic. Sometimes one of them would sing the verses and the other the chorus and, at other times, they would sing the verses and choruses together and all the way through. Some of the songs contained at least fifteen or twenty verses and it would take a long time to complete them. On clear still days all of the people living down along the mountain's side and even below in the valley could hear the banging of their hammers and the youthful power of their voices.

They were married on a Saturday in late September and their first daughter was born exactly nine months later, which was an item of brief and passing interest. And their second daughter was born barely eleven months after their first. During the winter months of that time he worked in a lumber camp some fifteen miles away, cutting pulp for $1.75 a cord and getting $40.00 a month for his team of horses as well. Rising at five-thirty and working until after seven in the evening and sleeping on a bunk with a mattress made from boughs.

Sometimes he would come home on the weekends and on the clear, winter nights she would hear the distinctive sound of his horses' bells as they left the valley floor to begin their ascent up the mountain's side. Although the climb was steep, the horses would walk faster because they knew they were coming home, even breaking into a trot on the more level areas and causing their bells to accelerate accordingly. Sometimes he would get out of the wood sleigh and run beside the horses or ahead of them in order to keep warm and also to convince himself that he was getting home faster.

When she heard the bells she would take the lamp and move it from one window to the other and then take it back again and continue to repeat the procedure. The effect was almost that of a regularly flashing light, like that of a lighthouse or someone flicking a light switch off and on at regulated intervals. He would see the light now at one window and then in the other, sent down like the regulated flashing signals his mares gave off when in heat; and although he was exhausted, he would be filled with desire and urge himself upwards at an even greater rate.

After he had stabled his horses and fed them, he would go into their house and they would meet one another in the middle of the kitchen floor, holding and going into one another sometimes while the snow and frost still hung so heavily on his clothes that they creaked when he moved or steamed near the presence of the stove. The lamp would be stilled on the kitchen table and they would be alone. Only the monogamous eagles who nested in the hemlock tree even farther up the mountain seemed above them.

There were married for five years in an intensity which it seemed could never last, going more and more into each other and excluding most others for the company of themselves.

When she went into premature labour in February of 1931, he was not at home because it was still six weeks before the expected birth and they had decided that he would stay in the camp a little longer in order to earn the extra money they needed for their fourth child.

There had been heavy snows in the area and high winds and then it had turned bitterly cold, all in the span of a day and a half. It had been impossible to get down from the mountain and get word to him in the camp, although his twin brother managed to walk in on the second day, bringing him the news that everyone on the mountain already knew: that he had lost his wife and what might have been his first-born son. The snow was higher than his twin brother's head when they saw him coming into the camp. He was soaked with perspiration

from fighting the drifts and pale and shaking and he began to throw up
in the yard of the camp almost before he could deliver his message.

He had left immediately, leaving his brother behind to rest, while
following his incoming tracks back out. He could not believe it, could
not believe that she had somehow gone without him, could not believe
that in their closeness he was still the last to know and that in spite of
hoping "to live alone together" she had somehow died surrounded by
others, but without him and really alone in the ultimate sense. He could
not believe that in the closeness of their beginning there had been
separation in their end. He had tried to hope that there might be some
mistake; but the image of his brother, pale and shaken and vomiting in
the packed-down snow of the lumber camp's yard, dispelled any such
possibility.

He was numb throughout all of the funeral preparations and the
funeral itself. His wife's sisters looked after his three small daughters
who, while they sometimes called for their mother, seemed almost to
welcome the lavish attention visited upon them. On the afternoon following the funeral the pneumonia which his twin brother had
developed after his walk into the camp worsened and he had gone to
sit beside his bed, holding his hand, at least able to be *present* this time,
yet aware of the disapproving looks of Cora, his brother's wife, who
was a woman he had never liked. Looks which said: If he had not gone
for *you*, this would never have happened. Sitting there while his
brother's chest deepened in spite of the poultices and the liniments and
even the administrations of the doctor who finally made it up the mountain road and pronounced the pneumonia "surprisingly advanced."

After the death of his brother the numbness continued. He felt as
those who lose all of their family in the midnight fire or on the sinking
ship. Suddenly and without survivors. He felt guilt for his wife and for
his brother's fatherless children and for his daughters who would never
know their mother. And he felt terribly alone.

His daughters stayed with him for a while as he tried to do what
their mother had done. But gradually his wife's sisters began to suggest that the girls would be better off with them. At first he opposed
the idea because both he and his wife had never been overly fond of
her sisters, considering them somehow more vulgar than they were
themselves. But gradually it became apparent that if he were ever to
return to the woods and earn a living, someone would have to look

after three children under the age of four. He was torn for the remainder of the winter months and into the spring, sometimes appreciating what he felt was the intended kindness of his in-laws and at other times angry at certain overheard remarks: "It is not right for three little girls to be alone up on that mountain with that man, a *young* man." As if he were more interesting as a potential child molester than simply as a father. Gradually his daughters began to spend evenings and weekends with their aunts and then weeks and then in the manner of small children, they no longer cried when he left, or clung to his legs, or sat in the window to await his approach. And then they began to call him "Archibald," as did the other members of the households in which they lived. So that in the end he seemed neither husband nor brother nor even father but only "Archibald." He was twenty- seven years old.

.He had always been called Archibald or sometimes in Gaelic "Gilleasbuig." Perhaps because of what was perceived as a kind of formality that hung about him, no one ever called him "Arch" or the more familiar and common "Archie." He did not look or act "like an Archie," as they said. And with the passing of the years, letters came that were addressed simply to "Archibald" and which bore a variety of addresses covering a radius of some forty miles. Many of the letters in the later years came from the folklorists who had "discovered" him in the 1960s and for whom he had made various tapes and recordings. And he had come to be regarded as "the last of the authentic old-time Gaelic singers." He was faithfully recorded in the archives at Sydney and Halifax and Ottawa and his picture had appeared in various scholarly and less scholarly journals; sometimes with the arms of the folklorists around him, sometimes holding one of his horses and sometimes standing beside his shining pickup truck which bore a bumper sticker which read "Suas Leis A' Ghaidlig." Sometimes the articles bore titles such as "Cape Breton Singer: The Last of His Kind" or "Holding Fast on Top of the Mountain" or "Mnemonic Devices in the Gaelic Line" — the latter generally being accompanied by a plethora of footnotes.

He did not really mind the folklorists, enunciating the words over and over again for them, explaining that "bh" was pronounced as "v" (like the "ph" in phone is pronounced "f," he would say), expanding on the more archaic meanings and footnoting himself the words an phrases of local origin. Doing it all with care and seriousness in much the same way that he filed and set his saws or structured his woodpile.

Now in this April of the 1980s he thought of himself, as I said earlier, as a man of seventy-eight years who had made it through another winter. He had come to terms with most things, although never really with the death of his wife; but that too had become easier during the last decades, although he was still bothered by the sexual references which came because of his monastic existence.

Scarcely a year after "the week of deaths," he had been visited by Cora, his twin brother's wife. She had come with her breath reeking of rum and placed the bottle on the middle of his kitchen table.

"I've been thinking," she said. "It's about time me and you got together."

"Mmmm," he said, trying to make the most non-committal sound he could think of.

"Here," she said, going to his cupboard and taking down two of his sparkling glasses and splashing rum into them. "Here," she said, sliding a glass towards him across the table and seating herself opposite him. "Here, have a shot of this. It will put lead in your pencil," and then after a pause, "although from what I've *heard* there's no need of that."

He was taken aback, somehow imagining her and his twin brother lying side by side at night discussing his physicality.

Heard *what?* he wondered. *Where?*

"Yeah," she said. "There's not much need of you being up here on this mountain by yourself and me being by myself farther down. If you don't use it, it'll rust off."

He was close to panic, finding her so lonely and so drunkenly available and so much unlike the memory of his own wife. He wondered if she remembered how much they disliked each other, or thought they did. And he wondered if he were somehow thought of as being interchangeable with his dead brother. As if, because they were twins, their bodies must somehow be the same, regardless of their minds.

"I bet it's rusty right now," she said and she leaned the upper part of her body across the table so that he could smell the rum heavy on her breath even as he felt her fingers on his leg.

"Mmmm," he said, getting up rapidly and walking towards the window. He was rattled by her overt sexuality, the way a shy middle-aged married man might be when taken on a visit to a brothel far from his home — not because what is discussed is so foreign to him, but rather because of the manner and the approach.

Outside the window the eagles were flying up the mountain, carrying the twigs, some of them almost branches, for the building of their home.

"Mmmm," he said, looking out the window and down the winding road to the valley floor below.

"Well," she said, getting up and downing her drink. "I guess there's no fun here. I just wanted to say hello."

"Yes," he said. "Well, thank you."

She lurched towards the door and he wondered if he should open it for her or if that would be too rash.

But she opened it herself.

"Well," she said as she went out into the yard. "You know where I'm at."

"Yes," he said, gaining confidence from her departing back, "I know where you are."

Now on this morning in April half a century later, he looked out his window at the eagles flying by. They were going down into the valley to hunt, leaving their nest with their four precious eggs for the briefest time. Then he recognized the sound of a truck's motor. He recognized it before it entered the yard, in the way his wife had once recognized the individual sound of his horse's bells. The truck was muddy and splattered, not merely from this spring trip up the mountain but from a sort of residual dirt perhaps from the previous fall. It belonged to his married granddaughter who had been christened Sarah but preferred to be known as Sal. She wheeled her truck into the yard, getting out of it inches from his door and almost before it had stopped. She wore her hair in a ponytail, although she seemed too old for that, and her tight-fitting jeans were slipped inside her husband's rubber boots. He was always slightly surprised at her ability to chew gum and smoke cigarettes at the same time and was reminded of that now as she came through his door, her lipstick leaving a red ring around her cigarette as she removed it from her mouth and flicked it out into the yard. She wore a tight-fitting T- shirt with the words "I'm Busted" across her chest.

"Hi, Archibald," she said, sitting in the chair nearest the window.

"Hi," he said.

"What's new?"

"Oh, nothing much," he replied, and then after a pause, "Would you like some tea?"

"Okay," she said. "No milk. I'm watching my figure."

"Mmmm," he said.

He looked at her from the distance of his years, trying to find within her some flashes of his wife or even of himself. She was attractive in her way, with her dark eyes and ready mouth, although shorter than either he or his wife.

"Had two phone calls," she said.

"Oh," he said, always feeling a bit guilty that he had no telephone and the messages had to be left with others farther down the mountain.

"One is from a guy who wants to buy your mare. You're still interested in selling?"

"Yes, I guess so."

"The other is about Gaelic singing. They want us to sing in Halifax this summer. This is the year of 'Scots Around the World.' All kinds of people will be there, even some of the Royal Family. We'll be there for a week. They haven't decided on the pay yet but it'll be okay and they'll pay our accommodation and our transportation."

"Oh," he said, becoming interested and cautious at the same time. "What do they mean by us?"

"*Us.* You know, the family. They want twenty of us. There'll be a few days of rehearsal there and then some concerts and we'll be on television. I can hardly wait. I have to do lots of shopping in Halifax and it will be a chance to sleep in without Tom bothering me. We won't even have to be at the theatre or studio or whatever until noon." She lit another cigarette.

"What do they want us to sing?" he asked.

"Oh, who cares?" she said. "It's the trip that's important. Some of the old songs. They're coming to audition us or something in two or three weeks. We'll sing *Fear A' Bhata* or something," she said, and butting her cigarette on her saucer and laying her gum beside it on the table, she began to sing in a clear, powerful voice:

Fhir a' bhata, na ho ro eile,
Fhir a' bhata, na ho ro eile,

Fhir a' bhata, na ho ro eile,
Mho shoraidh slan leat 's gach ait' an teid thu

Is tric mi 'sealltainn o 'n chnoc a 's airde
Dh'fheuch am faic mi fear a' bhata,
An tig thu 'n diugh, no 'n tig thu 'maireach;
'S mur tig thu idir, gur truagh a tha mi.

Only when she sang did she remind him somewhat of his wife, and again he felt the hope that she might reach that standard of excellence.

"You're singing it too fast," he said cautiously when she had finished. "But it is good. You're singing it like a milling song. It's supposed to be a lament for a loved one that's lost."

He sang it himself slowly, stressing the distinction of each syllable.

She seemed interested for a while, listening intently before replacing her gum and lighting another cigarette, then tossing the still-lighted match into the stove.

"Do you know what the words mean?" he said when he had finished.

"No," she said. "Neither will anybody else. I just make the noises. I've been hearing the things since I was two. I know how they go. I'm not dumb, you know."

"Who else are they asking?" he said, partially out of interest and partially to change the subject and avoid confrontation.

"I don't know. They said they'd get back to us later. All they wanted to know now was if we were interested. The man about the mare will be up later. I got to go now."

She was out the door almost immediately, turning her truck in a spray of gravel that flicked against his house, the small stones pinging against his windowpane. A muddied bumper sticker read: "If you're horny, honk your horn."

He was reminded, as he often was, of Cora, who had been dead now for some fifteen years and who had married another man within a year of her visit to him with her open proposal. And he was touched that his granddaughter should seem so much like his brother's wife instead of like his own.

The man who came to buy the mare was totally unlike any other horse buyer he had ever seen. He came in a suit and in an elaborate car and spoke in an accent that was difficult to identify. He was accompanied by Carver, who was apparently his guide, a violent young man in his thirties from the other side of the mountain. Carver's not-unhandsome face was marred by a series of raised grey scars and his upper lip had been thickened as a result of a fight in which someone had swung a logging chain into his mouth, an action which had also cost him his most obvious teeth. He wore his wallet on a chain hooked to his belt and scuffed his heavy lumberman's boots on the cardboard in Archibald's porch before entering the kitchen. He was by the window and rolled a cigarette while the horse buyer talked to Archibald.

"How old is the mare?"

"Five," said Archibald.

"Has she ever had a colt?"

"Why, yes," said Archibald, puzzled by the question. Usually buyers asked if the horse could work single or double or something about its disposition or its legs or chest. Or if it would work in snow or eat enough to sustain a heavy work schedule.

"Do you think she could have another colt?" he asked.

"Why, I suppose," he said, almost annoyed, "if she had a stallion."

"No problem," said the man.

"But," said Archibald, driven by his old honesty, "she has never worked. I have not been in the woods that much lately and I always used the old mare, her mother, before she died. I planned to train her but never got around to it. She's more like a pet. She probably will work, though. They've always worked. It's in the stock. I've had them all my life." He stopped, almost embarrassed at having to apologize for his horses and for himself.

"Okay," said the man. "No problem. She has had a colt, though?"

"Look," said Carver from his seat near the window, snuffing out his cigarette between his calloused thumb and forefinger, "he already told you that. I told you this man don't lie."

"Okay," said the man, taking out his chequebook.

"Don't you want to see her first?" asked Archibald.

"No, it's okay," the man said. "I believe you."

"He wants nine hundred dollars," said Carver. "She's a young mare."

"Okay," said the man, to Archibald's amazement. He had been hopeful of perhaps seven hundred dollars or even less since she had never been worked.

"You'll take her down in your truck later?" the man said to Carver.

"Right on!" said Carver and they left, the man driving with a peculiar caution as if he had never been off pavement before and was afraid that the woods might swallow him.

After they left, Archibald went out to his barn to talk to the mare. He led her out to the brook to drink, then to the door of the house where she waited while he went in and rummaged for some bread to offer her as a farewell treat. She was young and strong and splendid and he was somehow disappointed that the buyer had not at least seen her so that he could appreciate her excellent qualities.

Shortly after noon Carver drove his truck into the yard. "Do you want a beer?" he said to Archibald, motioning towards the open case on the seat beside him.

"No, I don't think so," Archibald said. "We may as well get this over with."

"Okay," said Carver. "Do you want to lead her on?"

"No, it's okay," said Archibald. "She'll go with anyone."

"Yeah," said Carver. "Perhaps that's a good way to be."

They went into the barn. In spite of what he had said, Archibald found himself going up beside the mare and untying the rope and leading her out into the afternoon sun which reflected her dappled shining coat. Carver backed his truck up to a small incline beside the barn and lowered the tailgate. Then Archibald handed him the rope and watched as she followed him willingly into the truck.

"This is the last of all them nice horses you had up here, eh?" said Carver after he had tied the rope and swung down from the truck.

"Yes," said Archibald, "the last."

"I guess you hauled a lot of wood with them horses. I heard guy's talking, older guys who worked with you in the camps."

"Oh, yes," said Archibald.

"I heard guys say you and your brother could cut seven cords of pulp a day with a crosscut saw, haul it and stack it."

"Oh, yes," he said. "Some days we could. Days seemed longer then," he added with a smile.

"Christ, we're lucky to get seven with a power saw unless we're in a real good stand," said Carver, pulling up his trousers and starting to roll a cigarette. "Your timber here on your own land is as good as ever, they say."

"Yes," he said. "It's pretty good."

" 'That Archibald,' they say, 'no one knows where he gets all them logs, hauls them out with them horses and doesn't seem to disturb anything. Year after year. Treats the mountain as if it were a garden.' "

"Mmmm," he said.

"Not like now, eh? We just cut 'em all down. Go in with heavy equipment, tree farmers and loaders and do it all in a day, to hell with tomorrow."

"Yes," said Archibald. "I've noticed."

"You don't want to sell?" asked Carver.

"No," he said. "Not yet."

"I just thought ... since you were letting your mare go. No work for the mare, no work for you."

"Oh, she'll probably work somewhere," he said. "I'm not so sure about myself."

"Nah, she won't work," said Carver. "They want her for birth control pills."

"For what?" said Archibald.

"This guy says, I don't know if it's true, that there's this farm outside of Montreal that's connected to a lab or something. Anyway, they've got all these mares there and they keep them bred all the time and they use their water for birth control pills."

It seemed so preposterous that Archibald was not sure how to react. He scrutinized Carver's scarred yet open face, looking for a hint, some kind of touch, but he could find nothing.

"Yeah," said Carver. "They keep the mares pregnant all the time so the women won't be."

"What do they do with the colts?" said Archibald, thinking that he might try a question for a change.

"I dunno," said Carver. "He didn't say. I guess they just throw them away. Got to go now," he said, swinging into the cab of his truck, "and take her down the mountain. I think he's almost got a boxcar of these mares, or a transport truck. In two days she'll be outside Montreal and they'll get her a stallion and that'll be it."

The truck roared into action and moved from the incline near the barn. Archibald had been closer to it than he thought and was forced to step out of the way. As it passed, Carver rolled down the window and shouted, "Hey, Archibald, do you sing anymore?"

"Not so much," he said.

"Got to talk to you about that sometime," he said above the engine's roar and then he and the truck and the splendid mare left the yard to begin their switchbacked journey down the mountain.

For a long time Archibald did not know what to do. He felt somehow betrayed by forces he could not control. The image of his mare beneath the weight of successive and different stallions came to his mind but the most haunting image was that of the dead colts which Carver had described as being "thrown away." He imagined them as the many dead unwanted animals he had seen thrown out on the manure piles behind the barns, their skulls smashed in by blows from axes. He doubted that there was anything like that outside Montreal and he doubted — or wanted to doubt — somehow more than he could what Carver had said. But he had no way to verify the facts or disprove them, and the images persisted. He thought, as he always did at times of loss, of his wife. And then the pale, still body of his quiet and unbreathing son, with the intricate blue veins winding like the map lines of roads and rivers upon his fragile, delicate scull. Both wife and son gone from him, taken in the winter's snow. And he felt somehow that he might cry.

He looked up to the sound of the whooshing eagles' wings. They were flying up the mountain, almost wavering in their flight. Like weary commuters trying to make it home. He had watched them through the long winter as they were forced to fly farther and farther in search of food and open water. He had noticed the dullness of their feathers and the dimming lustre in their intense green eyes. Now, and he was not sure if perhaps it was his eyesight or his angle of vision, the female's wing tips seemed almost to graze the bare branches of the trees as if she might falter and fall. And then the male who had gone on ahead turned and came back, gliding on the wind with his wings outstretched, trying to conserve what little energy he had left. He passed so close to Archibald that he could see, or imagined that he could see, the desperate fear in his fierce, defiant eyes. He was so intent on his mission that he paid little attention to Archibald, circling beside his mate until their wing tips almost touched. She seemed to gain strength from his presence and almost to lunge with her wings, like a desperate swimmer on her final lap, and they continued together up the mountain. In the dampness of the late spring Archibald feared, as perhaps did they, for the future of their potential young.

He had seen the eagles in other seasons and circumstances. He had seen the male seize a branch in his powerful talons and soar towards the sky in the sheer exuberance of his power and strength; had seen him snap the branch in two (in the way a strong man might snap a kindling across his knee), letting the two sections fall towards the earth before plummeting after one or the other and snatching it from the air; wheeling and somersaulting and flipping the branch in front of him and swooping under it again and again until, tired of the game, he let it fall to earth.

And he had seen them in the aerial courtship of their mating; had seen them feinting and swerving high above the mountain, outlined against the sky. Had seen them come together, and with talons locked, fall cartwheeling over and over for what seemed like hundreds of feet down towards the land. Separating and braking, like lucky parachutists, at the last minute and gliding individually and parallel to the earth before starting their ascent once more.

The folklorists were always impressed by the bald eagles.

"How long have they been here?" the first group asked.

"Forever, I guess," had been his answer.

And after doing research they had returned and said, "Yes, Cape Breton is the largest nesting area on the eastern seaboard north of Florida. And the largest east of the Rockies. It's funny, hardly anybody knows they're here."

"Oh, some people do," Archibald said with a smile.

"It's only because they don't use pesticides or herbicides in the forest industry," the folklorists said, "If they start, the eagles will be gone. There are hardly any nests anymore in New Brunswick or in Maine."

"Mmmm," he said.

In the days that followed they tried to prepare for the "singing" in Halifax. They had several practices, most of them at Sal's because she had talked to the producer and had become the contact person and also because she seemed to want to go the most. They managed to gather a number of people of varying talent, some more reluctant than others. One or two of the practices were held at Archibald's. The number in the group varied. It expanded sometimes to as many as thirty, including various in-laws and friends of in-laws and people who simply had little else to do on a given evening. Throughout it all, Archibald tried to maintain control and to do it in "his way," which meant enunciating the words clearly and singing the exact number of verses in the proper order. Sometimes the attention of the younger people wandered and the evenings deteriorated quite early and rapidly, with people drifting off into little knots to gossip or tell jokes or to drink what was in Archibald's opinion too much. As the pressures of the spring season increased and many of the men left logging to fish or work upon their land, there were fewer and fewer male voices at practice sessions. Sometimes the men joked about this and future make-up of the group.

"Do you think you'll be able to handle all these women by yourself in Halifax, Archibald?" someone might ask, although not really asking the question to him.

"Sure, he will," another voice would respond. "He's well rested. He hasn't used it in fifty years — not that we know of, anyway."

Then at one practice Sal announced with some agitation that she had been talking to the producer in Halifax. He had told her, she said, that two other groups from the area had contacted him and he would be auditioning them as well. He would be coming in about ten days.

Everyone was dumbfounded.

"What other groups?" asked Archibald.

"One," said Sal, pausing for dramatic effect, "is headed by *Carver.*"

"Carver!" they said in unison and disbelief. And then in the midst of loud guffaws, "Carver can't sing. He can hardly speak any Gaelic. Where will he get a group?"

"Don't ask me," said Sal, "unless it's those guys he hangs around with."

"Who else?" said Archibald.

"MacKenzies!" she said.

No one laughed at the mention of MacKenzies. They had been one of the oldest and best of the singing families. They lived some twenty miles away in a small and isolated valley, but Archibald had noticed, over the past fifteen years or so, more and more of their houses becoming shuttered and boarded and a few of the older ones starting to lean and even to fall to the pressures of the wind.

"They don't have enough people anymore," someone said.

"No," added another voice. "All of their best singers have gone to Toronto."

"There are two very good young men there," said Archibald, remembering a concert a few years back when he had seen the two standing straight and tall a few feet back from the microphone, had seen them singing clearly and effortlessly with never a waver or a mispronunciation or a missed note.

"They've gone to Calgary," said a third voice. "They've been there now for over a year."

"I was talking to some people from over that way after the call from Halifax," said Sal. "They said that the MacKenzie's grandmother was going to ask them to come back. They said she was going to try to get all her singers to come home."

Archibald was touched in spite of himself, touched that Mrs. Mac-Kenzie would try so hard. He looked around the room and realized that there were very few people in it who knew that Mrs. MacKenzie was his cousin and by extension theirs. Although he did not know her well and had only nodded to her and exchanged a few words with her over a lifetime, he felt very close to her now. He was not even sure of the degree of the relationship (although he would work it out later), remembering only the story of the young woman from an earlier generation of his family who had married the young man from the valley of the MacKenzies who was of the "wrong religion." There had been great bitterness at the time and the families had refused to speak to one another until all those who knew what the "right religion" was had died. The young woman who left had never visited her parents or they her. It seemed sad to Archibald, feeling almost more kinship to the scarcely known Mrs. MacKenzie than to those members of his own flesh and blood who seemed now so agitated and squabbly.

"She will never get them home," said the last voice. "They've all got jobs and responsibilities. They can't drop everything and come here or to Halifax for a week to sing four or five songs."

The voice proved right, although in the following ten days before the producer's visit Archibald thought often of Mrs. MacKenzie making her phone calls and of her messengers fanned out across Toronto, visiting the suburbs and the taverns, asking the question to which they already knew the answer but feeling obliged to ask it, nonetheless. In the end four MacKenzies came home, two young men who had been hurt at work and were on compensation and a middle-aged daughter and her husband who managed to take a week of their vacation earlier than usual. The *really* good young men were unable to come.

When the producer came he brought with him two male assistants with clipboards. The producer was an agitated man in his early thirties. He had dark curly hair and wore thick glasses and a maroon T-shirt with "If you've got it, flaunt it" emblazoned across the front. When he spoke, he nervously twisted his right ear lobe.

Archibald's group was the last of the three he visited. "He's saved the best for last," laughed Sal, not very convincingly.

He came in the evening and explained the situation briefly. If chosen, they would be in Halifax in six days. They would practice and acquaint themselves with the surroundings for the first two days and on the next four there would be a concert each evening. There would be various acts from throughout the province. They would be on television and radio and some of the Royal Family would be in attendance.

Then he said, "Look, I really don't understand your language so we're here mainly to look for effect. We'd like you to be ready with three songs. And then maybe we'll have to cut it back to two. We'll see how it goes."

They began to sing, sitting around the table as if they were "waulking the cloth," as their ancestors had done before them. Archibald sat at the head of the table, singing loudly and clearly, while the other voices rose to meet him. The producer and his assistants took notes.

"Okay, that's enough," he said after an hour and a half.

"We'll take the third one," he said to one of his assistants.

"What's it called?" he asked Archibald.

"*Mo Chridhe Trom,*" said Archibald. "It means my heart is heavy."

"Okay," said the producer. "Let's do it again."

They began. By the twelfth verse the music took hold of Archibald in a way that he had almost forgotten it could. His voice soared above the others with such clear and precise power that they faltered and were stilled.

> *'S ann air cul nam beanntan ard,*
> *Tha aite comhnuidh mo ghraidh,*

Fear dha 'm bheil an chridhe blath,
Do 'n tug mi 'n gradh a leon mi.

'S ann air cul a' bhalla chloich,
'S math an aithnichinn lorg do chos,
Och 'us och, mar tha mi 'n nochd
Gur bochd nach d'fhuair mi coir ort.

Tha mo chridhe dhut cho buan,
Ris a' chreag tha 'n grunnd a' chuain,
No comh-ionnan ris an stuaidh
A bhuaileas orr' an comhnuidh.

He finished the song alone. There was a silence that was almost embarrassing.

"Okay," said the producer after a pause. "Try another one, number six. The one that doesn't sound like all the others. What's it called?"

"*Oran Gillean Alasdair Mhoir,*" said Archibald, trying to compose himself. "Song to the Sons of Big Alexander. Sometimes it's known simply as The Drowning of the Men."

"Okay," said the producer. "Let's go." But when they were halfway through, he said, "Cut, okay, that's enough."

"It's not finished," said Archibald. "It's a narrative."

"That's enough," said the producer.

"You can't cut them like that," said Archibald, "if you do, they don't make any sense."

"Look, they don't make any sense to me, anyway," said the producer. "I told you I don't understand the language. We're just trying to gauge audience impact."

Archibald felt himself getting angrier than perhaps he should, and he was aware of the looks and gestures from his family. "Be careful," they said, "don't offend him or we won't get the trip."

"Mmmm," he said, rising from his chair and going to the window. The dusk had turned to dark and the stars seemed to touch the mountain. Although in a room filled with people, he felt very much alone, his mind running silently over the verses of *Mo Chridhe Trom* which had so moved him moments before.

Over lofty mountains lies
The dwelling place of my love,

One whose heart was always warm,
And whom I loved too dearly.

And behind the wall of stone
I would recognize your steps,
But how sad I am I tonight
Because we're not together.

Still my love you will last
Like the rock beneath the sea,
Just as long as will the waves
That strike against it always.

"Okay, let's call it a night," said the producer. "Thank you all very much. We'll be in touch."

The next morning at nine the producer drove into Archibald's yard. His assistants were with him, packed and ready for Halifax. The assistants remained in the car while the producer came into Archibald's kitchen. He coughed uncomfortably and looked about him as if to make sure that they were alone. He reminded Archibald of a nervous father preparing to discuss "the facts of life."

"How were the other groups?" asked Archibald in what he hoped was a noncommittal voice.

"The young man Carver and his group," said the producer, "have tremendous *energy*. They have a lot of male voices."

"Mmmm," said Archibald. "What did they sing?"

"I don't remember the names of the songs, although I wrote them down. They're packed away. It doesn't matter all that much, anyway. They don't know as many songs as you people do, though," he concluded.

"No," said Archibald, trying to restrain his sarcasm, "I don't suppose they do."

"Still, that doesn't matter so much either as we only need two or three."

"Mmmm."

"The problem with that group is the way they look."

"The way they *look*?" said Archibald. "Shouldn't it be the way they sing?"

"Not really," said the producer. "See, these performances have a high degree of *visibility*. You're going to be on stage for four nights and the various television networks are all going to be there. This is, in total, a *big show*. It's not a regional show. It will be national and international. It will probably be beamed back to Scotland and Australia and who knows where else. We want people who *look right* and who'll give a good impression of the area and the province."

Archibald said nothing.

"You see," said the producer, "we've got to have someone we can zoom in on for close-ups, someone who looks the part. We don't want close-ups of people who have had their faces all carved up in brawls. That's why you're so good. You're a great-looking man for your age, if you'll pardon me. You're tall and straight and have your own teeth, which helps both your singing and appearance. You have a *presence*. The rest of your group have nice voices, especially the women, but without you, if you'll pardon me, they're kind of ordinary. And then," he added almost as an afterthought, "there is your reputation. You're known to the folklorists and people like that. You have *credibility*. Very important."

Archibald was aware of Sal's truck coming into the yard and knew that she had seen the producers car on its way up the mountain.

"Hi," she said, "what's new?"

"I think you're all set but it's up to your grandfather," the producer said.

"What about the MacKenzies?" asked Archibald.

"Garbage. No good at all. An old woman playing a tape recorder while seven or eight people tried to sing along with it. Wasted our time. We wanted people that were *alive*, not some scratchy tape."

"Mmmm," said Archibald.

"Anyway, you're on. But we'd like a few changes."

"Changes?"

"Yeah, first of all we'll have to cut them. That was what I was trying to get around to last night. You're only going to be on stage for three or four minutes each night and we'd like to get two songs in. They're too long. The other problem is they're too mournful. Jesus, even the titles, 'My Heart is Heavy,' 'The Drowning of the Men.' Think about it."

"But," said Archibald, trying to sound reasonable, "that's the way those songs are. You've got to hear them in the original way."

"I've got to go now," said Sal. "Got to see about baby- sitters and that. See you."

She left in her customary spray of gravel.

"Look," said the producer, "I've got to put on a big show. Maybe you could get some songs from the other group."

"The other group?"

"Yeah," he said, "Carver's. Anyway, think about it. I'll call you in a week and we can finalize it and work out any other details." And then he was gone.

In the days that followed Archibald *did* think about it. He thought about it more than he had ever thought he would. He thought of the impossibility of trimming the songs and of changing them and he wondered why he seemed the only one in his group who harboured such concerns. Most of the others did not seem very interested when he mentioned it to them, although they did seem interested in shopping lists and gathering the phone numbers of long-absent relatives and friends in Halifax.

One evening Carver met Sal on her way to Bingo and told her quite bluntly that he and his group were going.

"No, you're not," she said, "we are."

"Wait and see," said Carver. "Look, we need this trip. We need to get a boat engine and we want to buy a truck. You guys are done. Done like a dinner. It matters too much to that Archibald and you're all dependent on him. *Us*, we're *adjustable*."

"As if we couldn't be adjustable!" said Sal with a laugh as she told of the encounter at their last practice before the anticipated phone call. The practice did not go well as far as Archibald was concerned, although no one else seemed to notice.

The next day when Archibald encountered Carver at the general store down in the valley, he could not resist asking: "What did you sing for that producer fellow?"

"*Brochan Lom*," said Carver with a shrug.

"*Brochan Lom*," said Archibald incredulously. "Why, that isn't even a song. It's just a bunch of nonsense syllables strung together."

"So what!" said Carver. "He didn't know. No one knows."

"But it's before the Royal Family," said Archibald, surprising even himself at finding such royalist remnants still within him.

"Look," said Carver, wiping his mouth with the back of his hand, "what did the Royal Family ever do for *me*?"

"Of course people know," said Archibald, pressing on with weary determination. "People in audiences know. Other singers know. Folklorists know."

"Yeah, maybe so," said Carver with a shrug, "but me, I don't know no folklorists."

He looked at Archibald intently for a few seconds and then gathered up his tobacco and left the store.

Archibald was troubled all of that afternoon. He was vaguely aware of his relatives organizing sitters and borrowing suitcases and talking incessantly but saying little. He thought of his conversation with Carver, on the one hand, and strangely enough, he thought of Mrs. MacKenzie on the other. He thought of her with great compassion, she who was probably the best of them all and who had tried the hardest to impress the man from Halifax. The image of her in the twilight of the valley of the MaKenzies playing the tape-recorded voices of her departed family to a man who did not know the language kept running through his mind. He imagined her now, sitting quietly with her knitting needles in her lap, listening to the ghostly voices which were there without their people.

And then that night Archibald had a dream. He had often had dreams of his wife in the long, long years since her death and had probably brought them on in the early years by visiting her grave in the evenings and sometimes sitting there and talking to her of their hopes and aspirations. And sometimes in the nights following such "conversations" she would come to him and they would talk and touch and sometimes sing. But on this night she only sang. She sang with a clarity and a beauty that caused the hairs to rise on the back of his neck even as the tears welled to his eyes. Every note was perfect, as perfect and clear as the waiting water droplet hanging on the fragile leaf or the high suspended eagle outlined against the sky at the apex of its arc. She sang to him until four in the morning when the first rays of light began to touch the mountain top. And then she was gone.

Archibald awoke relaxed and refreshed in a way that he had seldom felt since sleeping with his wife so many years before. His mind was made up and he was done thinking about it.

Around nine o'clock Sal's truck came into the yard. "That producer fellow is on the phone," she said. "I told him I'd take the message but he wants to talk to you."

"Okay," said Archibald.

In Sal's kitchen the receiver swung from its black spiral cord.

"Yes, this is Archibald," he said, grasping it firmly. "No, I don't think I can get them down to three minutes or speed them up at all. No, I don't think so. Yes, I have thought about it. Yes, I have been in contact with others who sing in my family. No, I don't know about Carver. You'll have to speak to him. Thank you. Good- bye."

He was aware of the disappointment and the grumpiness that spread throughout the house, oozing like a rapid ink across a blotter. In the next room he heard a youthful voice say: "All he had to do was shorten the verses in a few stupid, old songs. You'd think he would have done it for *us*, the old coot."

"I'm sorry," he said to Sal, "but I just couldn't do it."

"Do you want a drive home in the truck?" she asked.

"No," he said, "never mind, I can walk."

He began to walk up the mountain with an energy and purpose that reminded him of himself as a younger man. He felt that he was "right" in the way he had felt so many years before when he had courted his future bride and when they had decided to build their house near the mountain's top even though others were coming down. And he felt as he had felt during the short and burning intensity of their brief life together. He began almost to run.

In the days that followed, Archibald was at peace. One day Sal dropped in and said that Carver was growing a moustache and a beard.

"They told him the moustache would cover his lip and with the beard his scars would be invisible on TV," she sniffed. "Make- up will do wonders."

Then one rainy night after he was finished watching the international and national and regional news, Archibald looked out his window. Down on the valley floor he could see the headlights of the cars following the wet pavement of the main highway. People bound for larger destinations who did not know that he existed. And then he noticed one set of lights in particular. They were coming hard and fast along the valley floor and although miles away, they seemed to be coming with a purpose all their own. They "looked" different from the other headlights and in one of those moments of knowledge mixed with intuition Archibald said aloud to himself: "That car is coming here. It is coming for *me*."

He was rattled at first. He was aware that his decision had caused ill feelings among some members of his family as well as various in-laws and others strung out in a far-flung and complicated web of connections he could barely comprehend. He knew also that because of the rain many of the men had not been in the woods that much lately and were perhaps spending their time in the taverns talking too much about him and what he had done. He watched as the car swung off the pavement and began its ascent, weaving and sloughing up the mountain in the rain.

Although he was not a violent man, he did not harbour any illusions about where or how he lived. "That Archibald," they said, "is nobody's fool." He thought of this now as he measured the steps to the stove where the giant poker hung. He had had it made by a blacksmith in one of the lumber caps shortly after his marriage. It was of heavy steel, and years of poking it into the hot coals of his stove had sharpened its end to a clean and burnished point. When he swung it in his hand its weight seemed like an ancient sword. He lifted his wooden table easily and placed it at an angle which he hoped was not too obvious in the centre of the kitchen, with its length facing the door.

"If they come in the door," he said, "I will be behind the table and in five strides I can reach the poker." He practised the five strides just to make sure. Then he put his left hand between his legs to adjust himself and straightened his suspenders so that they were perfectly in line. And then he went to the side of the window to watch the coming car.

Because of the recent rains, sections of the road had washed away and at certain places freshets and small brooks cut across it. Sometimes the rains washed down sand and topsoil as well, and the trick was never to accelerate on such washed-over sections for fear of being buried in the flowing water and mud. Rather, one gunned the motor on the relatively stable sections of the climb (where there was "bottom") and trusted to momentum to get across the streams.

Archibald watched the progress of the car. Sometimes he lost its headlights because of his perspective and the trees, but only momentarily. As it climbed, swerving back and forth, the wet branches slapping and silhouetted against its headlights, Archibald began to read the dark wet roadway in his own mind. And he began to read the driver's reflexes as he swung out from the gullies and then in close to the mountain's wall. He began almost to admire the driver. Whoever that is, he thought, is very drunk but also very good.

The car hooked and turned into his yard without any apparent change of speed, its headlights flashing on his house and through his window. Archibald moved behind his table and stood, tall and balanced and ready. Before the sound of the slamming door faded, his kitchen door seemed to blow in and Carver stood there unsteadily, blinking in the light with the rain blowing at his back and dripping off his beginning beard.

"Yeah," he said over his shoulder, "he's here, bring it in."

Archibald waited, his eyes intent upon Carver but also sliding sideways to his poker.

They came into his porch and there were five of them, carrying boxes.

"Put them on the floor there," said Carver, indicating a space just across the threshold. "And try not to dirty his floor."

Archibald knew then he would be all right and moved out from behind his table.

"Open the boxes," said Carver to one of the men. The boxes were filled with forty-once bottles of liquor. It was as if someone were preparing for a wedding.

"These are for you," said Carver. "We bought them at a bootlegger's two hours ago. We been away all day. We been to Glace Bay and to New Waterford and we were in a fight in the parking lot at the tavern in Bras D'Or, and a couple of us got banged up pretty bad. Anyway, not much to say."

Archibald looked at them framed in the doorway leading to his porch. There was no mystery about the kind of day they had had, even if Carver had not told him. Even now, one of them, a tall young man, was rocking backwards on his heels, almost literally falling asleep on his feet as he stood in the doorway. There was a fresh cut on Carver's temple which could not be covered by either his moustache or his beard. Archibald looked at all the liquor and was moved by the total inappropriateness of the gift; bringing all of this to him, the most abstemious man on the mountain. Somehow it moved him even more. And he was aware of its cost in many ways.

He also envied them their closeness and their fierceness and what the producer fellow had called their tremendous energy. And he imagined it was men like they who had given, in their recklessness, all they could think of in that confused and stormy past. Going with their claymores and the misunderstood language of their war cries to "perform" for the Royal Families of the past. But he was not sure of that either. He smiled at them and gave a small nod of acknowledgment. He did not quite know what to say.

"Look," said Carver, with that certainty that marked everything he did. "Look, Archibald," he said. "We know. We know. We *really* know."